The Misplaced Spy

The Misplaced Spy

BY ELIZABETH ALTHAM

A ploughshare is a nobler object than a razor. But if your natural talent is for barbering, wouldn't it be better to be a barber, and a good barber—and use the profits (if you like) to speed the plough? However grand the job may be, is it your job? —D.L. Sayers, Gaudy Night

ISBN: 978-0-9824787-2-1

The Misplaced Spy is also available in standard CD audio format from Blue and Gold Media, LLC.

Printed and bound in the United States of America.

Cover illustration by B.J. Nartker.

Cover design by Sebrina Higdon.

Typesetting by Elizabeth Moors.

Blue and Gold Media, LLC
7431 E. State Street #116
Rockford, Illinois 61108
www.blueandgoldmediallc.com
info@blueandgoldmediallc.com

Dedication

*For my daughters, and in
loving memory of
Father Kevin P. Fitzpatrick.*

Contents

CHAPTER 1

But a stone had been dropped into the still pool of sleep.
  —*H.P. Sheldon, Old Man River's Geese*

DECEMBER 1 began in normal ways. It was a Saturday, which meant that nobody was rigorous about getting up or breakfast. On weekdays Mother keeps us on a pretty tight schedule because of lessons at home for Mary, Tom and Priscilla (when she's interested), and getting to the school bus for Martin and me; and on Sundays the timing is even tighter because of getting everybody ready for church (since Jane was born, that job has taken on cosmic proportions); so Saturday is her day off from nipping at our heels, as she says, and our day off from being nipped.

I had set my battery alarm clock anyway, in a vague hope rather than a real expectation of knocking off a book report before the Advent preparations absorbed my attention. It said 6:00 when it beeped; otherwise I couldn't have told the difference from the middle of the night. Our more-or-less renovated farmhouse sits on the town-ward corner of 21 acres in northwest Connecticut; when the winter solstice draws near it feels and looks a lot closer to the Arctic Circle than it is.

On this particular morning a heavy wind blew in from the north, carrying, to judge by the sound, sleet. I had left the alarm clock across my attic room from my bed, so that I could not just silence it and conk back out. The beep sounded a little uncertain, as if it was going to need a new battery soon. I stumbled over to the old dresser (Mother always has hopes, like mine about the book report, of refinishing such solid-but-neglected pieces of fur-

1

niture), stopped the noise and fumbled with a match and my oil lamp, which is my atmosphere of choice, since Daddy or Martin could run an electrical line up any day I wanted.

I dug out scruffy clothes in honor of Saturday, chores and the book report, and carried them down my narrow stairs to the bathroom I share with Martin (who sleeps in the other attic) and the little kids. A shower without a commentary is a rarity in our family, one worth getting up early for.

Down in the kitchen I scraped the grating of the coal stove back and forth to empty out the ashes and clinkers, opened the drafts and piled on three scoops of fresh coal. I could hear the chuckles and burps of the main heating system from the pipes out in the living room, and water running in my parents' bathroom above the kitchen, so at least one of them was up—probably both.

I ground up enough coffee beans for the first pot of the day, put a big, full kettle on the gas stove as the residuum of my civic duty, and dished myself out some cold cereal.

Northanger Abbey and my notebook were sitting on the kitchen table, which is huge, since it accommodates not only the eight of us and the odd guest for meals, but also schoolwork. I ignored the book as a job that called for at least one cup of coffee.

I really love Jane Austen. I finished *Pride and Prejudice* with a flashlight under the covers when I was 12, and *Sense and Sensibility* was all night, too—it would have been under the covers, except that lately my parents have given me more latitude about reading late, as long as it isn't too many nights in a row. The demands of keeping up with high school, as opposed to my mother, who taught me at home until eighth grade, and who used to let me coast a day here and there if I needed to, ensure that I don't abuse the privilege.

As I say, I love Jane Austen; but *Northanger Abbey* was giving me a hard time. Oh, I liked it as I read it; but it wasn't falling into place in my mind the way the other books had. I had finished it a week ago (we had our choice of books, and I wanted to do one off the beaten Junior English track), and I still had nothing specific to say about it.

Mary and Tom boiled down the back stairs, with Sioux Dawn,

the Brittany spaniel—she comes from a line of famous pheasant hunters, and Brittanies always have pretentious names; but we call her Susie—and Cousin Ribby, the calico cat, bounding like a whole sea of wriggling backs and waving tails around their legs. Mary and Tom are fraternal twins, and in their eleventh year they were fully capable of wreaking as much havoc as any household needs, even without the assistance of unregulated pets.

Cousin Ribby stroked herself against the bottom cupboard where the kibble is kept, and Susie did a polka at the kitchen door.

"Some pets," I observed, "have manners, dignity and decorum."

Tom made a flying dive into my lap.

"How boring," he said, digging his head into my middle. "Joanie, make cocoa! I'll show you where the groundhog denned in for the winter."

I was losing my taste for woodland lore, but Tom's green eyes and freckles were still irresistible. I deposited him gently on the floor, dumped some chow into Ribby's dish, released Susie to the joys of the morning, now coming up grey, still windy and definitely sleety; and set to work with sugar, cocoa and milk.

"Where?"

"Oh, you have to come and see. Doesn't she, Mary?"

Mary stepped up onto the low stool she uses for cooking.

"Joanie may be busy." She measured water from the kettle into a saucepan, oatmeal into the water. Her soft, straight hair, cut in a short bob at her request, fell before her pixie face as she stirred.

"I do have a book report." I mussed Tom's hair. "Tell you what. I want to visit Miss Peterson; she didn't seem very well when I saw her on Wednesday. Give me until around ten o'clock; maybe the weather'll be better by then—it can't possibly be worse—and we'll do the groundhog's den, and you come with me to the library, too, okay?"

Miss Estelle Peterson lived over the little village library she had been managing for nearly thirty years. She was a favorite friend of us all, and Tom and Mary readily accepted my proposal. I took my coffee and *Northanger Abbey* to the far end of the table, and tried to concentrate.

"Catherine Morland reads too many Gothic novels" (I wrote),

"and her imagination runs away with her; so much is clear. General Tilney neither murdered his wife nor hastened her demise—" no, hastening demises was a cliche— "nor particularly wished her dead," that was weak but it could stand for the moment, as I wanted to see whether I could make this idea play out.

"Henry Tilney's avowed liking for novels, on the other hand, is as much an affectation as other people's insincere contempt for them; he merely goes their pretended indifference one better, by showing indifference for the kind of affected taste that finds novels"—finds novels—oh, middlebrow for the moment.

"—middlebrow. 'Dear Miss Morland,' he reproaches Catherine. 'Consider the nature of the suspicions you have entertained. What have you been judging from?' Novels, obviously. And he proceeds to read her a merciless sermon—" Sermon? Let it go for now.

"—a merciless sermon, affirming the utterly staid nature—" no, "affirming the reliable stuffiness of their surroundings and acquaintance."

Still too wordy, but this was going to work. The idea was playing as I wrote.

"What happens next, the very next thing? Henry having persuaded Catherine of her folly in imagining his father capable of 'atrocities,' and Catherine having sunk into a misery of self-reproach, his father turns around and dispatches her home, companionless, by post, exposing her both to probable social reproach and to possible danger."

I looked it over. Companionless? I was starting to write like the novelists Austen derided. But at least I had an idea under cultivation. The plot gets back at the characters, if you like. I could call the essay, "The Revenge of the Novel," if I thought Mr. Denys would see the joke.

Daddy came into the kitchen with Priscilla on his shoulders.

"Duck for the doorway, Pitts," he told her, and she did. We call her that after Miss Priscilla Buckley at *National Review*, Mother's favorite magazine. Mother is also addicted to sporting fiction— she says the only view between a horse's ears she's likely to have in the rest of this lifetime is the literary kind—and she has a rare copy of a wonderful book Miss Buckley wrote called *Pitts Falls*.

It is about her youthful adventures, and I have often thought that, given our family's inclinations, it is a good thing that Mother sees literary merit, at least, in youthful adventures.

Daddy tucked our Priscilla into the baby seat that hooks onto the table, and Mary set oatmeal in front of her.

"O is for oatmeal," said Priscilla, and flipped some from her spoon to the far wall.

"She's really getting good, Daddy," said Tom, fetching a paper towel.

"Good grief," said Martin rather loftily, as he strolled in. "Only in the O'Connor family does the three-year-old know she can do what she pleases as long as she gives it a literary accompaniment. Did you make enough for everyone, Mary?"

Mary served up steaming bowls for him and Mother and Daddy, and I gave up on criticism and added a bowl of brown sugar and a pitcher of milk to the table. Mother came in issuing grumpy good mornings, dumped Jane into Daddy's lap, grabbed a mackintosh from the row of hooks at the door and ducked out for the newspapers at the bottom of the lane.

My mother is a wonderful mother, but even my father, who presumably loves her best, will tell you that she's no use to anyone until after a cup of coffee and some newsprint. That's simply what it takes to make the world swim into focus for her.

Mother and Susie came in dripping together and shook off by the door. Mother paused theatrically at the head of the table, newspapers cradled in one arm.

"Some rocket scientist," she said, "found it amusing to plant the jangly wheeled doggy just inside the nursery door."

She impaled Tom with a cold glare. He wilted.

"As the aforementioned rocket scientist no doubt foresaw, I tiptoed in last night to check on Priscilla and Jane before retiring to my well-earned rest, tripped over the aforementioned jangly wheeled doggy, and spent the next ninety minutes walking Baby."

She paused.

Tom wiggled miserably.

"Aw, Mamma, I am sorry. I just thought how funny it would be."

"It wasn't, not one little bit."

"I guess not. I am sorry." He was thoroughly dejected, as always when a brilliant idea went awry.

Mother sighed.

"Well, darling, I guess you won't do it again." She rumpled his hair resignedly with her free hand.

"No, Mamma, never, honest."

"See that you don't, there's a good boy." She gave his head a parting push and shared the sections of newspaper around; and chaos reigned pleasantly.

At last, "Who's going to help with Christmas cleaning?" asked Mother.

"Joanie can't," said Tom. "She promised to come see the groundhog's den, and that's an obelli- obelli—"

"Obligation," Mary said flatly. "And we're going to see Miss Peterson, because she's sick; but Joanie can do her share in the afternoon."

I felt a twinge of resentment at having my whole day thus arranged, but ordered myself to let it go.

Mother closed the *New York Times* book section, which Mrs. Tonypandy at the drugstore sends up by her son Fred on Saturdays to suit Mother's views on Sunday shopping (and her own convenience, as Daddy always observes).

"What's the matter with Miss Peterson?" she asked.

"I don't really know," I said. "When I went in on Wednesday to return some things and catch up on the shelving, she looked kind of greenish. She said she'd just had a bug, but she was sort of quiet and shaky, not really like her usual self."

Mother caught Daddy's eye.

"If the kids don't find her better today," she said, "maybe Michael should look in on her." Dr. Michael Brown is our neighbor to the north, and he brought all us kids into the world, except the twins, for whom he sent Mother down to Hartford; he is also a first-rate diagnostician, and writes sometimes for medical journals, when he's not too irritated at the fads of his profession.

Daddy nodded.

"I'll see him tonight at town committee," he said. "You kids give Miss Peterson a good looking-over, and let me know if he should stop in."

I felt "You kids" meant me, and I felt pleasantly grown-up to be trusted with such a responsibility. It wasn't much to worry about, really, since with Dr. Michael one could err on the side of caution, and not worry about the bill or about the doctor's temperament. The difficult part was going to be Miss Peterson's temperament, as she was not accustomed to interference.

"In fact," Daddy continued, "I'd hate to see Miss Peterson miss tonight's meeting, because she's been shaping up for a good fight with Elva Tonypandy over the candidates' subcommittee. Estelle Peterson knows everybody in town at least as well as everybody would like; if she took over candidate recruitment it could shake things up for the general benefit of the world. Elva, however, is not about to give up turf. It could be a good war."

"Really, dear," said Mother. "In a small community there's no such thing as a good war."

"Nonsense," said Daddy. "Small communities need the air cleared more than big ones do. We get ingrown, with political bad blood recirculating like the genes of the Hatfields and the McCoys."

"Not at the table, dear," Mother said automatically, her nose already re-submersed in the book reviews. Daddy chuckled.

I poured myself some more coffee and tried to attend to my book report. Daddy went down to his office, in the sort-of-renovated barn at the side of the road; Mother finished another section of paper, and she and the twins went to root preliminary Christmas things out of the basement, with Pitts and Jane to supervise. Martin sat in the dilapidated armchair by the coal stove, absorbed in a journal of mathematics. Conditions were ideal for insightful, creative thought, and I spent ninety minutes getting nowhere. The basic idea was there, but whether it was the germ of a worthwhile essay, or something that merited only a couple of paragraphs inside something else, I could not tell. A little before ten I dug Tom and Mary out of the tangle of tissue paper attendant on setting up the creche in the living room, and we bundled up to visit the groundhog and Miss Peterson.

The wind had subsided a bit, but a freezing mist fell so thickly and foggily that if we hadn't been that way a thousand times we'd have gotten lost crossing the rocky pasture south of our house. What with its winter-low azimuth and the thick cloud cover, the sun couldn't do much. It was a couple of hours short of noon, but it looked like dim twilight. There had not been any real snow so far; only a coating of semi-frozen slush adhered to the grass, mud and boulders. We huddled into our parkas and pretended not to start when trees rose out of the murk before us. Tom was holding to his secrecy, but I figured we were headed for the abbey grounds, which lie to the south and west of our property, covering nearly 300 acres in a rough parallelogram bordered by our farm, the town, the state highway and the state forest. On the highway, state forest and town sides the abbey lands are guarded by new barbed wire, because of liability rather than unfriendliness; on our side there is a high stone wall (We gather from old letters we found in our attic that a 19th-century farmer was worried about his daughters finding the nuns' company too congenial); but we all have keys to the one gate, and the abbess has always encouraged us to play in her woods.

"The land is a responsibility," she once explained, "and there are too few of us to pay proper attention to it." In the past couple of years she had gotten out only on the level paths in good weather, but when we visited her in the abbey parlor she liked to hear our reports on her flora and fauna; and she always detailed a couple of the more country-minded younger nuns to keep what track they could of things in the woods and fields.

Sure enough, we came to the stream at the edge of our property, and the little three-log footbridge to the wall and the narrow iron gate. The bridge was as slippery as one would expect, given the conditions, but we all made it over; and Tom used his big key, copied at the hardware store from the original, to let us through.

In the woods there was less wind, and also much less light. The sleet came down in patches around the trees. It was building up on the stones of our usual path up the side of the ridge, and turning to slick muck on the dirt in between. At the top of the first rise we passed the hidden beginning of our path to the fort we'd been developing ever since Martin and I were old enough to play in the woods. The younger kids had pretty much taken it over now; I noticed that Mary paused to adjust the branches of the rogue mock orange that shielded the beginning of the trail. It wasn't really necessary. The woods are very big, by New England standards, anyway; and I thought, as we scrambled up the rest of the ridge, that if we never showed anyone else the way our fort might very well stand empty until it rotted into the ground. We would all go off into the world, and no-one would come to clear the fallen leaves and branches from the roof, and the twins' little wild garden of Virginia bluebells and trillium would be overrun by poison ivy. (That was not an extra-creepy thought, by the way. The Connecticut woods are simply crawling with the stuff.) The seasons would go around, and no-one would come; we had built well, but eventually the walls would lean and buckle; and in twenty years, or thirty, there would be only a tangle of vines in a patch of shorter trees to show where we had built, and worked, and played.

I shook myself, and hurried to catch up with the twins. We had nearly reached the level of the abbey gardens when Tom and Mary turned off the path to the left. We navigated slowly along the side of the hill for about thirty yards, and Mary turned her usual serious face up to me.

"We must be very quiet now, Joanie. We don't want to disturb him. It's too nasty out here for him."

"I'll be careful," I said. A huge old maple had fallen downhill, leaving ridges and craters where its roots had come up. Tom dropped to his hands and knees, and waved me forward to look. In the dimness, with the sleet spraying into my eyes, I had to imagine that there must be a little, narrow, winding entrance into the earth among the upturned roots, for I could not really see it.

"How do you know he's there?" I whispered.

"Shh," said Tom. "We saw him go in four times, from our blind over there" —he gestured at some low shrubbery a couple of yards away— "and we stayed here the whole afternoon the last time, and he never came out."

"That was some dedicated woodcraft," I whispered. "Look, this is really neat, but I'm freezing. Let's go."

He nodded. We began to backtrack to the path. Mary stayed behind briefly, presumably to make sure we had not disturbed Mr. Woodchuck.

We toiled on up to the edge of the plateau, where the cultivated part of the abbey lands begin, and walked single file along the path through the turnip patch. Now it seemed darker out in the open, where we could see more of the sleet, and where there ought to be distances and weren't.

Then we were in the much smaller regular vegetable gardens. The nuns make a decent profit on their turnips, selling them to fancy grocers and even directly to a few very fancy restaurants, for nobody else in the state bothers to grow them sweet and spicy, and to harvest them small and tender; but the rest of the gardens are just for the abbey's own kitchen.

We came out onto the narrow drive over which Sister Stephen, eighty and stubborn, drives the little tractor and its trailer. The drive skirts the north and east sides of the abbey buildings and cloister. I wondered whether we ought to stop in. Permission or no, I felt funny about just strolling through this way. But it had taken time to get up the side of the ridge, and if we were to see Miss Peterson and make it home by lunch, we had better move along. I made a private resolution to come up the next afternoon for a visit, in case any of the nuns had noticed us walking through and not stopping, but also because it had been several weeks since I'd been to the abbey parlor.

Some of the kids in school think it is odd that the nuns are my friends, but I'm not thinking about becoming one. They're just my neighbors.

The main abbey drive let us out onto the state road, slick and miserable. There was no traffic. The puddles that had collected in the potholes and breaks had formed skins of ice.

In five minutes we reached the village square: a little green with the traditional gazebo-type bandstand, a general store-cum-post office, the hardware store, Mrs. Tonypandy's pharmacy, a gas station, the town hall (recently renovated by subscription more or less to its original 18th-century purity) and the library. Lights showed feebly from the store windows.

The library was dark, and the front door was locked.

"Miss Peterson must be really sick," said Tom.

"Nonsense," I said, trying to feel casual. "It's a wretched day. Look, Mr. Wall has closed the gas station, too." We could see a little glow from behind the curtains of his apartment over the garage.

"Let's go around," I said, and led the way to Miss Peterson's private entrance at the side. We waited a bit after knocking, for the stairs to Miss Peterson's apartment are long and steep; but there was no response.

"Look, she's probably fine, or she's gone out," I said.

"I'm going up to see," said Mary firmly. She opened the door. "You guys can stay down here if you like, but I'd appreciate it if you didn't go home without me."

I hated the idea of gate-crashing Miss Peterson, but there were thick flakes of heavy snow mixing into the sleet; and besides, I had seniority, for whatever that was worth. If Mary was going up, I was, too.

"Come on, Tom."

The stairs were lit by a couple of night lights plugged into the wall at the bottom and the turning. After the turn there were framed engravings on both walls, although we could not see of what. A window at the landing would presumably illuminate them during the day in better weather.

We paused at the top, shoving back icy hoods and skinning off gloves. Mary took a deep breath, and knocked.

"Go away, please, Joe."

Miss Peterson's elegant tenor voice just reached us. It sounded as if she were controlling discomfort, or even pain. We looked at each other. Joe was Joe Fredericks, I assumed, the town handyman, who did work for the library as well as the town hall. He had spent some time as a chef in New Haven, and sometimes, I knew, brought meals to Miss Peterson.

None of us could think of an intelligent thing to say. Mary knocked again.

"I am sorry to be unfriendly, Joe," said Miss Peterson, "but I am quite unwell. If you've brought food, I sincerely hope it will not be wasted, but I am not a fit audience for your lovely efforts. I simply need rest. Good afternoon."

"Miss Peterson," said Tom, "It's Tom O'Connor, and Joanie and Mary. We just came to—to visit you. May we come in?"

There was a long silence, then the sound of furniture moving across the floor inside. It sounded as if she was moving chairs, or tables, or something, away from the other side of the door. Had she barricaded herself in? Suddenly I felt very worried. If Miss Peterson was going—was becoming senile or incompetent, improbable as that seemed, maybe I had no business letting the little kids see it—see her.

Before I could decide to fabricate a reason to go home, the door opened.

Miss Peterson sank into the armchair closest to the door, evidently the last thing she had moved, and for a moment I did not recognize her. Chairs, tables, even a sideboard stood in disarray behind her. She huddled into the thick blazer that her field-hockey sort of sturdiness had pretty much filled a few days before, panting from exertion. Her mouse-and-grey hair escaped from its usual highly organized twist; a loose hairpin dangled from a lank strand. She'd always been handsome, never pretty; but now the skin sank and pulled over the square bones of her face so that it really took me a few seconds to be sure it was she.

There was a moment's shocked silence; then she shifted, and tried to straighten up.

"Well, children, it is good to see you on such a morning. Do close the door, Tom; and you and Mary move some of these things back in front of it, if you will. I—I—"

She seemed to drift for a moment; then her hands tightened on the arms of the chair, and she tried once more to push herself erect. She got her breathing under control, then.

"Joan, if you would be so very kind as to put on a kettle, we can have some tea. The milk may be off, but there is a lemon. Just give me a moment to sort myself out. I—I—have been a bit under the weather, as is probably evident."

None of us had moved.

"Tom! The door, if you please. There is a nasty draft from that window on the landing, and there may be—un—unpleasant people about on such a—such a morning.

"Tom!"

He cast a frightened look at me, and closed the door. I shook myself and said, "Miss Peterson, I'll be glad to make tea, but I hope you'll forgive the interference if I also call Dr. Brown."

"I will, for I may be old and sick but I'm not such a fool as to pretend I am well. However, the telephone has been out since last night. You just help me back into the sitting room, while the twins replace the fortifications, and go ahead with the tea. I am not going to expire in the next half hour, and you can call Dr. Brown from the abbey on your way home."

I helped her down the hall. Her hand felt hot and dry on mine. "That would be pleasant," she murmured. "I should like to see Michael. Yes, indeed. And perhaps he can call—" she broke off, and sank into the one armchair that remained in the sitting room. The tiny fireplace was dark, and a cold draft spilled down the chimney and across the floor. I chucked my parka in a corner, and tried to close the damper. It stuck for a moment, and then crashed down into place. I could hear the twins moving furniture, and the radiator clanked encouragingly.

"Thank you, Joan," said Miss Peterson. "Now we'll warm up a bit. You go make the tea, if you don't mind; and then I'll try to give you some sort of reasonable explanation for all these peculiar goings-on."

I looked at her doubtfully. She managed a smile.

"Don't worry. I'm not going anywhere. You get the tea, and then I'll explain."

The kitchen was tiny, but cheerful and orderly. Miss Peterson had not bothered with the little table and chair for her barricade. I put the kettle on, and found tea, sugar, lemon, a tin of English biscuits and—most improbably—an enormous quilted cosy for the teapot, appliqued with what could only be called duckies and bunnies. It had to be a keepsake, I thought, for it was utterly foreign to Miss Peterson's usual style.

She laughed when I brought in the tray. "Now you *must* think I've gone 'round the bend," she said. "Isn't it wonderful? It was a gift from the library volunteers, the first year I was here. On the floor, I guess, is the only place at the moment."

Tom and Mary had been waiting uncertainly in the hallway, and came in to the sitting room when I did. We sat cross-legged on the floor, and Mary handed tea and biscuits up to Miss Peterson. We munched, and she nibbled a little, and said,

"Well. Maybe the best way to explain all this is to say that there has been a most ridiculous mistake. As you know, I've been working for years on an annotated edition of Butler's *Lives of the Saints*."

We nodded. Some of the people in town made fun of Miss Peterson's book, because she had been working on it for so long; but Mother had told us that she was respected as a sound scholar, and could have had a comfortable post at a good university; apparently she simply preferred being a librarian in a small town, where she could rule her own little world.

"As you may imagine, I have had occasion in the course of my work to correspond with other—other investigators, to exchange information about Butler's sources and whatnot. Anyway, it happens that one of my correspondents has also done occasional work on other sorts of projects—I may as well say for the federal government, or all this explanation will be no explanation at all.

"The confusion arose when some—some agents, if you will, of another country, never mind which one, intercepted some of our correspondence and concluded that I was also a—a cloak-and-dagger sort of person."

She laughed in a kind of embarrassed apology.

"I do realize that that sounds improbable, and silly. But mistakes do happen. Unfortunately, my—my friend only managed to warn me last week that there might be some unpleasantness, and before I could think what to do, I'm afraid his obit appeared in the *Times*."

She looked at me pleadingly.

"I'm only telling you of this rather disagreeable event because I am going to have to ask you to be a bit circumspect." She emphasized the last word, glancing at Tom and Mary, and I understood that she was hoping the twins did not know what *obit* meant.

"You mean," I said, "he was—was—"

"Just so."

We looked at the twins. They appeared to have lost the thread of the narrative.

"You couldn't just tell these—these agents that it's a mistake about you? That you're not involved?"

"I could try; but how could I prove it? When I came down with this dratted bug I decided I had better just sit tight and wait for help. Last night I admit I did rather wish I could call Dr. Michael—"

She shuddered, and I noticed again how sick she looked. I had forgotten about that part of the problem while I was listening to the spy stuff. I could not tell whether to believe in all of the latter, but part of me felt distinctly worried about it.

"Are you assuming your phone is out because of the weather?" I asked, feeling foolish.

"I've considered the possibilities," she said, "and yes, I think it is the weather."

"Our phone is working," said Tom. "Miss Peterson, maybe the spies cut your line!" His eyes shone.

"We're on a different exchange," said Mary prosaically. "Besides, the wind could take down the one line from the street to the library, and nobody would know until someone tried to use it and called the phone company."

"Quite right, Mary," said Miss Peterson. "I am sorry that it's probably not so exciting, Tom; but if you and Mary and Joan will hike through the *sturm und drang* to call Dr. Michael from the abbey phone, you'll have completed quite a heroic mission."

She regarded him gravely. "We'll let Dr. Michael decide whether to call in a specialist."

Tom was delighted at being included in the cryptic mode, even though he obviously did not understand what kind of specialist she meant. The state police barracks, I thought, or the FBI. Tom jumped up, and began to put on his parka.

Mary looked doubtfully at Miss Peterson.

"Has anyone else tried to come in today?" she asked, and I kicked myself mentally for not thinking of this.

"No," said Miss Peterson, quite calmly, "and in this weather I shouldn't think anyone will."

"Will you be able to move the furniture back after we've gone," Mary persisted, "or shall we stop off and send Joe? He could—he could climb out the window afterward," she finished somewhat lamely.

"No, don't stop for Joe," Miss Peterson said, more forcefully than the occasion warranted, I thought. "I really must ask that you children not talk to anyone about all this—this nonsense; just send Dr. Michael over as soon as possible. All right?"

She looked at me.

"Maybe you don't really have to move the furniture back," I suggested.

"It might be somewhat imprudent in my present condition," she acknowledged, "but on the whole I think it would be more imprudent not to. You should worry a little less, Joan. Just give me your word that you won't tell anyone."

"Hold it," I said. "What about Trooper Daniels? If he's not at the town hall, we could call him from there, or from the drug store."

Miss Peterson laughed.

"Joan, you're not serious."

"I guess not. He probably wouldn't believe us, and even if he did—"

"Even if he did, he would think of a way to make an even bigger mess than we have now."

I couldn't think what else to do.

"All right," I sighed. "But I don't see how not to worry." Miss Peterson smiled.

"First of all, I am simply a little weak from having a bad bug. Second of all, skullduggery nearly always takes a while and it often misses its mark. What is it your father says, when a political campaign is not going well? 'Remember, the other side has problems, too.' Now, the weather's not getting any nicer as we chat, so you children get on the road."

I still felt miserably uncomfortable. I was sure that there was something else I should think of, something else I should do, some other way to handle the situation.

The twins. If there were dangerous people in the neighborhood, they should stay here. But they would never consent to miss an adventure for that reason.

"I can go much faster by myself," I said. "Tom, you know it's true. You guys stay here with Miss Peterson."

But Miss Peterson vetoed the suggestion even faster than the twins could voice their own protest.

"No," she said firmly. "They'll be better off getting home now. You'll all be late for lunch, as it is. Mary and Tom, go along with Joan."

So she did, in fact, think it possible that the—the spies, or whatever, might come to the library today. She had said not so we wouldn't worry about her.

Oh, brother.

Mary and I began to put on our parkas and gloves, too, and Miss Peterson rose to follow us all to the door. I could see her trying not to show what an effort it was. I didn't know which to worry about more, the Soviet spies (I don't know why I was assuming they were Soviet spies) or Miss Peterson's illness. The illness was more evident at the moment.

"Will you at least have some more tea and biscuits after we go?" I asked lamely.

She laughed again.

"To make you easier in your mind, Joan, I solemnly swear that I shall eat at least three biscuits within ten minutes of your departure.

"Oh, I ought to have thought of this. My friends may send someone to check on me. What's today, December 1? St. Eligius, it'll be St. Eligius."

I felt sick. She was delirious.

"No, no, I'm not hallucinating—not yet, anyhow. If you meet a stranger who's doing research on St. Eligius, it'll be a friend. Now, get!"

She shooed us out and closed the door. As we descended the stairs, I could hear a table moving slowly across the floor. The only thing between me and panic was not wanting to frighten the twins. I wanted to run back up the stairs and get behind the barricade of furniture with Miss Peterson. I wanted a grownup to be in charge like I hadn't wanted a grownup since I was eleven and had flu.

I was last out Miss Peterson's downstairs door. I closed it quietly behind me, and looked around. It wasn't quite noon, but the streetlights had come on in front of the town hall and along the little row of shops. The wind had risen again. It drove thick flakes of wet snow down from the north. It would be in our faces all the way home.

Mary took my hand, something she rarely does. It was awkward, holding hands with our heavy gloves.

"You scared, Joanie?" she asked.

"A little," I admitted. It was better than lying and having her know it.

"Me, too," she smiled. "You know what we have to do?"

"Get to the abbey, quick?"

"That, too. But I was thinking of what the Space Marines say in that book of Tom's."

"'Shut up and soldier?'"

She grinned and let my hand go. We started up the road.

CHAPTER 2

*In our position one's always interfering with people for
their good, you know. I'm sure it's a bad habit.*
—D.L. Sayers, Busman's Honeymoon

WE TRUDGED up the side of the square, Mary and Tom and I;
and I tried to think what I should do.

Call Dr. Michael from Mrs. Tonypandy's? From Mr. Wall's?
No, Miss Peterson had said to call from the abbey. Why?

Because at any phone in the village someone would be sure to
overhear the conversation, and there would be a risk of incompetent interference. What Miss Peterson needed was *competent*
interference.

We were passing under the last street light, our heads down
against the snow and wind.

"Excuse me?"

A tall figure materialized beside me. I gasped—nearly screamed.

"I'm so sorry to startle you."

It was a tall young woman, with rather elegant black features.
She wore a heavy parka like ours, and heavy boots and gaiters; a
large nylon knapsack hung from one shoulder.

I realized I was staring. So were Tom and Mary.

"I'm so sorry to startle you," she repeated. She had a soft, deep
voice, and she spoke in the cultivated kind of way that I associate
more with older black people, like Mrs. Matthews, my history
teacher.

"I saw you leaving the library," she explained, "as I was coming
up the road; but when I knocked there was no answer, so I thought
I'd ask you. Is it open? Is it generally open on Saturday?"

19

"Sometimes," I said guardedly. Who could she be? I felt I was going to be terrible at counter-espionage, if that was what this was supposed to be.

"I am trying to find a Miss Estelle Peterson," the young woman said. "I understand she is the librarian?"

"That's right," I said.

Impasse. We looked into each other's faces, tried to read each other's minds.

"Joanie!" Tom tugged at my arm. "Joanie! Let's go home. We're going to be late for lunch. Joanie!"

"In a minute, Tom," I said absently. I was trying to think, and I was getting nowhere. Did Soviet spies go around looking like Zulu princesses? I had the idea spies were supposed to be inconspicuous.

"It's such a rotten day," I observed, trying to sound casual. "Did you leave your car in the cross street? The sand truck may come up from Cornwall that way, and it's pretty narrow."

I was congratulating myself on my cleverness, but her face relaxed a little.

"No, I hiked up from the bus on Route 45. I don't have a car, I'm a graduate student. Do you know Miss Peterson? Can you tell me where she lives?"

And I am Rudolph the Red-Nosed Reindeer, I thought.

"Sure, we know Miss Peterson," said Mary. "Why are you looking for her?"

Good for Mary. I couldn't ask without sounding suspicious, which would make the might-be spy suspicious that Miss Peterson was suspicious; but a little kid could ask.

The princess/spy smiled at Mary, then looked at me.

"I'm doing some research on a Merovingian character called Eligius," she said. "Miss Peterson's supposed to have copies of some old articles from the *Revue des Questions Historiques* that would help me a lot."

I sighed with relief, and started to raise my arm, to point the way back to the library. But Mary grabbed my wrist.

"Eligius?" she asked, as if she thought the name sounded funny.

I stared at her. Did she think the young woman might be an enemy who had gotten hold of Miss Peterson's code?

"St. Eligius," the stranger said.

In the evergreen hedge next to the sidewalk there was a *thunk*, and the strange young woman gave a muffled cry and fell to her knees. She grabbed at Mary on the way down, and pulled her to the sidewalk.

"Hey," Mary protested. I heard someone running along the other side of the shrubbery, back toward the library. I thought the footsteps turned, then, into the side street; but a gust of wind interfered with my hearing.

"What are you doing?" demanded Tom.

The young woman was breathing fast, in short gasps. She let go of Mary, who scrambled back to her feet.

"Are you all right?" I asked, stupidly.

"I will be in a second, I think."

She eased herself into a more comfortable position, sitting on the curb, now, and glanced up and down the empty road.

"Did you see which way our friend went?"

"I didn't *see* anyone," I said, "but I think I heard him turn up the cross street."

"Umph." She pulled off her right gaiter, which showed a rough tear across the back. The heavy sock underneath was torn at the back of the calf, too; and blood was spreading around the tear. She looked up at me, and winked.

"He'd better watch out for the sand truck."

I had been completely obvious, then. I blushed.

"What are you going to do? Shouldn't we call Trooper Daniels?" For the second time that morning, I realized that that was a dumb idea even as I said it.

"Why not Sergeant Preston? Who the devil is Trooper Daniels?"

"The Resident State Trooper. North Salisbury is too small to have a police force, so we have a Resident State Trooper. He gets a house and a car, and he's pretty much it for law enforcement around here."

"Is he unusually intelligent for a state trooper?"

The twins and I laughed. It was a let-up from the scare.

"I see. No, I don't think we'd better call Trooper Daniels."

"But you're supposed to report gunshot wounds," I persisted lamely. "It's the law."

"Yeah, and you're not supposed to shoot people," she retorted, "and that's the law, too." She pulled a gauze pad and an elastic bandage, the tube-shaped kind that athletes use, from a pocket of her knapsack. She held the pad over the wound, and worked the elastic up onto her calf to hold it in place. I heard her hiss through clenched teeth as she drew it on. It must have hurt like anything. Whatever she was, this strange young woman was no chicken.

"There." She pulled the gaiter back on, stood up and tried the leg, regarding it with scientific detachment. "I think that'll be OK for a while, anyway. Can I persuade you now to tell me where Estelle Peterson lives? Like before Roscoe there with the gun finds her?"

I tried again to think, with no better result than I'd been having all morning.

"Look," I finally said, "OK, we did see her this morning, but she's not feeling well, in fact she has a terrible bug, and I don't think she's really up for company. You don't need to do your research on Saint Whoever this morning; you need to get to a doctor. We'll take you to our friend Dr. Michael Brown; he lives just up the road, and he's probably at home. If he isn't he soon will be."

"Actually, I don't need a doctor. I have some more first-aid stuff in my pack, and camping gear, too, if it comes to that, and it looks like it might, if you won't tell me how to find Miss Peterson. Have you seen any other strangers besides me this morning?"

I looked her in the eye. "No, which in this town probably means there aren't any, except for your friend with the gun, of course; and if he went the way I think he went, he doesn't know where she is, either."

I took a breath. "I'm not going to tell you how to find Miss Peterson. She's sick. She doesn't want to be bothered. Saint Whoever can wait until Monday, or until next year, for all I care." So there.

She surprised me by nodding agreement.

"All right. I'll wait until Monday morning, and see her at the library. What's the shortest way to the state forest?"

"To the *what*?"

"There aren't any motels or inns around here. I know, I checked before I came. So I need a place to stay until Monday. I'll camp out."

"In the middle of a snowstorm? You're hurt, you need medical attention."

"I just told you. I can give myself medical attention. Which way is the state forest?"

"Joanie." Mary tugged at my arm. I bent down. She whispered in my ear.

"The fort. We can take her to the fort. If she's a friend of Miss Peterson, we can find out and bring her back here. If she's—if she's not, we'll be able to tell—to tell whoever we're supposed to tell, where she is. It's better than having her wandering around loose."

I straightened up and expostulated. "This is a really stupid situation. We're standing here talking in the snow and wind, and I don't care what you say, you need a doctor, and my little sister wants to play cops and robbers, or spies, or whatever, and my mother is wondering what's become of us. All right. All right! You're not a graduate student, and I know it, and you know I know it. You're probably a friend of Miss Peterson, or a friend of her friends, and you're probably here to help her, or protect her; but right now you need some protecting, yourself, if you ask me, and if you *are* her friend, you don't want to go to her house right now, because whoever shot you might see you go there, and follow you in, and besides you couldn't get in, because she's got the door barricaded with all her furniture."

I realized as I said it how stupid it was, but my temper had run away. I was furious at having to make dangerous decisions on the basis of inadequate information, furious at having been frightened by the gunshot, furious at having seen the stranger pull Mary down—sure, it was no doubt to protect her, but the world had no business firing guns around Mary to begin with, or—or attracting gunfire to her vicinity. Or Tom's. Or mine, for that matter.

There was just the briefest pause.

"That's the most intelligent thing you've said so far," the stranger said approvingly. "You're quite right. Our friend with the gun will probably decide that it's easier to find her on Monday, too. I don't suppose you can give me the additional reassurance of knowing that she lives on a second floor or anything?"

I hesitated. My instinct was to trust this woman, but I wasn't trusting my instinct. Tom had no such qualms.

"Yup," he said cheerfully. "It'd take five KGB colonels or a bunch of plastique to get in there, and your friends don't want to use plastique if they can help it, do they? I mean, as you said, they probably figure they can wait until Monday and find her at the library, too, right?"

Tom grabbed her hand. What had made him decide about her? "Come on," he said. "You gotta come to our fort. It's really neat. It's much better than camping in the state forest. Come and see. Come and see."

I still felt horribly worried, but Tom's utter normalcy was somehow cheering. I still wasn't trusting my instinct, but I was almost ready to trust his.

We started up the road again, Tom still holding the young woman's hand.

"What's your name?" he asked.

"Agnes Breslin," she said. "Black Irish." She winked at me again.

"I'm Tom O'Connor, and this is Joanie, and this is Mary. We're twins, but I'm bigger."

"Yes," she said gravely, "I can see that. I imagine you're stronger, too, aren't you?"

She smiled over at Mary as she said it; Mary caught her eye and smiled back, enjoying the superiority of a feminine conspiracy on male vanity. I was deeply impressed. I knew black Irish wasn't supposed to mean Agnes' kind of blackness, but Irish certainly fit her in terms of charm.

"Let me take your pack," I offered. "You've got enough to manage with that leg."

She considered briefly.

"How far is it to your fort?"

"At this rate, about fifteen minutes, but some of it is rocky, and it'll be slippery. You'll need not to be worn out."

She unslung the pack from her shoulders, and dug down into it to pull something up from the bottom. She tucked whatever it was into her parka. A gun, I thought. Oh, Lord.

I took the pack. It was quite heavy. Agnes helped me to adjust it on my shoulders.

"Thanks very much. I've got some Tylenol, and some codeine, for that matter, but anything like that makes me groggy and I don't want to use them unless I have to. That helps a lot."

There was still no traffic at all, so we made our insane parade up the snowy road four abreast. Right after the village green, the abbey fence began on our left, and the first woods and pastures, the Golds', on our right. As I have said, it is a small town. Ordinarily I regard that as a blessing; as we tromped north with the wet snow driving in our faces, and forty imaginary KGB operatives following close behind, I thought how pleasant it would be to be able to stop at a house and ask to use a telephone. Only there aren't many houses in North Salisbury. The dirt lane leading to the Golds' house was at least as long as the distance along the main road to the abbey.

One thing was certain. Whatever promise Agnes extracted from us about not telling anyone about her or the events of the morning, I was going to have a formal mental reservation. The situation was definitely beyond the capacity of one teenager and a couple of imaginative little kids; and if you asked me, it was beyond Agnes' own capacity, too. I didn't know how high-level a spy she was supposed to be, assuming she was on our side—Miss Peterson's side, whatever side that was. Maybe she was shocky from the gunshot wound, and so not operating up to par; but I was far from sure that Agnes giving herself first aid in our fort and preparing to camp out for the next forty-two hours represented a complete assurance of Miss Peterson's safety—or of her own. She was in over her head as much as we were, and it was time to call for help. As soon as we got home, Mother and Daddy were going to hear the whole story, and they could decide whether to call the police, or the CIA, or whoever. Did the CIA have a branch office

in Hartford? They could jolly well send someone on a special
flight from Washington, if they had to. They had made this mess,
at least partly, and they could come and clean it up.

We got Agnes into the abbey drive without further incident.
"What is this?" she asked, as the abbey buildings came into
view. "New Foundation of St. Lucy, O.S.B.," I said. "Officially, you
are a trespasser. We have permission for ourselves, but not for
anyone else. So watch yourself."

"O.S.B.? Benedictines? Monks or nuns?"

I was surprised that she knew so much.

"Nuns. Real ones, not social workers in stretch pants. You'd better watch out."

Either she was a little cowed or she thought my warning unwor-
thy of reply. She was limping noticeably by the time we crossed
the turnip field. I offered her a hand at the top of the path, but she
shook her head.

Tom held us up just before the hidden turning to the fort.

"Just a minute," he said. "Agnes, do you believe in God?"

"Absolutely," she said readily. "Why?"

"Fine," said Tom. "Then raise your right hand, please, and
repeat after me. I, Agnes Breslin, do solemnly swear that I will
reveal the existence and location of this fortress to nobody at all,
not ever, unless a majority of the O'Connors say it's OK. So help
me God."

Lawyer's kid, he remembered to check for religion before taking an oath. She repeated it after him straight-faced. Mary held up
the branch of the mock orange, and Tom led her in. She was limping very heavily now. Mary and I followed.

The fort had begun as just brush, but when Martin was fourteen
he had dug deep holes for footings, and we had erected pressure-
treated uprights for the walls. They were otherwise still just brush,
but tightly woven, and they extended around the entrance to shelter the fireplace, which was open to the sky. The doorway and the
two windows had canvas curtains that could roll up, like a tent's,
and the roof slanted back to shed rain and snow. Agnes opened her
pack, and we brought our treasures out of the big sea-chest in the

back corner. I blessed Martin's determination that had gotten it up the path two years before. We were able to offer our guest a ground-cloth, an old-fashioned folding camp bed, a set of nested cooking pots and a little white-gas stove. There were a plastic box of Bisquick, one of dried apricots, a box of teabags and an unopened jar of peanut butter.

"This is positively palatial," said Agnes, unrolling a mummy-type sleeping bag on the bed. "I was not actually looking forward to the possibility of being out for a night or two at this time of year, even though I generally like camping; but this is going to be very nice."

"This is going to be very miserable," I corrected her. "You're wet, you're cold, you're injured, if you're not hungry you're going to be; and you don't have adequate means to remedy any of that. What are you going to *do* for the next forty hours?"

"I have a couple of good books in my pack," she said cheerfully.

"What about water? Is there a clean stream or something?"

"Just go back to the main path and down a bit," I said. "We've drunk it all our lives. It comes from a spring on the abbey ridge. Actually, Tom can fill one of those pots for you now."

Tom ran off to do that. Agnes put some medical stuff on the ground cloth, plunked herself down in front of it, and started doing things to her leg. I looked away. The wind was noisy outside now, but only a little draft made it through our walls.

"Obviously," Agnes said, "you had some idea before I turned up of getting help for Miss Peterson. Presumably she told you what she wanted you to do. No, I don't want to know what. She knows her own business.

"Equally obviously—ick, I thought there was some fabric buried in there, innnnf—ee—equally obviously, I have to ask you to give me a solemn promise not to tell anyone at all about me. I can't *make* you promise, of course—"

"You're not into hostage-taking?" I couldn't help it. I was still angry, and I remembered her gun. She wasn't so helpless, in some ways; and she was acting as if she simply depended on our mercy or our honor.

"No," she said rather tiredly. "I am not into hostage-taking."

Tom came back with the water; and Agnes watched him arrange the little camp stove.

"I am more sorry than I can say," she continued, "that you people got dragged into this mess, and I am trying to figure out how to resolve it without your having any more to do with it. I rather imagine Miss Peterson is doing the same. Now, will you promise, or do I have to get myself over to the state forest?"

"I promise," said Mary. She had found a ball of twine in the sea chest, and with that and her Swiss Army knife had been busy repairing the lashing of our low table; she looked up at Agnes as she spoke, and the look was little short of adoration. Good heavens. "I promise," said Tom, with equal fervor.

"Good grief," I said. "All right. I'm not going to be the proximate cause of your getting lost in the state forest and getting gangrene and getting amputated."

"You mean you promise, too?" she persisted. Had she read my mind about the reservation? What would she do if I refused? I couldn't imagine. She really didn't seem well-cast for a terrorist. In for a lamb, in for a sheep, or whatever, in respect of my formal reservation.

"Ok, yes, I promise." With a mental reservation. So there, Miss Cosmopolitan Spy. You can't do anything about a mental reservation.

"Thank you. Then you'd better get about getting whatever help you were going to get for Miss Peterson. Uh, was it competent help?"

"More competent than yours," I couldn't resist saying. Why was this woman irritating me so much? It wasn't just that I wasn't sure of her good faith as regarded Miss Peterson. It was her social polish, her adroitness. Nobody snows Tom, and especially nobody snows Mary. In spite of the apparent flub of getting shot, I had a feeling Agnes Breslin was very competent. I liked that, and I resented the hell out of it, too.

"All right," I said. "At least one of us will get back here this afternoon or this evening with some more food and whatnot. And we're going to ask you again about seeing Dr. Brown. I guess you're over twenty-one and we can't make you, but you think about it. And remember:" (at this I felt truly sophisticated, a world-class manipulator) "you extracted a promise from us, but you made an implicit promise, yourself, to stay here. You may think this is a New England town and not a wilderness, but there isn't anything much around here, and you could very easily get lost enough that nobody would know where you were until the crows found the remains in March. Stay put, OK?"

She surprised me again, by offering me her hand, gravely.

"OK. Thank you."

I thought fast as we made our way back to the main path. Back up to the abbey telephone, or home? The abbey, I decided. It was less than ten minutes away, and home was nearly twenty. If anything happened to Miss Peterson because of that extra ten minutes' delay in reaching Dr. Brown, I would never be able to forget it. I pushed down my glove to look at my watch. A quarter past twelve. Good Lord, what a morning.

We made it back up the ridge in record time, and trotted—we none of us had it in us for running, and the ice was spreading from the puddles to the rest of the ground—up the lane to the main entrance of the abbey.

Most of St. Lucy's was only built in the early '70s, but the fathers of three of the founding sisters were wealthy contractors and another was a heavy-duty investment banker—another sister, I mean, not another father. The walls are of the lovely silver-and-gold stone that you see at Yale and at some of the New Haven churches that were built in the '30s. The polished tile floors begin in the vestibule, and the door is of massy, polished oak. Sister Maura, one of the extern nuns, opened it, and we blew in on a burst of wet snow. The extern nuns are the ones who go out of the abbey enclosure to do business with the world—marketing the turnips, buying groceries and so forth.

"*Deo gratias*," said Sister Maura. "What a morning for a visit! Come in, children, come in. Did you want to see anyone special?"

Sister Maura is tall and spare, with a pleasant, homely face. She is somewhere in her fifties or sixties; it is difficult to tell about ages with wimples and healthy living. She led us into the abbey parlor, which is divided down the middle by an old-fashioned grille—a sort of fence extending from floor to ceiling. All our visits with these neighbors are conducted through the grille. We don't think twice about it. As Sister Maura explained once, many of the nuns who first took over St. Lucy's from its fading original order, and many who came in the first few years, were pretty much refugees from places that had gotten very worldly. Whether because the senior management of the Benedictines thought it best to have a safety valve for people who didn't want to be up to date, or because they sympathized with the retrograde tendency, the grille, the old habit, and the rest of the fourteen-hundred-year-old rule of which they are the most obvious signs are as secure at St. Lucy's as the laws of thermodynamics are elsewhere.

"You could see it as a great, big Do Not Disturb sign," Sister Maura once said, "except that anybody who wants us can always find us. The enclosure doesn't stop communication, really; it just damps down the random noise."

As always in winter, thrifty little fires burned on the twin hearths to either side of the grille; there were upholstered chairs on the public side, and sturdy plain ones on the cloistered side.

"Hello, Sister Maura," I said. "Could we use the telephone? It's kind of an emergency."

"I should think you could," said Sister Maura. "I'll get it for you, and call Sister Mark."

She fished a key from the bunch that hung at the waist of her black habit, let herself through the gate in the grille and picked up the telephone that stood on a little table on the other side.

"What number?"

I told her Dr. Brown's number, and she passed the receiver through the grille, and disappeared. I knew better than to try to prevent her from calling Sister Mark, the subprioress. At St. Lucy's, everything is automatically referred upward.

"Hello?"

"Mrs. Brown, it's Joanie O'Connor. Is Dr. Brown available, please?"

"Oh, hello, Joanie. No, I'm so sorry. He went down to Norfolk to do some errands, heaven help us in this weather. His nephew's coming for a couple of weeks—you remember Nicholas—and we needed more supplies. College boy's appetite, you know. It isn't an emergency, is it?"

"No, I mean, yes, but not in our family—"

Sister Maura and Sister Mark came in. Sister Mark is as little and round as Sister Maura is tall and thin. She is about the same age, with a sweet, pretty face, but she is nobody's fool. She watched me rather closely, I thought, as I spoke to Mrs. Brown.

"—It's a friend of ours, uh, two friends, actually; uh, it's kind of difficult to explain over the phone. When is he coming back?"

"Soon, I should think. He left quite early. Can I have him call you, Joanie?"

"I'm at the abbey now, but I'll be going home right away. Yes, please, I'd really appreciate it if he could call me there as soon as he can. Thanks a lot, Mrs. Brown."

"No problem, Joanie. You go on home and sit tight."

"Thanks, Mrs. Brown. Good-bye."

"Good-bye."

Sister Maura hung up the phone for me, and I looked at Sister Mark.

"We brought somebody to our fort," I told her. Tom started to protest, and I waved him off.

"I'll explain later," I told him.

"A friend of yours?" asked Sister Mark.

"A new acquaintance," I said, determined to be truthful. "We didn't know what to do with her, so we took her to the fort. I don't think she'll give you any trouble, but I wanted to tell you."

"And she needs a doctor?" Sister Mark asked, quite calmly.

"She says she doesn't, and she's a grownup; but I say she does," I said. "She might be there until Monday morning, though, if that's OK."

Sister Mark considered briefly.

"Perhaps someone should go and look in on her."

I had an immediate vision, over-imaginative probably, of a nun surprising Agnes and getting herself shot.

"No, no, I don't think that's necessary; if it's all right with you, we'll take responsibility for her, and see that she sees Dr. Brown, and see that she doesn't make a mess or anything."

"She won't make a mess," Mary said. "I can tell."

"Me, too," said Tom.

Sister Mark looked at us gravely. "I am concerned," she said, "that you may be trying to handle something rather difficult."

"We're trying to handle something beyond us," I said. "So we're going to get Dr. Brown, and whatever other help we need. I know it sounds silly, but please don't send anyone down there. It might be—oh, well, it might be dangerous."

She raised one eyebrow. Sister Mark was an elementary-school principal before she became a contemplative, and she can raise one eyebrow to very good effect; but she said only, "I see. Can we leave it like this? Will you undertake to come back here, let's say before noon tomorrow, to let me know that your—your friend is getting competent care? It is not exactly the height of camping season, you know."

"You don't have to tell me." I shivered. "I guess compared to most times and places that human beings have survived, she's got decent shelter and food and whatnot. But one of us'll be back by noon tomorrow, Sister, I promise. Probably we can even let you know when we come to Mass."

"All right, Joanie. You are decent, reliable children; and I shall trust your judgment until then."

I realized I had been half-hoping she would insist on intervening.

"Oh, thank you, Sister. We'll see you tomorrow. And thank you for letting us use the phone," I said to Sister Maura.

"Be careful going home," she said. Sister Mark caught her eye, and she came through the grille to see us out.

"Good-bye."

"Good-bye."

Outside was truly filthy now. The snow had turned back to heavy sleet, driving down hard on the north wind.

"Joanie, you told," said Tom as we headed for the turnip field for what I fervently hoped was the last time that day.

"I had a mental reservation," I said, slogging through an enormous half-frozen mud puddle because I was not attending to where I was going. "When I promised Agnes not to tell, I had a mental reservation. That means I could tell for a good reason."

"That sounds like a cas—cashew—"

"Casuistry," said Mary.

"Casuistry, shmasuistry," I exploded. "Let's just get home now, please, OK? We can talk about it when we get dry."

We descended the ridge path without another word, mostly sitting down. If we had tried to stand, sitting down is what we would have been doing anyway; so we slid and bumped our way from rock to slippery rock, while I wondered whether I was fit to have children entrusted to my care. I felt more like a child, myself, than I had in a long time. I wanted dry clothes, a fire, hot food, and above all a grownup to take over my worries.

I wondered also how many times I was going to have to half-tell the story before I could get rid of the whole responsibility. Surely Dr. Brown would call as soon as we got home, and I could turn the entire thing over to him.

We passed the turning to the fort, and I spared a thought for Agnes the person, as opposed to Agnes the problem. If Dr. Brown didn't take over—or Daddy, or both of them—I would come back right after lunch with supplies for her.

Daddy, Martin and Priscilla were already eating lunch when we came into the kitchen and began to shed our soaked and frozen outer clothes. Jane was presumably asleep upstairs. Mother was on the telephone; I thought it must be Dr. Brown returning my call, but Mother just shot me an angry look and went on listening.

"Joan, you are very late," said Daddy.

"I'm sorry, Daddy, we couldn't call. Miss Peterson's phone is out, and Daddy, I have to talk to you. It's important."

"Uncle Jerry had another heart attack this morning," he said. "We'll be leaving for Boston as soon as we've eaten and packed. Jane and Priscilla will have to come with us, obviously, and Mary and Tom. You and Martin may stay here on your own, if you will give us your solemn word that you'll keep up with school, avoid anything even a little bit hare-brained, and check in with Mrs. Brown every morning and evening. Is that understood?"

"Yes, Daddy. When will you be back?"

"I should think Monday evening, or Tuesday at the latest."

I couldn't tell how much he was angry at me for being late, and how much was worry over Uncle Jerry. Uncle Jerry is Mother's elder brother. He is a busy banker, and we are mostly stick-at-home people, so we don't see him much; but that doesn't mean we don't care about him. Now that I really looked at Mother, I could see that she was being remote and resolute, the way she gets on the very rare occasions that something really bothers her.

"All right, Mary," she said into the telephone. "We'll be there just as soon as we can. In this weather, there's no point in trying to predict when that will be. Hang on to your prayers, and we'll say some, too.

"—Yes, dear. 'Bye for now."

"Is he all right?" I asked her.

"Joanie, you are inexcusably late," she snapped.

"I'm sorry, Mother, really I am," I said miserably. "Miss Peterson's phone was out and we couldn't call. Is Uncle Jerry all right?"

"We won't know much for a few hours," she sighed. "If you're staying here, we'll call you as soon as there is anything to tell. I suppose I'd better eat."

She picked up a half sandwich from the platter on the table, looked unenthusiastically at it, and put it back down.

Tom and Mary had been conferring in whispers at their end of the table. Mary emerged as spokesman.

"Mother," she said, "We want to stay here with Martin and Joanie. We promise to be very, very good, and do our work, and go to bed. We love Uncle Jerry, too, but the hospital wouldn't let us see him last time, and we don't want to hang around the waiting room for a couple of days. OK, Mother?"

She was obviously trying to sound very serious and grown-up, but the effect was to make her seem younger than usual. If the situation had been less grave, I would have laughed at Tom, who was clearly suppressing his impulse to beg in the interest of diplomacy.

"No, Mary, I'm sorry," Mother said automatically. "All right, let me think a minute." She sighed again. I held my breath. I knew perfectly well that Tom and Mary didn't want to go to Boston in small part because they didn't want to sit in the hospital waiting room, and in large part because they didn't want to miss the Adventure of Miss Peterson and Agnes. In the question of whether I ought now to spill all the beans to Daddy and Mother, or manage on my own with Agnes and Dr. Brown, I was madly trying to balance off what I wanted to do (spill all the beans, pronto) against what I couldn't figure out about what I ought to do (my parents didn't need the burden of a new problem from the outside right now; or, however grumpy they were going to be about it, I should be brave and tell them everything and leave it up to them how involved they wanted to be).

In the end, cowardice won. I couldn't find the words to start the story. And as I was deciding to leave Mother and Daddy out of the problem of Miss Peterson and Agnes, I was fervently wishing they would insist on taking the twins to Boston. I didn't want to be thinking about their safety—or their socks and their bedtime, for that matter—while I was trying not to mess up my job of counter-espionage.

Mother's thinking lasted about a minute.

"Martin," she said, "are you willing to be completely serious about watching over the twins? You can drop them at the Browns', I imagine, for Monday, anyway; two more are hardly going to make much difference there, and we've taken care of their lot often enough. I'll call Louise in a minute. But if there is any problem, you or Joanie might have to stay home from school for one day, or at the most two, and I don't like that. What do you say?"

I tried like anything to telegraph No to Martin. He saw it, but of course he thought I just didn't want the responsibility. He looked a little surprised at me, and I felt misunderstood and frustrated.

"Sure, Mother," he said. "Please don't worry about it. It's no good for the kids to be stuck in the hospital waiting room, even if from their point of view it's just a matter of not wanting to be bored. It'll be Germ City, among other things. Joanie and I can take care of them, you know that. You just go pack, and go take care of Aunt Mary, and everything'll be fine here. There's plenty of food, we all have schoolwork to do, we'll go to Mass at the abbey tomorrow, and Monday if the high school is open we'll drop the twins at the Browns;' otherwise we'll just all sit tight right here. Now go pack.''

He sounded awfully mature at the end of this speech, almost as if he were somehow taking care of Mother. She looked a little surprised at him; so did I. I mean, I can remember Martin as a moderately rotten ten-year-old. But Mother half-smiled, and nodded.

"All right," she said. "All right. It's probably best, in fact, if you two—" she looked hard at the twins— "will absolutely be on your very best behavior."

"We'll be absolute angels, Mamma," said Tom, released at last from silence. "You'll see."

Martin rose.

"I'm going to make some space in my room," he said. "Tom can sleep with me, and Mary can sleep with Joanie."

"I'll go get my dolls," said Mary joyfully.

Daddy and I were left at the table with Priscilla.

"Joanie, a lot of this responsibility is going to fall on you," he said. "You haven't said anything. What did you want to talk to me about? You said it was important, and we just beat you up for being late and went making plans without your say-so. What's up?"

I looked at the worry lines around his mouth.

"It can wait," I said. "I do want to talk to you, but it can wait until you get back from Boston."

"Is it a boy?" he asked. I laughed.

"No, Daddy, it isn't a boy, and it can wait. It's OK, honest. We'll probably even have a good time, except for worrying about Uncle Jerry. What are the statistics on second heart attacks, do you know?"

"Not at all, I'm sorry. We can ask Michael. I have to call him, anyhow, to give him my proxy for town committee. Oh, and how was Miss Peterson? How selfish we are. I meant to ask Michael to check on her, if you thought it was necessary."

"She's not very well, Daddy. I think Dr. Michael ought to go see her as soon as he gets back."

"Gets back?"

This was why I was going to be a lousy spy.

"Uh, I didn't get a chance to tell you. We called him from the abbey, actually, but he wasn't home. Mrs. Brown said she'd have him call us here as soon as he got back."

"You mean she's seriously ill?" If he noticed the fact that having called Dr. Brown from the abbey we could have called home, too, Daddy forebore mentioning it.

"I don't know, Daddy. How can I tell? What do I know? I just thought she looked crummy, and—and somebody who knew something should check it out."

He nodded.

"So we'll wait for Michael to call. If he's not back by the time we leave, would you please tell him he has my proxy for town committee? I'll leave a form, in case anyone tries to be silly about it."

"Sure, Daddy, I'll tell him."

Daddy and Priscilla went to find paper for his proxy, and I was left alone in the kitchen. I vented some spleen on the coal stove, which was nearly out, and tried to think what provisions Agnes might need for a night at the fort.

Or could we bring her back here? With Mother and Daddy gone, and nobody to ask questions, why not? She ought to be willing to come; it wouldn't mean spreading knowledge of her existence or whereabouts any further, except for Martin; and if she trusted me and the twins she might as well trust him. It occurred to me then that Tom and Mary might already have thought of this, the little schemers. I was going to have a few things to say to them once Mother and Daddy were gone. Playing on my unwillingness to worry them, forsooth.

Mother, Daddy, Pitts and Jane packed into the car without much further ado. Mother had called Mrs. Brown about being the check-in person; Dr. Brown was still not home. Because of the weather we said our good-byes at the kitchen door.

"There are some new story-books," Mother told Martin and me, "on the top middle book shelf in the living room. They have pictures to color, and word lists for spelling. If the twins start to look like they need directed activity—"

"Please quit worrying," said Martin. "We're bigger and smarter, and it's only a couple of days. Give our love to Aunt Mary." He hugged her, and again I thought how mature he suddenly seemed. Mother hugged me, too.

"You two are two rocks. I don't really feel much worried. We'll call you tonight, or in the morning if we get in too late."

The four of us, and Susie, watched from the kitchen window as the car slid slowly down to the main road. They were gone.

CHAPTER 3

He had shown himself ready in a crisis, instant in action.
—John Buchan, Castle Gay

"ALL RIGHT, you two," Martin told the twins. "This isn't Liberty Hall. Settle down with something quiet and constructive, like coloring a map or learning some spelling words, pronto. And if you doze off for a nap in the process, so much the better."

"Not today, Martin," Mary said firmly. "There are spies out to kill Miss Peterson, and we have to rescue Agnes."

Because of Mary's unblemished record of unimaginativeness, I guess, Martin began by being ready to believe the whole story. The twins let me tell most of it, and Martin hardly interrupted, except for a suppressed exclamation when I came to the gunshot.

"Why the devil didn't you tell Dad?" he asked when I finished. "Oh, never mind, I understand. Oh, for crying out loud. What do we do now?"

"Obviously we have to bring Agnes here," said Tom. Just as I thought.

"We who?" said Martin. "Somebody has to be here to answer the telephone when Dr. Brown calls, and you guys should not go back out in that mess."

"Oh, yeah? Well, you didn't see Miss Peterson, so it shouldn't be you who talks to Dr. Brown; and Agnes doesn't know you, so if you go alone to get her from the fort she might shoot you. So Joanie stays here to wait for the phone, and you come with Mary and me to the fort."

"Like hell," I said; and before I could elaborate Martin agreed.

"Like hell, indeed. You guys are not going back out today. I can tell Dr. Brown about Miss Peterson, and your mysterious friend, too; Joanie can go retrieve the latter from the fort. (Sorry, Joanie, but I can't see any better plan.) And you, Agent ten and a half, and you, Agent ten and forty-nine fiftieths, are going to go upstairs and settle down for an hour. Now. Otherwise I will guarantee that the next time Mother and Daddy go out of town, you go with the babies."

"Aw, Martin—"

"Real spies know they need some down time now and then. Ask your friend Agnes. Come on. We'll wake you up if you're asleep when she gets here, and you can help with the debriefing. Now, march."

He showed me crossed fingers behind his back as he herded them up the stairs. Another mental reservation. I felt almost as relieved as I planned to feel when Dr. Brown stepped in.

Since Martin was being a hero and controlling the twins, I figured I might as well clear away the lunch dreck. I was browning some onions and beef to start a stew for dinner when Martin returned. He turned on the intercom, so that he could hear if the twins started to raise Cain.

"I put them both in my room," he said. "Easier to keep track of. Ten to three they're asleep in ten minutes, after the morning they had. That smells good." I dumped in some herbs and an ice tray of beef stock cubes from the freezer, covered the pot and set the fire low.

"If they wake up and you need to keep them busy," I said, "you can have them make bread. When Dr. Brown calls, I think Miss Peterson is more urgent than Agnes. I have dry liners for my boots, but can I borrow your parka? Mine is soaked."

"Sure. I think you're right. I don't like any of this, either, but I can't think of anyone else we can call, can you?"

"No, short of the CIA itself, and something tells me not to try that, at least not right away."

"Yeah, me, too, like for example they would think we were a couple of crack-brained kids. They must be like any other bureaucracy: what are the chances of getting through to the right person? And also, if Agnes is who she seems to be saying she is, we don't have any business going over her head. Be careful, OK?"

"Not to worry. Not much to be careful about, actually, except for the ice. See you when."

"Right-oh."

He settled back down with his mathematics, and I started to buckle on his parka.

"Martin?"

"Hmm?"

"Do you think we should let Agnes decide when to see Dr. Brown? Or whether to see him?"

"She was really set against it?"

"So I gathered."

He pondered. "Legally, he is required to report a gunshot wound."

"It could be anything."

"You don't really know that. You're not a doctor and you're not a cop."

"So we wait until she gets here to talk about it?"

"I suppose. I don't want to be an accessory to gangrene any more than you do, or an accessory to Dr. Brown's getting into trouble, or an accessory to your Agnes's getting into trouble."

"She's more Tom and Mary's Agnes, and she's already in trouble, if you ask me."

"You'd better get going."

"I go, I go, see how I go."

The weather was no better, but somehow I felt better for having Martin in on things. The snow and sleet had accumulated into a couple of inches of slush, and I couldn't tell what was slush-on-top-of-mud and what was slush-on-top-of-puddle until I stepped in them. I needn't have bothered with the dry boot liners.

Crossing the low field to the abbey wall, I asked myself why I had been so angry. The random events of the day had conspired to make my decisions for me, starting with the visit to the groundhog, although that certainly was nothing to get bent out of shape over. Neither was any other individual event, but the pattern was galling. In the light of the pattern, if you could call it a light, starting a stew was a kind of voluntary putting my neck in the yoke: better to take on one job than to have another put on me. It would have been simpler to thaw hamburger meat and rolls, but at least the stew was my own idea, and not something that happened *to* me.

The key stuck in the frozen lock of the abbey gate, and I wondered why I hadn't had the sense to foresee it. I couldn't imagine why Martin might have matches in his pocket, as nobody in our family smokes, but it was certainly worth checking, compared to hiking home for some. In the inner pocket there was a butane lighter. Why? I might have some fun later, twitting Martin. Meanwhile, I held the flame alternately under the lock and under the key. The metal housing at the top of the lighter grew threateningly hot, but I couldn't manage with my bulky glove. On the third try, the key turned.

I went up the path mostly on hands and knees, hauling myself over the slippery rocks and through the slush and mud, and wondering how in the world Agnes was going to make it down. Sitting and sliding, probably; actually, a bad leg might not matter so much for that form of locomotion, as long as she didn't go into an uncontrolled skid and hit something.

I made plenty of noise approaching the fort, and said, "Agnes?" when I was within earshot.

"Speak, friend, and enter," she called quite cheerfully from within.

I did. She had pulled the table over to the camp bed. A little flashlight sat upon it, and a couple of books and a mug of tea. She was propped up on an elbow on the bed, next to her sleeping bag, reading.

"You like Tolkien, then?" I asked, having located her quotation after a moment's thought.

"Everybody who isn't a beast likes Tolkien," she said. "I do admire your fort tremendously. It's quite tight to the wind—practically winterized. I suppose it would spoil the atmosphere if you piped in the water."

"So it would. How is your leg?"

"Miserable, but not life-threatening. How is Miss Peterson?"

I felt a pang of guilt, not having thought specifically about her for a couple of hours—except as part of the situation.

"We don't know anything. Dr. Brown was out. He's probably called my house by now, and my brother Martin will have told him."

"Brother Martin, eh? Would you like some tea? What else will Brother Martin tell Dr. Brown?"

"No, thank you. Nothing, for the moment, although we hope to persuade you to have him look at your leg."

"We, is it?"

"I had a mental reservation."

She stared at me for a moment, and I was afraid—not afraid of her gun or anything, just socially afraid.

But she laughed.

"Listen to the jejune Jesuit! So Brother Martin is coming up to talk to me, too?"

"We were hoping you would come down and stay at our house. Our parents had to go to Boston, so it's just us, and we won't tell anyone about you unless you want us to."

"The trouble with mental reservations is that I can't tell whether you're having one now. Maybe I ought to head for the state forest, after all."

"Oh, for crying out loud. Look, I really have no way of knowing that you are on Miss Peterson's side, that you aren't a KGB agent; but I think you are—I mean I'm practically positive you aren't—you know what I mean. I may not be ready to give you directions to Miss Peterson's house, but I'm certainly not ready to leave you to freeze in the woods, or to get gangrene, or whatever."

"Let me get your reaction to something," she said. "Do you know anything about the Church Committee?"

"Is that like a parish council?" I asked. "In my limited experience, parish councils are pretty worthless. They make life miserable for good priests, and aid and abet bad ones—supposing of course, that there are such things as bad priests." I didn't know any details about Agnes' religious convictions, except that she apparently had some, based on her reaction to Tom's oath.

"Of course there are. There are also bad senators and congressmen, from some people's point of view, anyway. The Church

Committee was a committee of the U.S. Senate that was supposed to be investigating abuses of the intelligence service."

"You mean spies and things?"

"I mean spies and things. The committee made public information about some of our officers and agents, people who were working under cover in foreign countries, that sort of thing."

"But why?"

"Senator Frank Church, and William Colby, who shortly thereafter became Director of the CIA, thought it might serve to correct what they saw as abuses of the intelligence privileges of secrecy and freedom of operation." She said it carefully, neutrally; and I couldn't tell just what she thought of it. I knew what I thought.

"The *Director of the CIA* helped to give them away? But that might have endangered those people. I mean, even if they were— were doing stuff I might not be too sure about—Were they? I mean, do you know?—even if they were, maybe some of them were acting in good faith, and they might have gotten into trouble where they were."

"Some of them got dead where they were. And no, they weren't; at least I don't think what they were doing qualified as abusive."

"But that's terrible. How come I never heard about this Church Committee? When did it happen?"

"Ten years ago. You've told me what I need to know; now I'm going to tell you a little of what you need to know. Are you sure you don't want some tea? You've been operating in the dark, haven't you?"

"And how. No, no tea, thanks. But what do you mean? What did I tell you?"

"You confirmed what I thought about your sympathies and your instincts. According to doctrine I shouldn't tell you, but I'm sick of treating you like furniture. It's what galls me worst about this business, the need-to-know garbage. Intelligence officers have to accept sometimes not knowing why things happen, but nobody gave you the chance to agree to those conditions before this morning happened. As far as I'm concerned, you need to know what's going on, having been practically shot at, and having been subjected to more pressure than should happen to somebody your age.

"The key you need to figure out most of what's going on around here is the fact that some people inside the CIA saw the Church Committee's performance as an opportunity to deal with some other, uh, inconvenient people inside the CIA. There's been a fight going on in the Agency since the '30s, sometimes overt, sometimes subtle; it's more complicated than this, but you can break it pretty much into three camps.

"Some people think the Agency should limit itself—or be limited—to gathering information, mostly or entirely in what they might call above-board ways, passive intelligence, if you like; that there shouldn't be much, oh, clandestine stuff, no complicated and expensive infiltration of other people's intelligence services, that sort of thing; certainly no wet work—no active interference in other countries, no assassinations."

I tried to decide what I thought about that.

"Well," I said, "I guess I wouldn't like to have to call the shots, if you'll excuse the expression, but some people ought to be assassinated."

"I couldn't agree more. Fortunately for world peace, I guess, I don't get to call the shots, either. Anyway, you can see how there would be gradations of opinion more or less falling into that camp.

"Then there are people who see fighting communism as an ongoing war between good and evil, no matter how cold public opinion and public policy say the war gets. There's no sense abandoning long-term counter-intelligence efforts, for example, just because some President or some Senator decides it's time to be lovey-dovey at a summit, or time to franchise Pepsi-Cola in Leningrad. That's sort of shorthand for the general thought, if you see what I mean."

"Yes, and I think it makes sense, although I'm not what you'd call sophisticated about intelligence. I mean, I wish like anything that there could be peace and harmony, and I don't think the average Russian means me any harm, but—"

I trailed off, not quite knowing how to finish my *but,* because

I've imbibed a lot of opinions from my parents, and some of them I haven't gotten around to filling in or checking out.

"But, is right."

"You said there were three camps."

"The third one is easy to describe. It's the moles."

"The what?"

"Little furry creatures who tunnel underneath the surface, so that just when you need a firm footing you step on empty space and break an ankle. You're supposed to be a country girl. You know, moles."

"You mean, Soviet agents inside the CIA?"

"I do."

"Wait, I've heard my parents talk about that. Uh, Hiss, Alger Hiss, right? And Philby, and, uh Burgess?" "Philby and Burgess were British problems; and Alger Hiss was not affiliated with the CIA, thank God, although he was an important player in the greater scheme of things, so to speak. Lots of people inside the agency would like to think it was all over with Alger Hiss."

"And it wasn't?"

"No."

The wind made itself heard outside the fort again, and I felt suddenly scared, scared in a way that trendy teachers and classmates had failed to make me scared when they talked about the greenhouse effect or the population explosion. I realized that without particularly thinking about it I had been going through life assuming that my country employed people as spies because it was sometimes necessary to know what other countries were up to; that all of those spies were fantastically intelligent and competent; and that of course they were all dedicated to preserving what was good about my country. It was horribly disquieting to learn that what I had vaguely thought of as a secure bastion might have some holes in it—or tunnels under it. That instead of outfoxing the Kremlin they were arguing with each other about whether or not to do so.

Also, I liked Agnes, somewhat in spite of myself, but she didn't strike me as super-competent, the way I thought our spies should be. She'd been in town five hours or so, and she still hadn't rounded up whoever was threatening Miss Peterson.

On the other hand, she knew things.

"So how does Miss Peterson fit in, and how do you fit in? I see the general picture you're showing me, but I don't see what we all have to do with it."

Agnes finished her tea, set the mug on the table, and reclined on the camp bed.

"How much do you know about Miss Peterson?"

"She's been here forever. From well before even Martin could actually read, I remember going to the library, and she was there."

"And before that?"

"I don't know, except that my mother, who is very particular about credentials, says that she is a serious scholar."

"So she is. But if anyone is going to tell you about the—the other side of her career, she should do it, herself. I rather think she will, eventually, after what's happened today."

"She said it was a mix-up with some other scholar who was also doing intelligence work."

"Does that make sense to you?"

"Not really."

"Let's just say that it's recently come to several different people's attention that Miss Peterson is in a position to identify the people who identified people to the Church Committee."

Now I could see some sense in things, even though it was a nasty kind of sense.

"So this is something out of something in her past? Your Mr. Colby, or whoever, doesn't want her to accuse the people who—who set up those agents who got killed?" "He wasn't my Mr. Colby, and in any case he's dead, no great loss." Her anger at that truly scared me, even though I knew it was not directed at me. "But yes, you have the general idea. Would you mind very much telling me whether you believe me?"

"Huh? Oh, you mean do I believe *in* you, don't you? I'm sorry, I was just wishing the grownups would behave themselves. Yes, I guess I pretty much believe you. And in you. I can't really believe the Soviets would send somebody like you to North Salisbury. I don't know why I still suppose they're completely competent, now

that I know we're not, but I do. Excuse me, that sounded awful."
She laughed.

"Don't worry about it. I've done a few things well enough that getting shot doesn't wreck my self-esteem, and neither do reasonable doubts from you. But you're right. They don't have the democratic process to worry about, or the need to operate in an essentially free and open society. On our side, of course—" she assumed an exaggerated air of uprightness— "On our side, we have Truth, Goodness and Rectitude."

"Wonderful. I'm cold. Let's go home."

"Oh, heavens. Let me think a second. Being here has some advantages, but I'm horribly out of touch.

"—Oh, all right. I'll tell myself that I like camping out so much, I decided against considerations of personal comfort. Actually, I do think it'd be better to be next to a telephone. And who knows? Maybe pretty soon you'll tell me how to find Miss Peterson."

"Maybe. Look, you can leave some stuff here. We can leave the bed out, and there'll be room in the chest. The path is awfully steep and slippery."

"Let me think again. Autonomy is wonderful, but if you make it complete you can't do much. How far is it to your house?"

"About twenty minutes, maybe more like twenty-five in all this ice."

"Ok. Give me a minute, will you?"

She nodded toward the door, just barely enough for me to get the signal. She wanted a moment's privacy, and didn't want to make me feel she was shutting me out. How well she gave such signals! It was probably part of the core curriculum in spy school—Non-verbal Communication 101.

"Of course."

I scooted out, and stood in the wet wind, watching the bare trees bend, and wondering how the adventure would shape. Oddly, in the turmoil of the weather, I felt a first glimmer of confidence that Providence might lend a hand, and that my blind efforts might not go for nothing.

"The Lord shakes the branches of the cedars of Lebanon," I murmured; and I remembered how, when Mary and Tom were very little, and afraid of the wind that swept down upon our old house from the north, Mother used to tell them that God sent the wind, and managed it, too, and provided for His creatures in its teeth. I looked up toward the old uprooted maple. The groundhog was safe in his house for the winter, and Agnes and I would shortly be safe in ours.

She emerged from the fort.

"All set. Lay on, MacDufff."

She carried a little knapsack that she must have taken from her big pack and filled with the things she most wanted. The gun, presumably, unless that was under her parka. And her toothbrush? The juxtaposition made me laugh.

"What is it?"

I hesitated, and then told her; and she laughed, too.

"You got it. I have my gun, and I have my toothbrush. What a world. Let's go."

She let me take the knapsack, and we both made it down the ridge on our fannies. After I let us out the gate and we set our faces up the rise to the house, I could see how badly she was limping. The gloom was deepening fast, but we could see the lights from the kitchen windows, tiny and far away from the bottom of the field. The wind continued to blow fierce gusts of sleet in our faces, and the footing was even worse than it had been on my trip out.

We were about fifty yards from the house when Agnes stepped in a chuck hole and fell.

"Oh, my Lord, that's done it," she said through clenched teeth. She got to her hands and knees and crawled one pace, and then sat up. "Joanie, I'm so sorry, but unless your brother is a cripple you'd probably better get him to help. I guess I've gone and sprained my ankle, on top of everything. I do apologize."

"Don't apologize, for heaven's sake. It's the moles, you know. They're everywhere."

She managed a faint grin, and wrapped her arms around her knees, prepared to wait.

"I'll be right back."

I half-ran the rest of the way to the house.

Martin still sat in the armchair by the coal stove. The intercom sat silently beside him, so the twins were asleep—and no wonder, after the morning they had had.

"Where's Agnes?"

"Down by the birches," I puffed. "She fell; she says she's sprained her ankle. You'd better come help."

He tossed aside his journal, and was into his boots and out the door almost faster than it takes to tell. He pelted down the hill much faster than I could go. I caught up with him having explanations, as Tom says, with Agnes.

"Look, lady, if I try to help you walk you're going to step in a declivity and break both our necks. Here's Joanie, she'll help you climb on. Climb on now, before we all drown and freeze."

He hunkered down in front of her.

"Excuse my back," he said, a little sarcastically, I thought, and I helped Agnes get up piggy-back on him.

"Hold onto my shoulders, not my neck. Didn't you have any uncles?"

"They were dead by the time I was old enough for this stuff," she snapped, and adjusted her grip.

"Maybe we should do a cross-hands carry?" I suggested lamely. "In all this dreck?" barked Martin. "Be serious. Just hold on, Agnes."

"I'm holding."

He rose and stumped up to the house with her; I trailed behind with the knapsack, wondering why her uncles had died. Not more crises, I thought. I wanted a quiet afternoon and evening, and things to sort themselves out. Providence seemed much farther away than it had back at the fort.

The telephone was ringing when we came into the kitchen. Martin dumped Agnes into the armchair, but I got to the phone first, anyway.

"Hello?"

"Joanie? It's Louise Brown. Did your parents get off all right, dear?"

"Yes, Mrs. Brown, they left a couple of hours ago. Uh, did Dr. Brown come back?"

"No, dear. He just called from Norfolk. He managed to drive

into a ditch on his way out of the Agway parking lot, and broke an axle, of all things. He'll be back in the morning, as soon as he can arrange transportation. *I'm* not driving down there. Most vexing, with young Nicholas due in by the four o'clock bus, supposing it gets here, of course. It's late now. I guess he can hoof it up from the village. I've left a message for him to that effect at Tonypandy's.

"Anyway, I told Michael you had a friend who needed to see him, and he said if it was urgent you should call Catherine Hardy down in Sharon. She has a four-wheel-drive, in case your friend hasn't. Would you like her number?"

"I guess so, Mrs. Brown, thanks."

I took the number, so that we could think about Dr. Hardy, whom we knew only slightly; but I couldn't imagine right then including her in our adventure.

"Uh, Mrs. Brown, Daddy said Dr. Brown was to have his proxy for Town Committee. What do we do about that?"

"Not to fret, dear. Frank McAllister called five minutes ago to postpone the meeting until Wednesday night."

I told Mrs. Brown we would check in with her at bedtime and in the morning, according to our parents' instructions, and hung up.

Martin had been helping Agnes off with her outer things. They propped both feet on a kitchen chair. Susie and Ribby had roused briefly from their communal bed by the coal stove, sniffed Agnes over, and decided they could wait to play with her after nap time.

"That looks like the devil and all," Martin said, as they eased the elastic bandage and gauze pad off her right calf.

"It feels like it, too," said Agnes. "Joanie, if you could give me that knapsack, I put some germicidal ointment in it."

"We can do better than that," I said. "Hang on a minute." I beat it upstairs.

Most of our serious first-aid stuff lives in our parents' bathroom. I took out a big bottle of Betadine, a fresh roll of gauze and one of adhesive tape, an ankle-shaped elastic bandage and some ointment, not having checked the expiration date on Agnes' tube. Mother raised us to be suspicious of expiration dates. A hot-water bottle might be useful for the sprain, and Tylenol for the pain.

Back in the kitchen, I gave the Tylenol to Martin to administer, and filled the bread-mixing bowl, which is by far the largest, with hot water and a liberal dose of the Betadine. I brought a lower chair over to between the armchair and the foot-chair, and put the bowl on it.

"This may be a bit awkward," I said, "but it's much warmer down here than upstairs, and it's only for a little while. Ick, that cut looks ugly. Dunk it in here, and let it soak. It's going to hurt. I'm sorry."

"Betadine?" said Agnes. "Oh, wonderful. Oh, yes, it hurts, uh-huh; I can just feel the bacteria in their dying throes. Nnnf. What is the story on your Dr. Brown? That was his wife on the telephone?"

I told her.

"Oh, good grief. I'll do fine indefinitely now, but what on earth do we do about Estelle Peterson?"

We looked at each other.

"Well," Martin finally said, "Nick Brown is due in on the bus, and he is a medical student. I know it isn't exactly a serious doctor, but at least he will know enough to be able to tell whether she ought to be in a hospital, or whether it's something that is going to fix itself. Right?"

"Maybe," I said dubiously. Nick used to spend his summers with his uncle and aunt, and we had included him as a marginal companion in some of our projects; but we hadn't seen him for a few years, and I was hardly prepared to vouch either for his political philosophy or for his medical competence.

Some kids grow out for a while, and then up for a while; Nick had been a spectacular example of growing up first, then out. He had always looked like a candidate for a nineteenth-century tuberculosis spa: thin, and with a tendency to melancholy, as if he were waiting for his red blood cell count to catch up with his height.

"Hold it," said Agnes suspiciously. "Who is this Nick?"

"Nicholas Brown," said Martin. "Dr. Brown's nephew. He's at the Yale med school; he's coming to visit for a week or two before exams. We used to know him fairly well, but it's been a while."

"So for all you know he could be a serious socialist, or a satanist, or a peace-and-brotherhood nummy-nummy?"

"I suppose," said Martin. "but it seems unlikely."

She sighed.

"If he is a normal Americano, he might be what we need. Can you get him over here and check him out?"

"I should think so," I said. "The Browns have four little kids, and Mrs. Brown is pretty much into staying at home at the moment. With Dr. Brown stuck in Norfolk, it could make sense for Nick to come over."

"Fine. I'm your long-lost cousin from Nepal."

Martin and I looked uncertainly at her for a second. She winked, and we chuckled. I realized again just what an effective thing Agnes' wink was. "How about a law school intern?" I suggested. "It isn't a permanent cover, and Nick'll be sure to mention you to his aunt—uh, as I suggested before, you are kind of conspicuous—unless we tell him not to, which would of course raise more questions than it would solve; but it's a decent temporary cover for deciding whether we bring him in on the story."

Agnes considered.

"It's risky, obviously. Blast. I can't think of anything better. I'm extremely unhappy about leaving Miss Peterson to herself. You think this Nick is likely to play out all right?"

"It's been a couple of years," Martin said, "but if I had to guess, I'd say yes."

"All right, then."

I realized that I had been noticing the twins making noise over the intercom without it really registering.

"Here come Chaos and Confusion."

Agnes glanced at her watch.

"I'm going to try to call in," she said. "Is there a telephone I can use away from the center of operations?"

"The office is too far for you," Martin said. "You'll have to use the phone in our parents' room. One of us can show you, and the other one can keep the twins busy."

Mary and Tom burst into the kitchen then, with all the rekindled enthusiasm that a long nap after lots of fresh air can give.

"Agnes!" Tom fairly capered around the kitchen. "You came! Oh, Martin, let's make a big fire, OK?"

Martin nodded at me.

"You guys go ahead," I said. "Agnes and I are going upstairs for a few minutes, and then I need some help with carrots and potatoes for the stew."

"We'll just nip out for some logs and kindling," Martin said. "Twins, put on your parkas."

Tom shot out with Martin to the woodpile, which was reliably dry even in this kind of weather, because of being raised on two steel bars and covered with a plastic drop cloth. Mary lingered. She shoved her hands in her pockets, and came to regard Agnes.

"How is your leg?" Her tone was faintly challenging.

"Nasty, but getting better," said Agnes levelly. "I like your house very much. I hope you don't mind too much my being here. I will try not to be a burden."

"Oh, it's OK," Mary said, still very serious. "Can you sing? Martin and Joanie are no use at singing for bedtime."

"I used to be the head of the altos at St. Peter Claver," said Agnes, with equal gravity. "Maybe I can sing for my supper."

"Can you sing *Die Lorelei* properly?"

"I think so. You can judge later on."

Mary nodded, apparently satisfied.

"Excuse me. Martin and Tom will bring in the wood, but men are no good at clearing ashes away to start a new fire, or at laying it properly; and they'd probably leave the damper closed."

Agnes nodded in turn. "It's the Y chromosome, poor things. I'll see you in a bit. Thank you for putting up with me."

Mary went out, and I began to help Agnes bandage her leg. The wound was deep and jagged, but it wasn't exactly bleeding, just sort of oozing. I washed my hands with dish detergent and the hottest water I could stand, then smeared Neosporin on the cut, as gently as I could.

"Nnf. Thank you."

"That's all right. Sorry."

"No, it's fine. Thanks."

"You should've gone into the diplomatic service."

"Why?"

"You figured out that Mary was the difficult one to win over."

"I like her, actually."

"So do I. I mean, besides her being my sister. She's very judg-
mental, but if she decided you were on her side, or she was on
yours, she'd go to the wall for you."

"I hardly think that will be necessary, but she's someone whose
friendship I'd value."

I had been speaking figuratively; it took me a second to realize
that in Agnes' world people probably did go to the wall, literally.
I shivered, and fastened adhesive tape around the edges of some
sterile gauze.

"There, that ought to do you for a while, although I still think
somebody credentialed ought to see it and probably stitch it
before it's too late and makes a big scar."

"It's already too late. It's just going to have to be Spook Chic at
the beach. Where's that telephone?"

I took her up to my parents' room, where children went only in
direst emergencies, and left her at the big table by the west window that held the phone and Mother's computer.

I stopped off to put away the first aid supplies, and Agnes was
back at the top of the stairs by the time I reached the bottom.

"My contact is out for the night," she said, and hobbled slowly
down. "I shall have to do some thinking. What about this Nick of
yours? He seems like the only avenue of actual action left available at the moment. I mean, if he proves reasonably trustworthy,
we can at least make some progress on the medical side."

"I'll call."

Martin and the twins had the living-room fireplace roaring, and
were at work on the Advent wreath. Agnes and I went into the
kitchen, and at her insistence I gave her some vegetables to clean
while I called the Browns'.

"Oh, Mrs. Brown, it's Joanie. We were wondering, if you don't
especially want Nick tonight, if he would want to come over for
stew."

"That would suit me, Joanie. I'm done in with chores and children, and ready to collapse as soon as the latter do. Nick just got

in; I'll ship him down in a few minutes. I'm sure he'll be glad of the company."

"Super. We'll check in in the morning, if we can count this as our evening call."

"Fine. Good-bye, Joanie."

"Good-bye."

If our mother sometimes thinks she has it tough with six of us, she must think of Mrs. Brown. At least when the courts are closed and there is no political meeting, Daddy is around to help—if not to do specific things, at least to take the personality pressure off, which is probably more important; but Dr. Brown can disappear for hours with no notice at all because sick people don't generally consider doctors' wives' convenience.

I stuck my head into the dining room. Tom had apparently gone out for more wood.

"Code Blue. Mrs. Brown's sending Nick down practically right away. If Agnes is going to be a law school intern, we need the details of her cover pretty fast."

Mary looked interested; Martin thought for a second.

"She can't be from Yale, because Nick wouldn't believe he'd never happened to see her in the street. Sorry, Agnes, you just don't blend in, you know."

"I know, but you don't have to keep saying it."

"All right, then, it probably has to be UConn. Nobody from out of state would bother looking over the shoulder of a country lawyer. Who is Nick likely to know about at UConn? Any guesses?"

"What about that philosophy of law fellow Daddy talks about sometimes?" I asked.

"Yeah, what's his name? Morris, Tom Morris. He got kicked out of Yale for not being socialist enough, or at least didn't get tenure, Agnes, did you ever hear of him?"

"Lord, no. What would I want with a philosophy professor? This is not going to work."

"Sure it is," said Martin. It's enough for casual conversation. It isn't going to occur to Nick that you're anything but what we say you are, and it's just until we figure *him* out. Morris wrote a book about Wittgenstein, right, Joanie?"

"I think that's right," I said.

"*Wittgenstein,*" Agnes groaned. "Come on, you people, this is ridiculous. I'm not going to pretend to know anything about Wittgenstein."

"You don't have to," Martin insisted. "I keep telling you, it's just a temporary cover. For an hour or so, until we can draw Nick out and find out about his—his ideology, or whatever. So you've heard Morris' book about Wittgenstein was really sound, and you can't wait to take his course next term. That's all."

"You win. It's a dumb idea, but I cannot think of a better one. I think I'm hungry. I lose fifty I.Q. points every twenty minutes when I'm hungry."

"Dinner'll be while," I said. "I'll make you a sandwich."

"Let me," said Tom, coming back in to plunk down the loaded log carrier. "I'm the best sandwich maker in the family."

"It's likely to be—uh—creative," I warned.

"I wouldn't complain about a creative sandwich for all the world," said Agnes, and Tom ran out to the kitchen. "I'm going to get some cider from the cellar, and warm it by the fire," said Mary, and she disappeared, too.

Agnes and I watched Martin mend the fire; my vague unease returned in full force, now that there was nothing to be about and doing.

"Miss Peterson is bothering the living daylights out of me," I said.

"Me, too," said Agnes.

"Do you really think," I flashed at her, "that I ought to have shown you to her door this morning? Do you really think that would have helped?" I was ready to accuse myself of bad judgment if anyone could show me the particulars; I also wanted specific weak charges to defend myself against, because I couldn't clear myself in my own mind, even though I couldn't think what I should have done differently.

She studied me for a moment.

"No," she finally said, calmly. "Do you? Your upset seems to go well beyond simple concern for Miss Peterson."

"I don't know what I ought to have done, and I hate being in moral limbo," I snapped. "I suppose you think decisions are always clear black and white, and all you have to do is figure out what's right and do it, or who's wrong and shoot him."

"By no means." She shook her head slowly and smiled ruefully. "Hardly anything is clear black and white. Most of the time you have to remind yourself that your premises looked good back when you were making a thorough examination of them; and up to a certain point, the small stuff to the contrary you have to regard as static."

"Oh, wonderful! And just where is that certain point? And do you warn your associates when you reach it?"

That was nasty and uncalled for, and I knew it. Her apparent calm and certainty had worn me down, had pointed up for me too clearly my own turmoil. I liked to think it was also the strain of honest worry over Miss Peterson—and even that thought made me mad, for it was uncomfortable asking myself why I was so angry.

But Agnes looked concerned rather than hurt, as if I were a confused student and it was her job to untangle the muddle.

"Let's see about your friend Nick," she said. "If he's all right, maybe we can do something about Miss Peterson tonight."

The doorbell rang, and her calm collapsed.

"Oh, Lord," she said. "Where do I live? What *town* is this university in?"

"Hartford," said Martin, heading for the door. "Farmington Avenue has apartment buildings and rooming houses. Take your pick."

Mary was coming in with a pitcher of cider on a tray with mugs. She continued on through the living room, reaching the front entry first, balanced the tray on one hip, and opened the door. A tall figure in an overcoat entered, swept off an improbable hat, and bowed over her hand.

" 'Ullo, 'ullo, 'ullo,' " said Nick. "Awfully kind of you to have me on such a night, and what a lovely fire. Miss Mary, you are more charming than ever; and Miss Joan, well, my humblest compliments."

None of us could speak for a second. Nick tossed his hat and topcoat on the back of the sofa, revealing an unbelievably sober tweed jacket and creased twill trousers. He came to stand before Agnes' chair.

"Always a distinct pleasure, Martin; and who is this? Maiden, let this friendly rooftree count as introduction, as in more gentle times."

Martin recovered his senses and spoke.

"Uh, Nick, this is Agnes Breslin, who's interning with our father from law school. Oh, I'm sorry—" he was evidently spurred by Nick's performance to unusual decorum— "Agnes, may I introduce Nicholas Brown?"

Agnes got a firm grip on her gravity, and held out her hand.

"Mr. Brown, I am so pleased."

Nick did his thing with her hand, and accepted cider from Mary.

"The next round will be hot," she said.

"Honored, Miss Breslin. Thank you, Miss Mary. What a night. And what in the world has happened to you, Miss Breslin? If I may be so bold?"

Martin, Agnes and I stared helplessly at each other, for there were Agnes' legs, stretched out to a spare chair with miscellaneous bandages.

Tom burst in from the kitchen, carrying a large platter that overflowed with most of a loaf of French bread, liberally stuffed.

"Oh, Nick, Agnes got shot by the KGB and sprained her ankle, could you look at it, you're practically a doctor, and they're after Miss Peterson, too, and do you want some sandwich? It's probably more than Agnes can eat, if she wants to leave room for dinner."

CHAPTER 4

THERE was a moment's dead silence.

"By Jove," Nick said at last. He surveyed all our guilty countenances, and smiled.

"Miss Breslin, you will permit me?"

And he set his cider on the table, and began pulling tape off Agnes' right leg.

"Pheee-yew. The KGB, was it?"

"Well, actually, just KGB sympathizers inside the CIA," I said, as if that would help matters.

Agnes looked furiously at me.

"Them," said Nick. "Hnf. Well, this is nice and clean, although it ought to have been stitched a few hours ago. Not much point now, and it'll leave a nasty scar on a, forgive me, a pretty leg."

Agnes jerked away from him.

"You need a little more detachment in your bedside manner, *Mr.* Brown," she said coldly.

"I do beg your pardon," he said humbly. "You have a bad chill, though, Miss Breslin. I should counsel bed, and soon, with a hot water bottle if possible."

At that, some layer of control broke in Agnes, and she began to shiver as if at his suggestion. She let him replace the bandage.

"No," she said. "There's still Miss Peterson."

"Tom," said Martin, "get more wood."

"But," said Tom.

"Now," said Martin. "And Mary, assemble bowls and spoons. That stew will be ready by the time the table's set, and everyone is ready for it."

"You're not kicking me out," said Mary, as Tom left. "I know how to wrap a hot water bottle best, and you people are too caught up in games to take proper care of Miss Peterson."

"Miss Peterson, the librarian?" asked Nick.

I turned to Agnes.

"Do you want to try to vet him now, or shall we wing it?" I asked.

Agnes produced a calm cooler even than Nick's, and a convincing air of authority.

"Mr. Brown," she said firmly. "You reacted rather strongly to the suggestion of conflict, shall we say, within the intelligence community. Would you mind telling me why?"

"They're breaking a trust, aren't they?" he asked, and eyed her with a persuasive air of simplicity. "Like a doctor who engages in fancy poisoning. The ones who really believe we'd be better off not actively resisting the Soviets are lying to themselves about the implications of the Lubyanka, or else they have such a low opinion of human nature that they think Lubyankas are necessary, or else—"

"That will do, thank you. It appears you are exactly what we need around here."

"—and the ones who are plain old moles are—well, they're fair game, what?"

"Wait a minute," said Mary. "Nick, you can't shoot a gun straight, can you?" "I can shoot very straight, as it happens," said Nick. "Unfortunately, I am unarmed at the moment."

"No problem," said Mary. "You take Agnes' gun. You and Martin can stay the night with Miss Peterson, or stake out her house from the outside, whichever Agnes thinks is best."

"Hold it," said Agnes. "Mary, you have all the makings of a splendid tactician, especially the willfulness, but let me think a second, would you?"

"Sure. I'm right, and you'll realize it. You have to get some rest, somebody has to stay with Tom and me, and Joanie has already been out too much today. I'll get the stew, now."

Mary went out to the kitchen. Tom dragged in another enormous load of logs in the carrier, and Martin and Nick helped him off-load it. I sat and thought about Martin playing spy while I played baby-sitter.

"She's right," Agnes told me. "The plan has the additional

merit, from your point of view, of keeping me out of the loop with Miss Peterson. I wonder whether Mary thought of that. Probably." She sighed, and shivered again.

I couldn't think of an answer. If Agnes was who I thought she was—who she said she was—it was nasty for her being kept under suspicion, especially now, with Nick being let in on the game so precipitously. She was, moreover, the only certified professional among us, and it seemed foolish on that score to withhold information from her.

Mary came back with bowls, spoons and napkins; and I roused myself to locate a ladle and an insulated pad in the sideboard for the stew. We shared around cider, and said grace, and suddenly everyone was hungry, and nobody said much for a few minutes. The fire cracked and spat, and the Advent wreath sat in the middle of the table, its candles waiting for tomorrow.

When second helpings were served, we filled Nick in on Miss Peterson's illness and the shooting. The obligation of delivering a clear narrative dispelled some of the social constraint, although I took pains to conceal from Agnes the location of Miss Peterson's apartment, more from inertia than from conviction. She said nothing about the obvious circumlocutions, and it occurred to me that this sort of water-tight-compartment behavior was normal in her line of work.

"Unless anyone has thought of anything I haven't," Nick said, "Martin and I may as well stake out Miss Peterson's place from the inside. Is there any reason to suppose that her illness is anything but a bad bug?"

It took me a second to realize what he meant, and then I felt nasty all over, like on the one occasion I'd been on a New York City subway, in August.

"It has occurred to me that she may have been poisoned," said Agnes, quite calmly and clinically. "There simply isn't enough evidence available just now to decide that question."

"We can at least take precautions in case that is the case," Nick said. "We'll bring some of this admirable stew for her supper, supposing she has not yet had any, which seems likely; and also complete provisions for breakfast. Unless you wish," he said to Martin, "to undertake differential sampling with me of the contents of Miss Peterson's larder?"

"You mean, you eat some of this and I'll eat some of that, and we'll see who gets sick?" Martin asked.

"Well, we're both bigger than she is, and if it hasn't killed her, I guess it wouldn't kill us; still, I'd just as soon skip the experiment, if there's another way."

"It's time you got going," said Agnes rather tartly, and we brought the remains of the stew into the kitchen. Martin saw Nick move to assist Agnes, and forestalled the rebuff that was sure to come by doing it, himself. He settled her in the big armchair. I fetched some plastic containers and Martin and I began to pack food.

"I shall have to call my aunt," said Nick. "May I use the phone?"

"Right there," I said, "unless you want privacy."

"Not at all; thank you. "Aunt Lou? Nicholas here. Still no sign of Uncle Michael?"

"—No, I should have called the road impossible, myself. Aunt Lou, it is awful out there, and I'm so enjoying talking to Martin; if you don't think there is any risk of appearance of impropriety, would it be all right if I stay over here tonight?"

"—Of course. And in the unlikely event that anyone pays a call, I shall do the gallant thing and disappear."

"—Oh, all right. Of course, you're right. You get some rest, too."

"—Good night."

"What an appalling pack of half-truths we're piling up around here today," I observed. "Speaking of moral philosophy, what about church for you two tomorrow? And what exactly did your aunt say?"

"Probably I should stay with Miss Peterson while Martin goes to church," Nick replied. "Unless you also harbor unsuspected talent with firearms?"

Martin shook his head.

"I shall make shift somehow later in the day. Perhaps the roads will improve, and I can get down to Norfolk."

He favored me with a look of mock longing.

"My aunt, Miss Joan, said you could take care of yourself. Alas. She also said I shouldn't be an idiot, and if somebody does come calling I should endeavor to behave like a normal person. There is no sense of romance left in the previous generation, none."

Agnes looked at him witheringly for me.

"I do not like," she said, "not one little bit, giving you my gun. I don't suppose you are licensed to carry in this Godforsaken state?"

"As it happens, I am," Nick said, "and as a matter of fact, at least as far as the Second Amendment is concerned, Connecticut is not so bad, not yet, anyway. Could I see it, please?"

Agnes sighed, and halted over to her knapsack, and drew out a small revolver. She flipped it open to show the empty chambers, and gave it to Nick.

"You abuse this, Mister, and you're on my list. It's a short list, and you'll go right to the top." "A chief's special," said Nick with evident satisfaction, and sighted it at an imaginary malefactor, and slipped it into his jacket. "I wouldn't dream. I suppose you have some ammunition for it?"

"No, I just wave it at people and they melt away, like water on a witch. Here."

I looked away, unaccountably embarrassed. Handing over the gun seemed almost intimate, as if Agnes and Nick were actors compelled to play a love scene. I noticed that Tom and Mary were staring, and wondered yet again whether I was qualified to have children entrusted to my care.

It was a big relief when Martin and Nick left. The twins and I made short work of the dishes, with Agnes back in the armchair, saying nothing. Ribby sat in her lap, though, and Susie next to her; and she seemed to appreciate the company. Then we all returned to the fire.

"What about singing?" asked Tom, and I was embarrassed again, because I usually sing alto, and it isn't exactly first-class alto. But Tom brought out some songbooks, and it was easier to go along than to resist. It turned out that Agnes could handle anything between first tenor and second soprano, and sight-read beautifully, to boot; so we got on well for an hour or so, with me contributing most of the sour notes, even in songs I knew well, out of annoyance. We sang folk songs, and madrigals, and hymns, while Susie and Ribby dreamed on the hearth; and after a while I forgot to be irritated. Agnes was obviously enjoying herself. Was this cold-bloodedness about Miss Peterson? I thought about it, and thought not. First of all, she wasn't acquainted with her; and it is difficult to keep direct, personal worry about a total stranger in the forefront of one's consciousness for very long. Second of all, in her job Agnes had had to become accustomed to having even friends in danger, and also to not knowing how things were going on another part of a project. The need-to-know business, against which she had complained this afternoon: I could see some sense in it. You cannot have people continually on the strung-tight emotional ragged edge about things they cannot help.

At eight o'clock I dictated bed. The twins' protests were obviously just formalities, a sort of a reserving of their right to object. They both wanted to sleep in Martin's attic— "So you and Agnes can talk if you want to," said Mary, and I thought, too, that any theoretical marauder would have far to go before finding them there. So we threw fresh sheets on Martin's bed for Mary, Martin having already put up a cot for Tom, and plugged in the intercom transmitter. We'd use the receiver's battery pack in my attic.

Tom and Mary said their prayers, alternating God-blesses at the end, as is their habit.

"God bless Agnes," said Mary, whose turn it was to go first.

"No, Agnes is mine," said Tom.

"It's my turn to go first, and I say God bless Agnes," said Mary.

"You can say God bless Agnes, too, Tom," I interposed, "and tomorrow it's your turn to go first."

He sighed.

"Oh, all right. God bless Agnes."

If Agnes was moved by this display of devotion, she gave no sign.

"God bless Mother," said Mary.

"God bless Daddy," said Tom, and so forth, down to the pets.

"Now, Agnes is supposed to sing '*Die Lorelei*,' Mary said firmly;

and Agnes did. It sounded just as lovely and lyrical and haunting as it is supposed to sound, and never quite does when I sing it.

> *Ich weiss nicht was soll es bedeuten*
> *Dass ich so traurig bin . . .*

There was a brief silence when she had finished, and then Tom said,

"Thank you, Agnes. Oh, Joanie!"

"Go to sleep, dear. What is it?"

"I forgot to say, God bless Miss Peterson. That's terrible. How could I forget?"

"Because you're tired, dear. Don't fret."

"God bless Miss Peterson, then."

"Yes, indeed, Tom. Now go to sleep."

We left the door open a bit at the bottom of Martin's attic stairs, so a little light would come up from the hall for them.

"What about you?" I asked Agnes. "You must be done in. Do you want to give up now?"

"Not just yet," she said. "Would you mind keeping me company by the fire for just a bit?"

"I'm not sure all these stairs are good for your injuries," I said, "but I guess you're over twenty-one, and I'll be happy to sit up with you for a while. How about some herb tea?"

"That would be wonderful, thank you."

I fed the animals while the kettle got hot, and let Susie out for one more merry romp in the sleet. Ribby went to re-occupy Agnes' lap as soon as her chow was gone.

"If she bothers you, kick her off," I said when I came in with the tea.

"No, it's pleasant to have her," said Agnes. "Thanks, that smells good. Heavens, what a day it has been."

"Uh, don't you have lots of exciting days in your line of work?"

She chuckled.

"No, actually, you'd be surprised. Mostly I sift through papers and come up with dead ends, or read reports on people following people around on the chance they might do something interesting, and they don't."

"What is the Lubyanka?"

"It was a famous prison and house of horrors in Moscow."

"Was?"

"It's been closed, and more modern facilities opened elsewhere. Your friend's heart may be more or less in the right place, but his information is a bit out of date."

"You—you were never there, were you?"

"No, but someone I used to know went there once, and never came back."

"Oh, Agnes, I shouldn't have pried. I—"

"That's all right. Actually, I was imprecise before, when I said the need-to-know rule bothered me the worst. I've been feeling ground down and strung out for a year or so, and what is really getting to me is not knowing, most of the time, how things turn out at the end. The—the friend who died in Russia was an accidental exception. I only found out about him by accident, I mean. The doctrine is, we're supposed to do our jobs, and assume our superiors are doing theirs, and not mind that we don't find out the results. I simply cannot stand the thought that some damned bureaucrat, or some damned diplomat, or some politician, or the fellow that the fellow I work for reports to, is making an error of judgment, or engaging in systematic errors of philosophy, or neglecting a fact, or something."

So I had been making good guesses about spies in general, but not about Agnes. Or maybe it bothered them all, sometimes.

She sipped some tea, and slowly swirled the rest around in her cup.

"I am wondering more and more whether I am really cut out for this work. I began it because I was raised to try to make the world better, and it seemed the most direct method. But I do not trust all of my superiors, and I doubly do not trust their political managers."

"Because of the Church Committee?"

"In large part. But if the Church Committee were an anomaly, a strange accident, I could shrug it off. It wasn't, though. It was a symptom of widespread rot. And I resent the hell out of putting my life on the line so that the rot can rot away whatever I manage to accomplish."

*"The ground that we take
The Grand Senate gives back
Rather more often than not."*

"The what?"

"Sorry. It's a song from one of Tom's science fiction books."

"It is apt."

"So what are you going to do?"

"Probably what they say in the French Foreign Legion. Shut up and soldier."

"I didn't know that was where that came from."

The telephone rang in the kitchen, and I ran for it.

"Hello?"

It was Mother.

"Darling, we just wanted to let you know we're here safe. There isn't really any news."

"He's—he's all right so far?"

"As all right as anybody could expect, I guess. At the moment we just have to wait. Are the twins behaving?"

"Yes, really well. They're in bed, and I think even asleep."

"Wonderful, dear. It probably is best for them to stay with you, as long as you can take it."

"No problem so far, Mother." Well, not exactly from the twins, anyway. She gave me the hotel phone number, and we hung up. I went back to Agnes, who had been looking through the books on a little table by her chair.

"My mother," I explained. "The reason my parents had to go to Boston was that my uncle had a heart attack. There isn't really any news, though. She just called to check in."

"Is your mother a teacher?" she asked, indicating a couple of teacher's manuals.

"No and yes. She teaches the little kids at home—taught Martin and me, too, until we started high school."

"Why?"

"It's a long story. It's not that unusual, actually; people tend to think it's just crazed anti-social types who home school, but lots of perfectly normal people do it. I mean, I guess we generally qualify as a normal family."

"A little large, maybe."

"I guess, by some standards." I felt a bit defensive. "We like it."

"Obviously. So public elementary schools aren't good enough for you?"

"Academically, you mean? That's part of it. Did you go to one?"

"Yes."

"Was it good enough for you?"

"No. But there wasn't any alternative."

"So we're lucky. I mean, you evidently weathered the experience all right, but why should children have to who don't have to, if you see what I mean? We were all reading by the time the schools said we were ready for kindergarten."

"Yes, I could have skipped the part about slowing down and not going too far too fast. But what about socializing and sports and so on?"

"There have always been at least a few other kids around, like Nick; and Tom and Mary fit in well with the Browns' children. And we've had each other. Martin's generally been decent to me."

"I can see that he's a good egg."

"Thanks. Besides, you of all people ought to sympathize with parents not wanting to subject their kids to the average public school teacher's liberal social and political agendas."

"Maybe. Or maybe I think my kids, if I had any, would be able to make up their own minds. I haven't thought about it much."

"I think it would be rough on a little kid to hear one thing at home, and another at school."

"They're going to have to deal with the world sooner or later."

"Sure, but why not give them the wherewithal to deal with it before you chuck them out into it? Besides, we are dealing with it, at least Martin and I are. We go to the regional high school, and we get along all right most of the time."

"Why did you switch?"

"We started to think about it because Martin is good at mathematics, I mean really good. There was no way Mother could keep up with him. She's fine with algebra and geometry and trig, but he packed it away faster than she could dish it out. She didn't want to make him wait while she figured out calculus, and besides, even that wouldn't have kept him going long."

I stirred up the remains of the fire.

"He could've gone over to the university a few days a week; the math department there was willing to have him; but he was only thirteen, and the bus schedules were awful, and there is one teacher at the regional high who is still a little ahead of him on some things. So he and Mother and Daddy decided he should try the high school and see if it worked out. It's been pretty good, on the whole, although a few of the courses have been deadly—history, especially, which we've tended to emphasize around here."

"What about you?"

"Well, after Martin was there for a year, my parents asked me if I wanted to try it, and I decided I did. I don't know. I don't have any special teacher, the way Martin has Mr. Abrams; but I'm glad I'm doing it. It is interesting to see how other people think—or don't think, sometimes."

"You don't have a special field of interest yet?"

"Oh, sometimes I think literature, but it's too soon to tell. I don't have the kind of outstanding talent Martin has, the kind that shows up obviously and early."

"I know what you mean. I sometimes wish I'd been born a prodigy, so that choices would be clearer."

"You mean career choices?"

"Mm."

"Agnes, where did you grow up?"

"Somewhere south of here, as should be obvious."

"I'm sorry, Joan. I shouldn't be sharp with you. I guess I'm tired, mentally as well as physically. I don't feel like talking about my childhood right now; the contrasts with this—" she waved her arm around our dining room— "are a little uncomfortable. And I'm trying to think through the Estelle Peterson problem, and not getting very far. Maybe morning will bring clarity."

"Shall we head for bed? There's already a cot in my room. We set it up this afternoon, when we thought Mary'd be sleeping up there."

"Thanks. Listen, I don't really think anybody could possibly have figured out where I am, but I'm a little nervous about how much our friend from this morning may have heard of our conversation, and figured out since. Especially with the twins here. Are there dead bolts on the outside doors?"

"Yes. I'll just let Susie in, and lock up. Uh, do you want to come to Mass with us in the morning?"

"I'd like to, but I think it would be foolish with these legs."

"Probably so."

Susie was still enjoying herself in the kitchen yard, and the sleet was still pelting down. I shook the box of biscuits at her, and she consented to come in. I fixed the coal stove to keep warm all night, and rubbed Susie with a big towel. She slurped some water from her bowl, and settled down in her bed. She would undoubtedly be in Tom's before midnight. Ribby came in and sniffed her, and shook a paw, the way cats do when they encounter something unpleasant.

"Oh, all right, Ribby." I shot the bolt on the kitchen door and picked up the cat. "I don't blame you. I wouldn't want to sleep with her, either. Good night, wet dog."

I checked that we had locked the front door after Martin and Nick. It was strange to think of Martin bedding down on Miss Peterson's floor, strange to think of myself as the senior family member on the premises. You couldn't get much safer, I reminded myself, than having an actual professional spy in the house—a spy, myself replied, without a gun, who had gotten herself shot and sprained her ankle in the space of four hours. I shook off the thought, and went to find Agnes, and to fill a hot water bottle for her.

A sound, or a worry, or a dream woke me in the middle of the night. Ribby was still curled against my middle, out cold. Agnes was standing by the north window, looking out.

"Agnes?"

She started, and turned. I could see her shoving something into the pocket of the old bathrobe I'd lent to her. Another gun. Maybe it was time I decided she was on the side of the angels, and nearly as competent as she ought to be.

"I imagined I heard something outside. I checked downstairs.

Probably it was just my own nervous system humming along on stand-by. I'll go back to sleep if you will."

"Is your hot water bottle still hot?"

"Satisfactorily warm, thank you. Good night."

She got back into the cot.

"Good night."

Should I have had the twins sleep with us? No. There wasn't room, short of complete panic conditions; and if I let myself think these *were* panic conditions, I should have to conclude I ought to be getting outside help. Susie would let us know if anyone so much as touched a door or a window; and nobody would. It was just my nervous system, humming, too. I reminded myself that I wasn't going to solve anything by staying awake, and making myself fuddled tomorrow. It was disquieting to have someone sleeping with a gun in my room—and reassuring, too. I decided to trust Agnes' judgment, and pulled my funky old comforter up to my ears, and tried to go back to sleep. I could hear Agnes moving around.

"Agnes?"

"Yes?"

"What happened to your uncles?"

"They were teaching Sunday school, and there was a bomb."

"Oh, God. How can you not hate everybody?"

"Because it would be stupid. I'm out for the lies and the liars, but how could I hate Tom? Or Mary? Go to sleep."

"Do you think they're in Heaven?"

"Who?"

"Your uncles."

"Do you?"

"Yes."

"Then go to sleep."

I didn't have any right to push any further. I didn't say anything more, but it was a long time before I went to sleep.

CHAPTER 5

THE conventual Mass is at eight on Sundays, out of consideration for the families that attend; but the twins and I had to scramble, anyway, to get there on time. We went around by the road, and it was nearly impassable, even with boots. There was a thick sheet of ice over every surface—the road, the grass and weeds at the side of the road, the trees. The sky was a silent, heavy grey, under which the air ought to have been warmer.

We would not ordinarily have seen many cars so early on a Sunday; but there were none at all. I had not checked the temperature before leaving, because it was an obvious case of simply wearing the warmest stuff one had; I was sure it was well below twenty, though, because the insides of my nose felt sort of adhesive. There wasn't any wind at all, but the trees still creaked with the cold. Strange, for the second of December.

We overtook Mrs. Brown and her kids at the abbey door, but there was time only for a fast good morning, which was just as well, since I had not thought to develop a reason for Martin and Nick not being with us. I had managed not to tell an outright lie so far in this business, and I wanted to keep that record going.

The public side of the abbey chapel opens right off the foyer, opposite the parlor. There are five wide pews, and then another grille in front of them, like the one in the parlor. On the other side of the grille is the chapel proper; we can see the choir stalls for the senior nuns, and the pews for the juniors and postulants, at a right angle to ours; if we sit at the left-hand side of our pews, we can just see the altar.

Martin was kneeling at the right-hand end of the front pew, leaving the better view-point open for the little kids. I went in first and knelt next to him, and Tom and Mary followed. The Browns filled the pew behind us. The introit began immediately, and I thought I couldn't wait through the long Mass to learn the news of Miss Peterson, to tell Sister Mark about Agnes, to be *doing* something. But the chant rose, pure and clear, the apparently effortless product of terrific discipline. Whatever the text, for me the subtext of Gregorian chant is always the same: *You have something more important to do than to pay attention to this? Stop hurrying.*

Ad te levavi animam meam:
Deus meus, in te confido,
Non erubescam: neque irredeant me inimici mei:
Etenim universi, qui te exspectant,
Non confundentur.

None of them that wait on Thee shall be confounded. Did Miss Peterson wait on God? I rather thought so. And Agnes? I was less certain. And I? Only when cornered; only when left with nothing positive to do, and even then, only sometimes.

Until you re-calibrate, chant seems to take forever. It insisted that I shut up inside. A third-rate literary critic, I could not make a clear tale out of a plain essay assignment. A third-rate spy, I could not even manufacture and sustain a simple fabrication. But I could pay attention to the wisdom of the chant, and shut up for an hour. So I did, if not for my own sake, for Uncle Jerry's, and for Miss Peterson's, and Agnes'.

When it was over, I took my time over my thanksgiving prayer, hoping Mrs. Brown might be gone by the time Martin and I reached the foyer; but after a minute I could hear Tom's voice and the Brown children's. Martin caught my eye, and I knew it was no good. Fine: he could explain his separate arrival, and Nick's absence, too.

Mrs. Brown was much occupied with sorting boots and mittens. I wondered how to look as if I had a reason to stay around until she left, so that I could ask to see Sister Mark. I stopped Martin by the chapel door.

"How is Miss Peterson? Is Nick still there?"

He nodded.

"She's not too good. Nick doesn't know what's wrong, and he's pretty sure it's not immediately life-threatening, but he insists she's got to get real medical attention. Where's Dr. Brown? And where's Agnes? Back home?"

I explained about Agnes' legs.

Martin shook his head. "We have to think out loud together," he said, "and figure out how to start some serious detective work. But Agnes can't travel all the way to Miss Peterson's, and Miss Peterson definitely can't walk any distance at all, and she shouldn't be left alone. Brother. It's as bad as Dad, trying to get town committee together all in one place."

"Look, I have to see Sister Mark, and let her know Agnes is gone from the fort; and I don't especially want Mrs. Brown to see me going into the parlor. We're already acting plenty suspicious as things stand now. What do you mean, detective work?"

"Nick thinks it might really be poison, after all. It'll take some time to figure out how to figure it out, and then some more time to figure it out, if you see what I mean."

"What do you mean, figure it out? This is nuts. Nick may have Lord Peter Wimsey delusions, but you're supposed to have some sense. If Miss Peterson's been poisoned, we go to the police."

"What police? Trooper Daniels? And with what evidence? And what'll the fellow who shot Agnes do while Trooper Daniels is fooling around? Wait politely? He's here, whoever he is, wherever he is, to get Miss Peterson, remember? And do you want to try explaining that one to Trooper Daniels, a mysterious and incidentally unreported shooting on top of a theoretical but as yet unproveable poisoning?"

He waited for it to sink in.

It did. It felt like a Mack truck running over my fragile confidence.

"Well, the duty nearest to hand at the moment is Sister Mark. I promised I'd check in with her this morning."

Martin shook his head furiously, and I was about to expostulate when I realized he was warning me that Mrs. Brown was approaching.

"Good morning, Martin; Joanie. Isn't it fun? We're as stuck as stuck can be; if the power would only go off we could pretend it was a hundred years ago. Where is my scapegrace nephew? Did he keep you up all night and then turn immobile?"

Mrs. Brown has a thick brown braid of hair down her back, and her clothes are just a little arty. She wears cast-offs from her college roommate, who is a set designer in New York and obliged to Keep Up. The clothes suit her, though, setting off her delicate features, and supporting her rather larkish air.

"Good morning, Mrs. Brown," said I.

"Good morning," said Martin. "I was just telling Joanie she ought to relax and enjoy it."

I looked furiously at him. His aplomb was really unforgivable, in the circumstances. Too much contact with Nick's new persona.

"Here's an off-the-wall question for you," he continued, leaning nonchalantly against the foyer one. "Can you think of anyone who might have a quarrel with Miss Peterson?"

Mrs. Brown looked mildly concerned, but not at all surprised.

"Oh, dear, don't tell me there's been more mischief."

"*More* mischief?"

"Oh yes. Didn't you know about the *asperula odorata*?"

"The *what*?"

Was this not the first occasion of poisoning, then?

"*Asperula odorata*, my dear: sweet woodruff. Estelle Peterson's been trying to grow beds of it under the shade trees in the front yard of the library. She always hated the variegated hosta that'd been there forever (can't say I blame her, nasty stuff); and last Spring she rooted it out, and set out a few hundred asperula plants. It's lovely, actually, and a good choice for the location. Well, Estelle worked so long and hard at those beds, and along about, oh, July, it must have been, they were really starting to look very nice. The asperula was spreading happily, and it does smell so good when the sun hits it—I guess a non-gardener might not think much of it, but it *is* nice. Anyway—Joe, you give that boot to Frank, put your own on, and go ask Sister Maura if there's anything you can usefully shovel to make amends for disturbing her house. I'll save some lunch for you, if you're lucky. March.

"Sorry, where was I? Oh yes, Estelle's asperula. Well, one morning last July Estelle came out to put some letters in the box, and found the asperula gone. Not just torn up: apparently whoever did it knew that it was reasonably tough stuff, and could be re-planted, if Estelle got to it quickly. It was all gone, all of it, pulled out and disappeared as neatly as if a gardener had disposed of weeds, *and* enough lime dug in to keep Estelle busy with manure and pH paper the rest of the summer."

I felt nasty again, as when the idea of poison had first appeared. "That isn't just mean," I said. "It's a complicated, thought-out kind of mean."

"Indeed. What made you ask? We couldn't think who would have the motive *and* the imagination, short of Virginia Crawley, of course, and this just wasn't her style, if you see what I mean. Too—well, too stealthy."

"I should say not," said Martin, thoughtfully.

I thought not, too. I didn't know Mrs. Virginia Crawley well, although she had been on Town Committee with Daddy forever; but I agreed with Mrs. Brown's assessment. I couldn't imagine Mrs. Crawley pulling out asperula in the middle of the night.

"But why think of Mrs. Crawley at all?" I wondered.

"Well, because of Trooper Daniels and the parking ticket, of course. Do you children miss all of the good gossip? Oh, dear, at what point does gossip become a sin? I always forget."

Mrs. Brown looked fuddled, and fished vaguely in her skirt pockets, as if she might find a catechism there.

"I'd like to hear about it without any malice at all, Mrs. Brown," said Martin, "which makes it not a sin. There's apparently been a bit more mischief, and we—I mean Miss Peterson, of course—would like to figure out who, and—and make peace, if at all possible."

Mrs. Brown studied him a little more intelligently than I liked.

"Hmm," she said. "Well, it is a very good thing that you O'Connors have made the effort to be friends with Estelle. She seems quite self-sufficient, of course; but it isn't always easy even for a woman of considerable intellectual resources to be all alone. Hmm."

And she looked at Martin in the same disquieting way.

"I guess you know your business," she said. "It's a silly little story, but it's also the sort of thing that keeps bad blood circulating in a little town."

Daddy had said the same thing the morning before.

"It must have been around the middle of June, because I remember everyone was a little high-strung getting ready for the middle school graduation. Ginnie Crawley had picked up the library curtains from the cleaners down in Norfolk, and she'd left her car at the curb while she ferried them inside. They're pretty heavy, I guess, so it is easy to understand her not parking down in the next block.

"But you know the street in front of the library *is* a No Parking zone, and *wouldn't* you know Trooper Daniels would happen to come along just as Ginnie was struggling through the library door with a huge load of curtains. Apparently he started to write out a ticket, and she started to object; and by the time she'd gotten inside and dumped her cargo and come back out, he'd tucked the ticket under her windshield wiper.

"He bent it, of course, I mean the windshield wiper, not the ticket—"

"Oh, Lord," said Martin. "Was it the pet Porsche?"

"Of course it was the pet Porsche. Ginnie went ballistic. Estelle apparently heard the explosion, and came out to try to arbitrate. Ginnie seems to have decided Estelle was taking Trooper Daniels' side, although I rather imagine she was just trying to calm things down. She should have saved her breath. Michael came along just as Trooper Daniels was arresting Ginnie for interfering with an officer, my dears—oh, dear, am I enjoying this too much?

"The Porsche was towed, and Ginnie had to ride with Trooper Daniels to the state police barracks in Canaan and be *booked*, if you can imagine. Michael talked her into going just in time; he could see Resisting Arrest in Trooper Daniels' eye. He followed in our car with Estelle, in case Ginnie needed bond posted, and to bring her back; but she was released right away on a promise to appear, as you would expect.

"Well, Ginnie wrote a truly amazing letter to the Library Board, accusing poor Estelle of going along just to witness her discomfiture, and of deliberately escalating the dispute just when she, Ginnie, was on the verge of persuading Trooper Daniels to be reasonable. Said she wanted to resign from her position at the library—"

"Excuse me," I said. "Isn't Mrs. Crawley just a volunteer at the library?"

"Oh, yes; but you'd never know it from the letter, which I had the pleasure of entering in the Board's minutes. She said *she* intended to rise above petty personal conflict, implying that Estelle would not, and would Continue in Her Duty in the General Interest. She also enclosed a copy of her letter to the State Police Commissioner, which I must admit included some accurate general observations about Trooper Daniels; but I imagine they were lost in the noise of her specific complaint.

"Mercy, look at the time. I must collect those children before they dismantle the abbey stone by stone. The denouement was deflating, of course. Ginnie paid the parking ticket under heavy pressure from Leo Ely, and the more serious charge was dismissed. Estelle, thank God, has a pretty healthy sense of humor; otherwise Ginnie's high-minded rising above petty personal conflict would surely have driven her nuts within a week."

Mrs. Brown zipped her parka and tilted her head to one side. "There's your story, Martin. Now, where's mine?"

"Oh, Mrs. Brown. Fact is, I've promised not to tell. Suppose I promise to get special permission to tell you by—oh, by Christmas?"

"Serves me right for blabbing. All right, but I'll hold you to that. Now where are those dratted offsprings? Oh, I meant to say, would you like to be relieved of yours this morning? Of Mary and Tom, I mean. They can come back with us and play until you want them."

We were suitably grateful; I murmured something true about a book report and needing fewer distractions for a few hours. Martin went off with Mrs. Brown in search of the twins. I fiddled with a boot until they were out of sight, and then went into the parlor.

Martin joined me there while I was waiting for Sister Maura to find Sister Mark. He was grinning.

"Did you swear the twins to silence? Were they furious?"

"Yes, and furious is not the word. They both realized right away that they had to act delighted to go to the Browns', *and* that it was just retribution for their wrangling to stay behind when Mother and Daddy went to Boston. They couldn't say anything about why they wanted to be home this afternoon, any more than we could say anything about why they should have gone to Boston yesterday."

"They'll have plenty to say when they get home."

"That's OK. The look on Tom's face was worth it."

He stood up.

"Good morning, Sister Mark."

"Good morning, children. Sit down. How and where is your mysterious friend?"

Martin deferred to me, as having seen Agnes more recently.

"She's at our house, and she says she's all right, although I have my doubts. Oh, I suppose she'll be fine, really; but I'll feel a lot better about it when Dr. Brown's seen her. He's stuck in Norfolk, did you hear?"

"No, and I don't blame you for feeling uneasy. The Abbess had spoken to Sister Andrew, the Infirmarian, about having her here if necessary. Would you like to pursue that idea?"

I looked at Martin, and got no wiser.

"I guess not for the moment, Sister, although it is awfully kind of you. Our—friend is a grownup, at least technically; and Dr. Brown ought to be back today, unless the roads stay too terrible. Could we leave it open for now?"

"That seems reasonable."

"Sister," said Martin. "I have an idea. I wonder—do you suppose—well, I know this will seem an odd coincidence, but the fact is there's someone else who maybe ought to come and stay with Sister Andrew, if she'll have her."

"Another mysterious friend?" Sister Mark sounded as if she saw the theoretical humor of the situation, but she looked rather stern.

"More mysterious than you might think. It's a strange story—I mean, it's another strange story, but it's Miss Estelle Peterson."

"Miss Peterson, the librarian? I know her by sight, of course; she often comes to the abbey for Mass; but I am not at all acquainted with her. If she is ill, shouldn't she be under a regular doctor's care?"

Martin looked at me. Apparently he wanted me to be the one to break both Miss Peterson's oath of silence and Agnes', or he wanted me to give him instant absolution for doing so, himself. It seemed reasonable, in the circumstances; but I was hamstrung by the thought that promises are for when it seems reasonable to break them—otherwise, you wouldn't have to have the promise at all.

I shrugged.

Martin sighed, and began the narrative. Sister Mark interrupted him almost at once.

"Just a minute. Agents of the United States intelligence community are trying to kill Miss Peterson? Or double agents, you are saying? There is no sense in telling such a story twice. I shall find the Abbess."

She left, and Martin turned to me.

"Supposing the Abbess agrees to have Miss Peterson here, we ought to be able to have a real conference back at the house by —" he consulted his watch— "well, it's 9:45 now, let's say by noon, allowing for getting her here over the bad road, and then for us and Nick to get back home. Or do you want to go back now, and fill Agnes in on Mrs. Crawley? Detection's not exactly her line, but she may as well be thinking about it."

"Why are you trying to get rid of me?"

"Because you are having compunctions."

"Are you trying to spare me my conscience, or yourself my recriminations?"

"Yes."

"Tough. I'll stick, thank you. You know, Dr. Brown is probably arriving home this very minute."

"Probably, but I don't think we can responsibly count on that. Besides, he can perfectly easily visit Miss Peterson here. Doctors and such are allowed in the abbey enclosure."

"I know. But don't try to make me like this."

"If you have a better idea, let's hear it."

"I haven't. But that doesn't mean I'm not entitled to an opinion about this one. Did you notice that Mrs. Brown didn't ask again about Nick, for one thing? She knows something's up. And how *is* Miss Peterson going to get here, with the road the way it is, for another?"

"So Mrs. Brown knows something's up. She'll ask us about it before she goes calling Boston and worrying Mother and Daddy. I expect we can use Sister Stephen's tractor to bring Miss Peterson here. It won't be fast, and it won't be comfy, but it won't skid, either. Better ten minutes' exposure to the cold, and we can bundle her up, than staying where she is."

"What about a regular hospital, then? I mean, there are helicopters and things for emergencies like this."

"In books, people get shot in hospitals all the time. You know, somebody goes in for a ulcer or something, and there's a security failure. Besides, we probably can't even produce any security at all, remember?"

"Oh, bother. You're being reasonable, but I still don't like it, and I don't know what I'd like better.

"Look, poison is not Mrs. Crawley's style, and people don't try to kill people over a parking ticket."

"There was a substantial additional humiliation involved, remember; but I tend to agree with you. Here comes the Abbess, I guess."

She walked slowly, largely because proper use of her four-footed cane entailed small steps, and at five-foot-nothing she'd never had much of a stride; but her absolute uprightness reminded me, as always, of C.S. Lewis' description of an angel: the world seemed to take its referent plane from her, rather than she from it.

We stood, of course. The senior nun who came behind her helped her into a chair by the grille.

"Good morning, children. Sister, these are Joan and Martin O'Connor. Children, Sister Andrew. Sit down, all of you."

"How do you do, Sister?"

"How do you do?"

"Sister Mark has been telling me such an extraordinary story," said the Abbess. "Dear me, yes. Let us take it from the top, shall we?"

We did. Both nuns listened intently, and neither gave the smallest sign of what she was thinking as we went along. Sister Andrew was not much larger than the Abbess, and about half her age, I guessed. She had a notably fair, clear skin, large green eyes like Tom's, and a snub nose well covered with freckles. I could easily imagine her on a tennis court or a mountain face, for there was a tough fitness about her bearing.

". . . So, anyway," Martin concluded, "we thought, I mean I thought, maybe Miss Peterson could stay here a bit, that is if you don't mind. We could get one of those helicopter ambulances to take her to a hospital, but you know what always happens in books when people that people are trying to kill go into hospitals. . . ."

He trailed off. This analysis, which had sounded so unanswerably tight when he gave it to me, sounded like the product of a fevered adolescent imagination when he presented it to the Abbess. There was a moment's silence. The Abbess nodded to herself several times.

"Hmm," she said. "Sister, you have not been here so very many years. Do you recall this Church Committee?"

"Yes, Mother."

"It was as the children and their friend said?"

"Yes, Mother, essentially so."

"Hmm." She nodded again. "Sister, this must be your decision. I do not see much real risk, but there is material responsibility. Do you wish to undertake to care for Miss Peterson, provided, of course, that if you find she needs more expert care we can make other arrangements?"

Sister Andrew smiled slightly.

"Mother, may I ask you something?"

"Certainly."

"If you were in my place, would you do it?"

Mother Abbess smiled widely.

"Like a shot, Sister. Like a shot."

Sister Andrew smiled wider, too.

"Thank you, Mother. May I go ask Sister Stephen about her tractor?"

"Certainly."

Sister Andrew made the traditional bow to the Abbess, nodded to us and left the parlor.

Martin and I hardly knew whether to look at each other.

"Uh, Mother," I said. "Thank you. I—"

"Nonsense, child," said the Abbess. "This is not a personal favor. People think we are unworldly, simple. Bah. We do not leave our judgment behind us when we walk into the cloister. For hundreds and hundreds of years abbots and abbesses have made judgments about the right of sanctuary. Besides, in a closed community, we had better develop judgment, or we should be at each other's throats every day.

"Now, Martin, you go to Miss Peterson's home with Sister Andrew. She has been through the town only once, on her way here—let me see, eight years ago; she will need a navigator, to say nothing of not being shot by your enthusiastic friend Nicholas. One of you will have to walk back—back here? Back to your home? Back here, I think will be best. Yes. Joan will stay and read to me until you return."

She gave a great, pacific smile that, if she had been anyone else, would have dared anybody to think of an objection to her plan.

CHAPTER 6

Never mind Why; Why never gets you anywhere.
—D.L. Sayers, Busman's Honeymoon

WE WENT home by the road, which was still icebound. The sky was still muffled, too; but the air felt warmer, and there was occasional variation in the dim daylight, as if the clouds were at least moving around. Now and then a few flakes of snow drifted down.

On our way, Martin and Nick told me about the ferrying of Miss Peterson. They had bundled her onto the tractor seat, a cocoon of blankets liberally stuffed with hot water bottles from the abbey. Sister Andrew drove standing on the left-hand running board; Nick rode shotgun, so to speak, on the right-hand one; and Martin kept up behind at a jog trot most of the way to the abbey drive.

"It would have been nothing but ridiculous," he said, "except that every moment I expected to hear a shot. I couldn't shake the thought that they'd go for Sister Andrew first—why, I don't know, unless Miss Peterson happened to be behind her in their line of sight."

"I was thinking the same thing," said Nick. "The driver, of course, is the obvious primary target; and it would have been fairly clear to an intelligent observer that she was officering the expedition. The really appalling part was that I couldn't stop picturing us trying to explain a wounded nun and a sick librarian to— oh, Heaven help us, to your Trooper Daniels."

Sister Andrew, apparently, managed the entire affair quite calmly.

"She was thoroughly serious," said Nick, "and she gave orders

85

as if she was assuming we'd follow them, and we did, of course; but I have a sneaking suspicion she was enjoying it tremendously. A lark, you know."

He shook his head. "I call it unseemly. A cloistered nun. She should have been scared. She should have been—have been—"

"A fainting flower?" I snapped. "Don't be an ass. Discipline and duty are discipline and duty, whether you're in the 82nd Airborne or the O.S.B."

"Did you really read to the Abbess all the time we were gone?" Martin asked hastily.

"No," I said, feeling very small that my brother was performing social interventions because of my temper. Nick was just trying to be witty. "We, uh, we talked about books. She knows a lot. It was very interesting."

"Did you talk about your essay?" asked Martin.

"Yes, and I don't want to tell you about it, OK?"

"Joanie, I hope you are not developing a poetical temperament."

"Lay off, will you? Yes, we talked about some of my ideas, and I'm still thinking over what she said, OK? I don't want to talk about it yet."

"Many people are willing to accept temperament in a poet, but in a critic it is unforgivable. A critic must be rather more civilized than the next fellow."

"I said, lay off!" If this had been five years before, we could have resolved it by throwing things at each other. As it was, we turned into our drive in resentful silence. Nick looked distinctly uncomfortable, and I was mad enough to be glad he could think of no soothing small talk.

Susie met us half way up the lane. Her yelps of joy evidently alerted Agnes, for the latter opened the door as we approached.

"She told me a while ago that it was a capital crime around here not to let her out. I couldn't get her back in. I hope it's OK."

"Of course it's OK," said Martin. "In, wretched puppy."

"The telephone rang once," Agnes reported as we shucked parkas and pried off boots. "That is, it rang ten rings. I didn't answer it."

"Could've been Mother," I said, glad to have a reason to say something non-surly. "She says ten is enough to let a person get to a phone, and not enough to irritate someone who doesn't want to bother. Why don't you call her, Martin? I did the check-in last night.

"Sure. Pull in another chair from the dining room, Nick, and thaw your toes at the coal stove."

I went upstairs. I really did want to be alone, to think over what the Abbess had said.

At first, she had had me pull *The Consolation of Philosophy* from the shelf on my side of the parlor, and read to her. But my attention drifted, and she asked me about school.

I explained to her my idea about *Northanger Abbey*. It sounded as lame as Martin's theory about the dangers of hospitals. But she picked up the ball immediately, and ran with it a bit, and then handed it back to me, to see what I could do. I fumbled a little, but she had turned things just enough so that I could see more clearly how the thought could play out.

"Now it will be dull for you, writing the essay," she said. "But every discipline has its—well, has its discipline. You have the makings of a first-rate critical mind, and you will offer up the exercise to—to—just who is the patron of critics? I shall investigate, and let you know when you come to inquire about your friend Miss Peterson, shall we say Tuesday? And you will bring me your essay."

I hadn't had the nerve to tell her that it wasn't due for another week, that I had been just fooling around with it.

You have the makings of a first-rate critical mind. Was this a calling, of the kind Agnes and I had discussed? I sat on the edge of my bed, and tried to feel around my insides for the resonating note of vocation; but I got only dissonance and discord. I gave it up as a bad job, and fished a fresh spiral notebook from my bottom bookshelf. If Martin and Nick wanted to play sleuth, we could at least attempt order. Correction: if we were all there was available to play sleuth, we had better attempt some order.

Down in the kitchen, Martin was carefully turning an enormous mound of scrambled eggs in one skillet, while sausages fizzled in another.

"Joanie, you could drain those and make some toast. Nick is on coffee and condiments detail."

"Right-oh," I said, and did, anxious to make amends for my crabbiness.

"What was the news in Boston?"

"He's stabilized, and the blood-chemistry things that show the dead bits after a heart attack are settling down. They haven't decided what to do, but he's pretty much out of immediate danger."

"Thank God."

"Yes, indeed. Mother and Dad are going to stay with Aunt Mary for a few more days, as long as everything is all right around here." He made a wry face.

"Yeah. What were you supposed to say? That we need them back here right away because of a terrible emergency, only of course they shouldn't worry because it isn't urgent?"

"I know, I know. But didn't you ever have the feeling you should have done something differently, even if you can't think how?"

"In the past thirty hours, constantly."

"You've done fine, Joanie."

"Me?"

"You. Come on, let's eat."

We wolfed for a while, and it began to snow in the moderate manner that means serious business in our part of the world. The great big flakes that swoosh down rarely amount to much, but the little ones that just come calmly down are like an inescapable fate.

When everyone was provided with second cups of coffee, and the boys with third helpings of toast (there's no use pretending about the appetite of the semi-adult male), we got down to business.

"If nobody minds, let's impose a little order on this thing," I said. "I'll make a table for your suspects, and you can fill in motives and opportunities and whatnot."

"Don't forget method," said Nick. "When once you know How, you know Who."

I overlooked the pomposity, and amended my table.

"You'll need a separate section for a timetable," said Martin, "with people's movements and alibis and things."

"What good does an alibi do for poison?" Agnes objected. "It can sit around for days or even weeks before she gets around to eating it. The criminal can be anywhere he happens to be when she happens to get around to it."

"Probably," said Nick. "But we still have to find out everybody who gave her anything to eat or to drink in the period preceding her falling ill."

"Or anybody who could have slipped something into something she already had around to eat or to drink," said Agnes, "which broadens the search considerably."

"It needn't necessarily," said Martin. "We got a fairly complete account from Miss Peterson of her doings, right, Nick?"

"What about getting alibis and timetables from everybody for the time Agnes was shot?" I asked.

"No good," Martin said kindly. "We don't have any official status to make that kind of investigation, and if we tried it somebody would have Trooper Daniels down on us in a half an hour."

"Which is the last thing we need," Agnes said. "I'm afraid Martin is right, Joan. The shooting would be a lot easier to investigate, but we cannot do a thing with it."

"It seems so unfair," I said. "It's like the bad guys have the law on their side, practically, just because we have to keep everything quiet."

"That's normal in intelligence," Agnes smiled at me. "Don't waste emotional energy on it. Besides, in this case the likeliest suspect is the one we can't find. Let's look at the menu."

Nick pulled an untidy collection of lined yellow paper and torn envelopes from an inner pocket. Agnes groaned, and he smiled.

"As Joan said, let us impose some order upon chaos. The victim is not exactly a Sloane Ranger, consuming a tidbit in this club, a morsel in that bar. The opportunities are limited.

"Let's see, Tuesday, Monday, Sunday, Saturday. Miss Peterson became ill Monday night. We asked her about things beginning on Friday; Lord knows this probably isn't complete, but it is a beginning. We can ask her more later on.

"Here we are. Joan, you are prepared to generate order? Friday, that is ten days ago, now: November twenty-fourth. Breakfast: toast and coffee. The bread, the coffee (she drank it black, no sugar) and the butter all from previously opened supplies. This means either a) someone managed to introduce something during her work-day on Thursday, and it did not act until Monday—a pair of extreme improbabilities—or b) that meal was what we may call clean.

"Elevenses, if you will, in the kitchenette off the library office. My initial vote, by the way, is for that kitchenette, although probably not so early on. Anyway, Friday elevenses: a glass of milk—the last of a quart carton—and the end piece of a coffee cake Mrs. Virginia Crawley had brought a few days before. Mrs. Crawley had, herself, ingested some significant portion of the said coffee cake; but of course it is possible that there was something in the end portion only.

"Luncheon at one, with Leo Ely, in Norfolk, at The Elms."

"Wow," I said.

"Nice, what?" said Nick. "But unless you wish to include Leo Ely on your list of suspects, an easy meal to mark off as clean. On second thought, perhaps we should be developing habits of thoroughness. Include him in, as somebody would say."

"Yogi Berra," said Martin.

"Right, of course. At four o'clock—"

"Hold it," said Agnes. "Who is Leo Ely?"

"State senator," I told her, "for us and Salisbury proper, and Norfolk and most of Canaan and Lakeville. Pillar of the community. Everyone thinks his first name is Senator, nobody bothers to run against him. In real life, so to speak, an accountant, although he's pretty rich and probably doesn't need the money." Agnes nodded noncommittally.

"At four o'clock," Nick repeated, "a cup of tea, again in the library kitchenette; and here we begin to have something approximating an evidentiary trail, as the quart of milk then opened was still there this morning. My able colleague and I secured a sample, which I have taken the liberty of placing in the refrigerator here."

"Good heavens, I hope it's marked with a skull and cross-bones," I said.

Nick raised an eyebrow.

"Certainly not. It is nearly always fatal to theorize ahead of the facts. It is contained in a plastic pill bottle, such as pharmacies are accustomed to use to dispense prescription medications, and it is denominated, 'exhibit A.'"

"Of course it is," I said, and then hoped I had not sounded nasty.

"Silly me."

"Ahem. The tea and the sugar were in like case to the coffee and so forth of the morning, previously opened and previously, presumably, harmless. We secured samples. How unfortunate that Miss Peterson did not foresee our inquiry, and set aside small quantities of each upon each occasion they were used. The library kitchenette is so much more accessible than the kitchen of her apartment, and she does seem to take her tea there so often. It would be convenient, if that turns out to be the—ah—the avenue, as it were, of harm, to know at what point the contaminant was introduced. However, we can hardly expect a normal, healthy-minded victim to take such precautions in the interest of simplifying a subsequent investigation."

"Could you possibly get on with it?" asked Agnes. "I have a telephone call to make in a few hours."

Nick cocked an eyebrow at her. "I should keep both legs elevated, if I were you, Miss Breslin," he said, in the friendliest manner. Her mouth tightened, but she plunked both feet up on an empty chair.

"Most sensible. Now, Friday supper. Eggs, scrambled soft, toast, canned beetroot and tea. Miss Peterson seems to be going out of her way to establish herself as middle-class English, or perhaps lower middle-class. Is that a clue, or an insight, or an irrelevancy?"

"I don't know anything about her background," I said. "She seems always to have been what she is."

"Martin?"

"Nada."

"Might be worth checking later. Probably just a distraction. The beets are the safest objects of the whole four days, having been opened on the spot and at the moment. It is notoriously difficult to introduce odd things into sealed cans. Eggs are in similar case, for all the loose talk about hypodermic syringes that goes into detective stories. The first six you try break, don't you know; and unless you are armed with replacements of the appropriate size and color, you are sunk. To say nothing of the mess involved. I think we can clear the eggs merely on the ground of elapsed time, along with the rest of Friday's rations; but there may be poisons whose effects appear long after any associated food is ingested. We shall have to check that point, as a general precaution. In any case, we have the last egg of the carton—well marked, Miss Joan, well marked."

"And the tea from the apartment kitchen?" asked Agnes. "And the milk and bread?"

"Captured, bagged and tagged," said Nick cheerfully. "Saturday breakfast. Ready for a brand new day, Miss Joan? Splendid.

"Here we are. Breakfast, coffee and toast. Lunch, roast beef on rye with onions and Russian, if you will forgive the expression, delivered by my uncle, as it happens, from that wonderful new delicatessen in Norfolk. No, no, Miss Joan—" as I began to protest— "Neither can I feature Uncle Michael as a poisoner, much less, supposing the impossible possible just for the moment, as a poisoner sufficiently stupid to make a semi-public delivery of food to his victim."

"Semi-public?"

"Mrs. Crawley was filling in on the desk, so that Miss Peterson could complete her budget for next year. Of course, my uncle might not have foreseen her presence."

"He is on the committee," Martin observed, "just as your aunt is."

"I'm not going to listen to any more of this," I said, trying to keep my voice calm. "Even if he had a motive, and he couldn't possibly have, Dr. Michael is simply not capable of murder."

"I wouldn't be too sure of that, under different circumstances," said Nick. "And remember, as we are all of us amateurs, we are going to bind ourselves to the sensible rule of ignoring motive, as much as possible."

"What circumstances? You're nuts."

"Oh, Uncle Michael wouldn't kill for money, or for revenge, or for jealous passion, of course. None of that stuff. But for justice, maybe, in an extreme case; or to save an innocent life."

"Those don't exactly count as murder, do they?"

"We're getting off the track again," Agnes observed. "Let's finish this part of the exercise first, and then we can play around with theories and interpretations."

"Sensible again, Miss Breslin. Tea around four, in the library kitchenette."

"Oh, Lord," I said. "Mrs. Crawley."

"Possibly," said Martin. "As you said this morning, poison's not her style, really. You'd expect her to be too proud for it, somehow. If she felt justified in killing someone, she wouldn't take the sneaky route. She'd also have had to walk right through Miss Peterson's office to get to the kitchenette. Miss P. says she didn't see her go through; but she could have been too absorbed to notice."

"I still don't believe it," I said.

"No more do I," said Nick, "although for other reasons. Anyhow, dinner sounds perfectly lovely. Joe Fredericks seems to have thrown together tournedos chasseur and petits pois, and delivered them in one of those styrofoam covered plates the environmentalists love so well. Hidden depths for the town handyman."

"Joe has worked a few times as a chef in New Haven," I said, "when he's stopped drinking. He always ends up back here after a few months, and the selectmen give him his job back, because nobody else can fix everything the way he can."

"So Martin explained. Miss Peterson says he took to bringing her the occasional fancy dinner upon his latest return, about a year ago. Have you, in fact, begun your list of suspects, Miss Joan?"

"Let's get through this part first, and then we can go back."

"You're not making the list for a grand jury, you know. Writing a name is not an accusation. Never mind, we'll do as you say."

He was right that I felt reluctant to write a person's name under my neat heading, even Joe's.

"On Sunday Miss Peterson went to Norfolk to church. Anyone

know why, when there's a perfectly good one here in the village? I got the impression she diverted me when I asked; dashed if I can tell you how. Part of the training, Miss Breslin, or natural talent?"

"Will you get on with it?"

"Hmm, Miss Peterson was more deft at the deflection of a question. Never mind.

"She broke her fast at the doughnut shop on Route 12. That she excused this on grounds of sudden and unusual hunger suggests nobody would have expected her to be there. A cinnamon doughnut for the record, though, and a glass of milk. Then home for eggs as before. Dinner, a minestrone courtesy of our friend Joe Fredericks. A sample in your refrigerator for form's sake, Miss Joan. Readily discernible ingredients: beef stock, onion, celery, tomato, elbow macaroni and some odd beans, rather like deformed limas; fava beans, perhaps.

"Why only for form's sake? Have you decided Joe couldn't have done it?"

"Not at all. But if he did, the tournedos are more likely, the evidence having been entirely consumed."

"Oh. The soup could even be a blind."

"Just so. Nevertheless, a sample rests in your refrigerator, Miss Joan

"Monday breakfast I shall leave you to guess."

"Coffee and toast," Agnes and I chorused.

"Got it in one. Lunch, a bit of left-over soup, warmed upstairs. She was beginning to feel a little low, as she said; and she left Mrs. Crawley to man the library while she went up for the minestrone.

"At four she made herself a cup of tea, looked at it, and poured it down the drain. She is quite sure that she was ill before she made the tea, and that she drank none of it. She recalled quite clearly making it with the intention of preserving routine, of fending off discomfort; and she recalled looking at it, and realizing she could not drink it. After that, it was crackers and water until Joan and the twins saw her yesterday. I have the remains of the cracker box, but my guess is that it is clean."

"Why?" Agnes demanded.

"She was sick enough Monday night, by her own description,

that if she had been ingesting more of whatever it was for four days, she would be worse now, at least I think so. Moreover, Miss P. is quite certain she had none of the crackers until after she became ill."

"But what exactly is wrong with her?" I asked. "Is she sick to her stomach?"

"No," said Nick. "The only identifiable symptoms are extreme weakness, shortness of breath and loss of appetite. I think the difficulty in breathing is from an ordinary heavy cold, not related to the main complaint. I'm not sure, though. I'm not a doctor. Sometimes I wonder if I—" he trailed off.

If you ever will be one, or if you should be one, I finished for him, silently. So, Nick was suffering uncertainty about his calling. Just now, because of Miss Peterson, or generally? Did anybody really know what he ought to do in the world, or were there any real oughts about it?

"How can we get all this stuff tested?" Martin wondered.

"Barring the state police," I said, "and I guess we're all agreed we're barring the state police, maybe the prosecutor's office?"

Martin sat up straight.

"Not exactly," he exclaimed, "but that's the right track. The regular prosecutors would be all over us in a second if they half believed us, and make as much of a hash as Trooper Daniels, supposing they didn't turn it right over to him, and they might well do. But what about Len Laurio?"

"Of course," I said.

"Hold it," said Agnes. "Len what?"

"Len Laurio," I repeated. "He's a retired cop from Bridgeport who does private investigator things on accidents and icky divorces and so on, just short of enough to reduce his Social Security check. Daddy uses him sometimes, and so do lots of other lawyers around here. Martin's right. I'll bet you anything he could get our samples into a forensic lab without any official reports or questions or anything."

Agnes whistled softly.

"I'm beginning to wish I had you people around more often," she said. "That's pretty good. Where does he live?"

"Way off in the woods, south of Canaan," said Martin. "He has a little cabin, no electricity, no phone. When people want him, they go find him; otherwise he hunts and fishes and reads."

"I don't remember the map all that well," said Agnes, "but I think we can't get there from here, right? Not without a car, and maybe not even with one, in this weather."

"Well, it could be done," Martin replied, "but it wouldn't be much fun. We can check our map in a minute, but I'd guess it would be about eight miles each way through the state forest, with plenty of ups and downs. There's a pretty decent trail running more or less east and west; one could pick it up a ways in from the abbey land, and as I recall it'd put you out on Route 7, not far south of the turnoff for Len's cabin. Not much fun, as I say, in this weather, but I could do it, or maybe Joanie. But she shouldn't go alone in all this."

"Nobody should go alone in all this," said Nick. "Why don't we put that expedition down as one thing that probably ought to be done tomorrow, and wait and see what else we have on before we start arguing about who goes?"

"Now you're being sensible, Mr. Brown," Agnes said with a hint of humor. "Joan, you are still taking notes? Then you're in charge of bringing us back to that point later. Martin, would you and Nick please go back to your conversation with Miss Peterson for a minute? I am wondering about something you said. You said she hadn't noticed Mrs. Crawley going through the library office to the kitchenette. The way you said it kind of implies that maybe she, Miss Peterson, was thinking along the lines of opportunities for poison, too. Did she say so? Or am I reading in too much? And what, incidentally, do we know about Mrs. Crawley in general?"

"Do you mean, could she be a KGB agent, or rather a KGB mole in the CIA?" I asked. "Not remotely possible. Her family's always lived around here, back scatey-eight generations. You know, Smith College and the League of Women Voters and you name it. She'd be president of the garden club, if we had a garden club."

"So what?" asked Nick. "Look at Alger Hiss, if you can stand it, or what's his name in England. Blue blood goes necrotic practically every chance it gets."

"If we start to argue about the social psychology of treason," said Agnes, "we'll be here all night, or more likely all month. What do you know, I mean really *know,* specifically about Mrs. Crawley's sympathies and associations?"

"The League of Women Voters," I replied, "as I said. She's actually some kind of big shot in it on the state level, but according to what Nick said that doesn't cut much one way or the other. She's about as liberal a Republican as they come, and she's always been on the Republican town committee. She and Daddy are always fighting—completely politely, but always fighting.

"Uh, and Smith College, as I said; we always hear about the reunions."

"Hmm," said Agnes. "She could have picked up anything there. But what does she do for a living?"

"Clips the coupons on her bonds, as far as anybody knows," said Martin. "Her husband died, what, about ten years ago?" I nodded.

"He was kind of a nothing, anyway. You know, like Mrs. Rachel Lynde's husband."

Agnes chuckled.

"So she does her civic stuff, and her library routine, and her car? And as far as you know, she's never had an actual job? Does she travel?"

"A couple of times a year," I said. "first-class trips to artsy places or exotic places, stays in a palace in Florence or in that tree-top thing in Kenya."

"As a suspect, not bad," said Nick. "Wouldn't you say, Miss Breslin?"

"Not too bad," said Agnes noncommittally. "Did Miss Peterson say what she thought?"

Martin and Nick looked at each other.

"N-no," said Martin. "Not exactly. I mean, Nick was asking her what she'd eaten, and she was going along with a pretty meticulous list; but I wouldn't like to have to guess whether she thought it was along the lines of an allergy, or a spoiled can, or poison. Nick?"

Nick shook his head. "I wouldn't like to have to guess, either.

She's—not cagey, exactly; more like keeping her own counsel, and maybe even humoring us a little, too."

Agnes nodded. "Now, how about those prescription medication bottles? Local pharmacy? Anybody know the pharmacist?"

"I surrender," said Nick. "You're good. I only thought of that when I was using the fourth empty for a food sample, which brought it home rather forcefully, her name being printed on it. Dilantin, twenty milligrams, very low dose. I fancy she had one nasty call at some point in the past, and browbeat her doc—not my uncle, incidentally; a Dr. Gerow all the way down in New Haven is on the bottles—she browbeat him into tinkering the titer down because she didn't like the possible side effects or the symbolism. That's just a guess, obviously, based on what little I saw of her personality."

"Excuse me," I said. "What's Dilantin, and what do you mean, a nasty call?"

"Standard treatment for epileptic seizures," said Nick, not at all loftily, bless him. "If she were having them often, or if her doctor thought she was in serious danger, the dose would be a lot higher."

"Uh, did you get a sample of that, too?" I asked, fumbling for my page with the food samples.

He nodded. "We kept a couple, and delivered the rest to the abbey along with the patient. Is Tonypandy's a local chain? I just don't seem to recall anything about it."

Martin and I laughed.

"Mrs. Tonypandy is about as independent as they come," he said. "Um, I would say somewhere in her late fifties, been here as far back as I can remember; been in her late fifties as far back as I can remember, too."

"Meee-ow," said Nick. "A saucer of milk, old thing?"

"No, he's right," said I. "She just doesn't change. I swear she wears the same faded floral house dress—you remember house dresses, Agnes? You know, what a certain kind of aunt would wear, with maybe the smock kind of apron on top? And the figure to suit. I'm *not* being catty, that's simply the truth, it has got to be the same dress every day, or else she has several, all identical. She's open from six until ten, every day, and of course nobody should criticize because it's awfully nice to have a pharmacy available like that, in such a remote place. Except sometimes she disappears, and the store is shut."

"Disappears?" Agnes sat up straight.

"Once or twice a year, for maybe three or four days," said Martin. "Not like a store closing for vacation, no sign in the window saying when it'll open again. Just dark, and the door locked. And then she comes back, and she's crabby enough, as far as I know, nobody has ever asked where she's been."

"I would guess," said Agnes, "from my one look at the town, she lives over the store?"

"Oh, sure, there are generally lights at night," said Martin, "but that doesn't signify, as somebody would say. Her son, Fred, lives there, too."

"She is a widow? Divorced?"

"Widow, I think, although I don't know why I think it. I suppose I've always assumed it."

"And you have no idea where she comes from?" Agnes asked.

Martin and I shook our heads at each other.

"Sorry."

"Well, Suspect Number Two," said Nick. "Got her, Joan? Who's next, Miss Breslin? How about our quondam New Haven chef, now handyman?"

"In a minute," Agnes said. "Let's cover the rest of the medical ground first. Tell me more about this Dr. Brown."

I stood up.

"I'm sorry. I won't have any part of this. You can go ahead and play your sleuth game, if you want to, but not even as a matter of theoretical possibilities will I consider Dr. Michael as being maybe a spy or maybe a poisoner."

"Joan," said Nick. "Agnes doesn't know him."

"Well, I do."

"Please listen. We need your brain around here. The only hope we have of figuring out what is going on, and of doing something about it, is if we keep all our brains engaged. The moment you get that kind of mad, part of your mind gets less functional. We're all mad, mad at the situation, furious that anyone would dare to raise a hand against somebody so essentially good and civilized as Miss Peterson; and I don't know about you, but every time I stop being furious about that I get outraged at the betrayals within the intelligence community. But we can't do anything if we stop thinking."

"Thinking about Dr. Michael as a suspect is a waste of time and energy."

"Not necessarily." He held up a hand to forestall what I was about to say.

"Assuming right now that he is totally outside the category of suspects, thinking him through may give us something on somebody else. It may shed some light on the general situation, or make us notice some fact that we need to establish. I know we've said this before, but it's really important: we are amateurs. We don't have the—the feel for a situation like this that somebody would who'd seen a hundred of them. With all due respect, Miss Breslin, I suspect this is not the sort of problem you generally confront."

"No, it isn't," said Agnes. "Nick is right, Joan. Please, let's just get through all this, so we can figure out what to do. I think not doing anything is getting on all our nerves."

I noticed that she said, "Nick," and sat down, more because that was an interesting event than because either one of them had persuaded me.

"All right," I said stiffly. "Let's get on with it."

Martin counted off what facts he knew.

"Dr. Brown bought his home here at the same time my parents bought this farm, that must be about twenty years ago. He had joined the practice of an older doctor who'd been around here forever; my father did the legal work for him when the older man retired and Dr. Michael took over. I guess the file would be down in the office, although I can't imagine it would have anything of interest. My father also did the closing on Dr. Michael's house.

"Um, I think he married Mrs. Brown right after medical school, and then went into—was it the Army, Nick? Actually, you probably know more about the earlier parts."

"The Army, yes. Korea, in fact. Uncle Michael had spent some time there in his teens, as his parents were missionaries."

"Uh-oh," Martin started to say, and tried too late to suppress it.

"What do you mean, uh-oh?" I asked.

"Uncle Michael volunteered for Korea because he cared about the place, having been there and formed attachments," Nick said calmly. "That doesn't mean the attachments were Red, and Agnes isn't going to jump to that conclusion. He's been a Goldwater Republican forever, as far as I know; in fact I do happen to know that that's how he and Aunt Lou met, in conservative politics."

"None of this is conclusive either way," said Martin, "and I don't think anything we know about anybody around here is going to be."

"Probably not," said Agnes. "But I can probably have somebody run checks on our possibilities, and it is wise to have all of us know as much as each of us knows, if you see what I mean, in case something turns up that makes four out of any of our twos. You see, if Miss Peterson had not fallen ill, and if I had not gotten shot, I could have played cat-at-the-mousehole, waiting for whoever to come and find her—and then *I* should have found *him*. A bit crude, perhaps, but not terribly dangerous, particularly if I kept the advantage of surprise.

"But as matters stand now, I shall have to engage in this old-fashioned detective work. It isn't my strong suit, and I am not exactly in top form for the leg-work bits, so to speak; but it is the best avenue available at the moment. Who is left? Your handyman, and Senator Ely."

I started a suspect table for Joe Fredericks with a sense of relief. He seemed utterly unlikely, for one thing; and I didn't particularly care about him, for another.

As it turned out, we knew very little about Joe.

"Do you know any of the restaurants at which he has worked?" Agnes asked.

Martin and I thought hard, and came up negative.

"How old is he? Where does he live? Do you know where he lived before, or while he was in New Haven? Might he have mentioned a neighborhood, at least?"

"I suppose he's in his early thirties," I said, and thought some more. "I am pretty sure I have never heard which restaurants, or which neighborhoods. I think I remember him being around as far back as I can remember anything." I looked at Martin.

"I can't do any better," he said. "Miss Peterson may know more. Since he sometimes does fix things in the library, he may sometimes have talked to her. And he does bring her food. He lives in a little room over the old garage in back of Mr. Wall's. It's got a kitchen, obviously, but it must be pretty tiny. That's just a two-bay garage."

"The New Haven connection is a point of possible interest," Agnes said. "There is an active Communist Party office there. If they have ever actually run agents out of it, though, they have done a good job, for we don't know about them."

"I know the place," Nick said. "It's pretty lame, or at least you'd say so until you found out that there's somebody around who'll believe anything. They sponsor speakers sometimes, you know, the Assistant Minister for Something or Other of the People's Republic of Albania. And they trot out a few candidates for local races. It's pretty difficult to imagine them actively involved in counter-intelligence, or counter-counter-intelligence; unless the useful idiot business is a cover."

"It's pretty unlikely," Agnes said.

"Speaking of idiots," I said, "something's bothering me. Maybe I'm being too elaborate, but I'm not trying to defend Joe. It just seems that nobody would be so dumb as to first make a habit of bringing food to someone, so that lots of people know about it, and then to try to poison that someone. Nobody's that dumb, right?"

Nick nodded. "You'd think not, wouldn't you? Unless everybody assuming as much gave you a cover. We haven't examined the most obvious possibility."

"Which most obvious possibility do you have in mind?" I asked.

"Whoever it was that shot—shot our esteemed associate, here," he said, indicating Agnes with a half-bow, "may well be a complete stranger to all of us, and is presumably the same person who poisoned Miss Peterson, if poison it was. Isn't it more likely that there is one person running around North Salisbury trying to do murder, than two?"

"But how?" I asked. "We know what she ate. How could a stranger have put anything in her food?"

"Mrs. Crawley's coffee cake, for one possibility," said Nick. "As I recall, the coat closet is off to the left of the front door of the library, well away from the outer desk."

I nodded.

"So what?"

"So think about Mrs. Crawley coming in with the cake. Where does she put it while she's hanging up her coat? On the floor next to the closet? I think not.

"She walks in the door, continues to the desk, deposits the cake and whatever else she may be carrying—shopping parcels, perhaps, or even her purse, since this is a small town with little in the way of random petty crime—then she walks over to the closet and hangs up her coat. Anyone who happened to be in the library, someone who had been there a hundred times or a total stranger, could spot the opportunity and do the deed in a jiffy. He would have to be quick, but not impossibly quick."

"But then it could be anybody at all," I said.

"Not quite anybody," said Martin. "It would be someone who would be unusually interested in Miss Peterson's subsequent health, someone who might visit the library to enquire after her, someone who might be surprised enough to find it open tomorrow—if we could get it open—that he would stop in to fish for information."

"It seems like a long shot," Nick said.

"Long shots are the only shots we have available at the moment," said Agnes. "Obviously we would like to know whether the coffee cake was a commercial one in a sealed package, or a bakery one in an open bag. As to your second point, Mrs. Crawley would not ordinarily open the library and man it on her own?"

"I don't remember Miss Peterson ever being sick enough not to be there, herself," I said, "but no, I don't think Mrs. Crawley would do that. I don't think she even usually goes in on Mondays."

"Perhaps we can talk her into it," said Agnes. "We can appeal to her pride. I gather she is not without that quality?"

Martin snorted.

"But then if she is the poisoner," he said, "and I still can't believe she is, she won't be surprised to find the library open. Maybe we can open the library? I mean, if we explain the situation to Miss Peterson and she gives us permission?"

"Not bad," said Agnes. "Maybe. Maybe we ought to hold that one until Tuesday, though. We have an awful lot to do tomorrow, already. For your list, Joan?"

I nodded, and scribbled.

"Now, your Senator Ely."

"He's a bit of a throwback," Martin said. "I imagine the type is more common in more traditional societies—I mean in places where it's more likely that someone of just average ability will have all the advantages of wealth and education. I like Senator Ely as much as the next fellow does, but even his most ardent admirer would admit there's not much in the way of raw brain power there. On the other hand, he does more with what he's got than lots of people do who're born more talented. I guess it's character; of that, he has plenty. But I can't imagine him having hidden depths. It's just Senator Ely, no matter how deep you go."

"It's just turtles, Mr. Churchill," Nick murmured, "all the way down."

"Exactly," said Martin.

"We'll see," said Agnes.

"I was thinking," Nick said, "that in spite of what we have said about ignoring motive, as all good story-book detectives should, we have been thinking more like spies than like detectives. Wait," he said, as Agnes began to protest.

"Wait. It's given me an idea for the—the interviews we've probably got to do. The idea has the same drawback that this whole line of thinking has, but it is a good cover for gathering gossip; and all good detectives gather lots of gossip.

"It would have to be Martin or Joan, as you will see in a second. The story is a social studies project on McCarthyism."

"*On what?*" demanded Agnes.

"On McCarthyism. You know, those terrible days we hear so much about, when nobody was safe from a fraudulent accusation of Communist sympathy, or fellow-traveling, or even actual Party membership. Well, Martin or Joan goes around with this project, to see how McCarthyism would work in a community, you see? Asks about people's—what were your words, Agnes? Asks about their associations and sympathies."

"No, this is even better," said Martin. "We could ask about who might launch an accusation because of a grudge. That makes it sound more like the assignment of a liberal social studies teacher."

"Then it would have to be you," I said, "because Mrs. Matthews is not that kind of a liberal; I mean she isn't the kind who assumes everybody McCarthy accused was innocent just because he accused them. And besides, we're ruling out local grudges, remember? It was a spy who shot Agnes, or a mole, and the same spy or mole poisoned Miss Peterson, if she's been poisoned, of course. So what do local grudges matter?"

Martin sighed.

"You're right, of course. I was getting carried away. I guess the associations and sympathies business is better. But we're all still letting ourselves get completely carried away with the motive thing. I say our best shot is Len Laurio and the food samples."

"Of course it is," said Agnes. "But one or two of us can handle that, and the others will do better to do something, rather than chew fingernails up to the elbows. Moreover, when you start asking questions, as often as not you find something useful, even if it isn't what you thought you were looking for. It is a decent cover, Nick."

She had done it again. This time Nick did bow, very gravely.

"Somebody has to look after the twins," said Martin.

"And of course we are assuming that school will be closed on account of the weather," I said.

"Is that probable?" asked Agnes.

"I'd say so. Nearly everybody has long bus rides, and half the school board realizes it's dumb to risk an accident, and the other half won't risk the embarrassment of an accident. We can check the radio in a bit, or Mrs. Brown may know; we have to call her soon about reclaiming the twins."

"Here is the probable plan, then," said Agnes, "unless anybody can think of a better one. I'll get my friends busy checking our list of possibilities, assuming I can reach them on the phone this afternoon or this evening.

"Tomorrow, I want to talk to Miss Peterson. Someone ought to, assuming she's up to it; we want to know about that coffee cake, and about any strangers who might have been in the library when Mrs. Crawley brought it; and the abbey is about as far as I can go; and there are—other things, things I want to discuss with her, myself.

"Martin will deal with the social studies project, interviewing Mrs. Crawley, Mrs. Tonypandy, Joe Fredericks, Dr. Brown if he has returned and Leo Ely, if possible. I gather he lives the farthest away?"

"A couple of miles north on the highway," Martin said. "All the rest are fairly easy walks."

"If you cannot leave the twins with Mrs. Brown, or back here with me, that may let him out for now," she said. "You ought to have them with you for the others, though."

"Hold it," he began.

"Hear me out. One, you cannot drop them on Mrs. Brown all day without arousing her suspicion. She is no doubt perfectly trustworthy, but there are already far too many people knowing far too much of this business. Two, they are sufficiently distracting that most people will be put a little off guard if they are about—quite possibly enough so that they will say things they would not otherwise say. The twins needn't be in earshot for the actual conversations, in fact it is better that they not be; their presence in the vicinity, however, may very well be useful. I cannot imagine that they would be in any actual danger. And three, the most unfortunate consequence of their having been around for the shooting and the visit to Miss Peterson is that if we don't give them something to do, they will assuredly think of something on their own, probably with disastrous consequences."

I could see where this was going, and I was not going to be sent off on a long walk in the woods with Nick without a protest.

"Look, Agnes," I said. "You're in charge, and I'll do what you think is best, and I'm not trying to get out of a hike in the snow, but why can't I do the interviews part?"

"You aren't cold-blooded enough," she said. "Of the lot of us, you have the worst poker face, the least sense of the game as a game. It isn't that we care less, but we can pose better. Ok?"

"I suppose. So Nick and I go to Len Laurio's?"

"Listen, sport," said Nick. "Try not to be too downcast. You know the way, you're in charge, and I'll tell you funny stories."

I couldn't tell how much he guessed about my mixed feelings, but at least I could be friendly and polite. I tried on an amiable smile, which very obviously only made matters worse, for Nick looked puzzled.

"It would be best," Agnes said, "if you could leave before dawn, to minimize the chance of anyone seeing you go. Nick, you should go back and stay at your aunt and uncle's house tonight, I think?"

He nodded.

"Then you need to cobble up a story for an extra early departure. Why do people go out before dawn?"

Nick held his thumbs together in front of his mouth and made a rude noise.

"I beg your pardon?"

"The noble duck, Miss Breslin. The noble duck. I shall help myself to Uncle Michael's twelve-gauge, and head off for Little Mudge Pond. Perfectly reasonable behavior for a fellow contemplating his medical boards. I shall come home skunked, and Aunt Lou will have a little fun, which she entirely deserves. Uh, I should like to leave the waders and gun somewhere, perhaps at your fort, Martin? Not much fun for packing up hill and down dale, if one cannot anticipate the pleasure of using them."

So it was arranged. I called Mrs. Brown, who undertook to ship the twins home for dinner. The schools were shut for tomorrow, she told me, and the high school at least through Tuesday, due to a blown boiler; and town committee was now postponed indefinitely.

"Nick says to tell you he's on his way," I said.

"Nick who? Oh, you mean my scapegrace nephew? Well, it'll be nice to have a little more or less adult company around here. Michael is staying over in Norfolk again tonight, as there's a man says he can replace the axle tomorrow. Did your friend get to a doctor, dear?"

"Uh, yes, Mrs. Brown, thanks," I said, figuring that the abbey infirmarian ought to count. "She's doing fine. I'm sorry for all the trouble and messages."

"Not to worry, Joan. Talking of messages, Sister Maura called here just a minute ago to let Nicholas know there's going to be a Mass at 5:00; she'll probably be trying your place next. I'll keep back dinner 'till 6:30 or so, if you wouldn't mind telling him."

"Of course, Mrs. Brown."

"Now, you promise to let me know if you run into any trouble?"

"I promise, thanks, Mrs. Brown."

"We've enjoyed having Mary and Tom. If you need to get rid of them again, please really do feel free."

"Oh, thanks, yes, I will."

I told Nick about the Mass. I am always interested to see how the Mass obligation takes people older than me, but he exhibited neither relief nor irritation. Sister Maura did call, then, and I told her Nick would be there. He left right after that, murmuring something about not being up for the twins' energy level, and wanting to talk to the infirmarian. Martin went to do something about dinner, and Agnes and I wandered into the living room to look for books. I picked out John Buchan's *The Free Fishers* to take my mind off adventures in nasty weather, and Agnes chose Chesterton's *The Everlasting Man*, defying me by a look to comment upon it. I wouldn't have dreamed; I wanted nothing more than an hour's peace. The twins came back and tried to pick a fight about being shipped off to the Browns', but we told them about their mission for the morrow, and they subsided into building a fire.

Dinner was quiet, considering the twins. Martin had broiled three small chickens, so that we would have plenty left for lunch on the trail. Before we began, Mary moved the Wise Men a few inches across the library table in the living room, westward toward the creche. We lit a candle on the Advent wreath, and Martin asked Agnes to read from Isaiah. Agnes still had not gotten through to her people on the phone, and she was worrying about that, and still fighting off shivers from the excursions of the day before. Martin and I were worrying about what we Should Have Done Instead, and Mary and Tom were worn out from playing with the Browns all day.

I was supposed to meet Nick at 5:30 at the gate to the abbey grounds, so I left the washing up, the twins' bedtime and entertaining Agnes to Martin. I packed some things into a small knapsack and left it in the kitchen, so that I could put in Miss Peterson's food samples in the morning.

CHAPTER 7

Everyone has a second-rate streak somewhere, but
there are many lucky ones to whom circumstances have
been so kind that nothing has evoked it.
—*Angela Thirkell, High Rising*

THE TWINS insisted that they could easily walk as far as Senator Ely's house and back, so Martin decided to begin his investigations with him. It was still snowing moderately when they set out, but the plow had been through and it was not very cold.

Senator Ely's house was built by his father between the world wars. It sits back a good thirty yards from the state highway, with beds of roses well organized in front and behind. Its bricks look like solid comfort, and that is what is inside, too. Senator Ely and a housekeeper had looked after his ailing mother for fifteen years after his father died; and now Senator Ely looked after the old housekeeper. They were sitting on either side of a cheerful fire, reading, when the new housekeeper let in Martin and the twins. Two elderly cocker spaniels dozed on the hearth.

In those days Senator Ely was very big and nearly fat, but not in an ugly way. He just looked as if he would be better suited in breeches and a fancy waistcoat than in ordinary trousers and an old tweed jacket. He was quite ready to believe in Martin's social studies project. The old housekeeper never lifted her nose from her book.

"One of these years," Senator Ely rumbled, "someone is going to get around to doing something about that school board. Bet you can tell me all about those innocent victims of McCarthyism, and you never heard of Thermopylae."

"Well, actually, sir," Martin replied, "I do know a little about Thermopylae. Mother had us do the Greeks and the Romans a few years ago, before we started the high school."

Senator Ely snorted.

"Of course, of course. Forgot about your mother. Admirable woman. Ought to make her dictator of education. Solve the budget and the curriculum all in one.

"Well, well. Want me to help you with this foolishness, do you? Tell you who are the reds in town, eh, beginning with your teacher? Can't leave him out. Hurt his feelings, make him think we don't realize he's an inn-tell-eck-shoe-all."

Once Martin realized his cover was working, he began to enjoy the interview.

"Well, sir, if you don't mind, something along those lines."

"Might as well be a little sophisticated about it. You can forget the regular Democrats. Solid working people, God and the Constitution, not a subversive among 'em. You want the summer people, though, the New Yorkers and the professional types, and your teachers? Party line. Tax, spend and reg-you-late, and don't forget you-knee-lateral disarmament. No sense making extra trouble for yourself on account of my sense of humor, though."

"I guess we'll leave the teachers out, sir, if that's OK with you."

"Of course, of course. Your project, not mine, thank God. Let's see.

"Ah, Ginnie Crawley. You know Ginnie Crawley?"

"Yes, sir."

"Over-educated er—" he glanced at the twins, who were not pretending very hard to be concentrating on the spaniels. "Hmph. Over-educated, anyway. She's a Republican because the Democrats won't put up with her. Same problem as all those parlor pinks. Can't believe ordinary folks can run their own lives. Got the permanent mad on against the world you'd expect from a social worker when the bee-nighted po' folks ignore her good advice. Mark my words, Martin, a few more Ginnie Crawleys and the Republicans are done for in this state. Toryism, that's what it is; and yankees won't stand for it.

"Where was I? Is Ginnie a real red? Probably not, but if somebody wanted to he could make a case. That's your project, isn't it? Even did the World Peace Council a few years back, she did. Ever heard of that? Get your papa to tell you. Suits your project down to the ground. Meetings in godforsaken Budapest and whatnot.

"Who else? You want to get ridiculous? Look at Estelle Peterson. If she's a red I'm the Queen of Sheba, but some people wouldn't mind making her out one. Keeps to herself, even on Town Committee. Self sufficient, doesn't show any signs of suffering from not having married, and some men find that annoying. Smart woman, too, and that causes resentment. Bookish, of course, ha.

"Estelle Peterson . . ." he mused. "Ha. Estelle Peterson can't drink gin and tonic. Offered her one right here, after a Town Committee meeting, must have been five years ago; you'd think I'd offered her strychnine.

"You know something else funny? Not for your project, but just to give you an idea. You know I'm executor of her will. Of course you don't, your papa wouldn't tell you. Well, I am; and she came down to Norfolk last Sunday on purpose to tell me she'd made a codicil, leaving half her estate in trust for the benefit of the widows and orphans of intelligence officers. Ours, that is. Now, isn't that funny, seeing you're doing this project now? Seems her nieces and nephews are through college and taking care of themselves, so she figured she'd take care of someone else. Not a big fortune, but enough to help some people who probably need it. What do you think of that?"

"It seems very unusual," Martin said.

"Doesn't fit the red stuff, and as I said, I wouldn't want you to put it in your project. Interesting, though. People are interesting. Why I keep working. Ha.

"Who else? You want some more, Martin, or just a couple from each person you talk to?"

"No, that's wonderful, Senator. Thank you so much."

"Don't you want some coffee before you go? It's still coming down out there."

"No, thanks. As long as school's closed, I want to get through a couple more interviews today."

"Say, you should ask Ginnie Crawley. Maybe she'll tell you I'm a red, heh, heh."

"That's great. Uh, you wouldn't mind?"

"Mind? It'd be hilarious."

So Martin, Tom and Mary said good-bye to the Senator and his housekeepers, and headed back toward town. Mrs. Crawley's house is up a side road from the state highway, and they had time to call on her before lunch.

"Wow, Martin," exclaimed Tom, as soon as they were back out on the road. "Maybe it really is Mrs. Crawley, after all!"

"Or maybe," said Mary, "there was something else about Miss Peterson's will, something Senator Ely didn't like."

"Quiet, both of you," said Martin. "I want to think." So the twins played Call of the Wild all the way to the turn-off for Mrs. Crawley's house, and Martin thought.

Mrs. Crawley was at home, too; a snow day is a wonderful day for sleuthing, because people tend to stay put. It was some time, however, before she answered Martin's knock; and when she did open the door it was obvious that she had been crying.

"Uh, hi, Mrs. Crawley," said he. "We caught you at a bad time, I'm sorry. We'll come back another day."

"Nonsense, Martin. You look like the answer to the maiden's prayer. Come in, come in. I'll make something hot. Put your wet things over there, if you would, and sit down. I shan't be a minute."

They sat on the edges of a pair of sofas that faced across an enormous expanse of coffee table, and looked around. It was an old house, as old as ours, but better cared for than ours probably ever had been. The plaster was a soft rose color, the elaborate woodwork pale cream. There were beautiful old rugs on the highly polished floor ("the kind of rug you walk around," Martin said later), and the furniture was all like Mother's one Queen Anne table, the one we are not supposed to dent.

They heard Mrs. Crawley go into the kitchen, and then upstairs. "I'm going to play this one differently," Martin whispered to the twins. "Don't contradict, don't act surprised, and for heaven's sake don't break anything. In fact, don't even touch anything."

Mrs. Crawley was back in the kitchen, and they heard cupboard doors. She returned with a large tray.

"I know you won't deny me the pleasure of giving you some cocoa," she said. There were also little butter cookies in elaborate shapes, with elaborate fillings; so while Tom made a perfect pig of himself, and Mary wrinkled her nose at him, Mrs. Crawley and Martin talked.

Or rather, Mrs. Crawley talked. "She hardly stopped to breathe," Martin said later. "She almost seemed feverish, or drunk—no, not drunk, she was more precise than normal, not less so. Wired, I guess is the word."

"I'm so very glad you came by," Mrs. Crawley had trilled, "for I admit I was feeling a bit lonesome. You would think I would be used to it by now, and ordinarily I am perfectly self sufficient. The silliest thing set me off, though. I was wondering a bit about Estelle Peterson, all alone, poor thing; and I decided to give her a call, and make sure she was getting along all right, what with the weather having things so shut down. It occurred to me that—that she might not see a living soul from one day to the next.

"Well, I couldn't get through, and I couldn't get through; and finally I called the telephone company, and they said there had been a report of trouble on the line, but they wouldn't be able to send anyone out to see about it until tomorrow at the earliest, the ice had taken down so many lines.

"And that did it, isn't it silly? Somehow finding that I couldn't casually turn to—casually call someone up and ask how she was getting along—well!" She gave herself a little shake, entirely for Martin's benefit, he thought, and made a little show of brave cheer.

"You didn't come out in all this to listen to my foolish little tale of woe, did you?"

"Actually, Mrs. Crawley, we were just out for a hike in the weather. When I heard school was closed, I decided to take advantage of the opportunity. Our parents are in Boston, and Joanie and I are taking care of the twins; so I thought I'd let her have a little peace for a couple of hours. We passed the turnoff, and thought we'd stop by; after a couple of hours in the snow, we were kind of ready for a friendly face, too."

"I'm so glad," she said. "When are your parents due back?"

"Oh, tonight, unless the roads are totally impossible."

Tom started to speak, but Mary overrode him.

"Tom, if you eat one more cooky you won't eat lunch, and Joanie will have your guts for gaiters."

Tom subsided, and drained Martin's cocoa by way of consolation. Mary glared at him, but forebore to pursue the issue.

"Aren't they droll," Mrs. Crawley exclaimed. "Where your mother gets the energy, I cannot think."

"You know, Mrs. Crawley," said Martin, "that reminds me. Mother has been saying how you brought some fantastic cake or something to some social event or other, I forget which; and she keeps wanting to ask you if you'd actually found a first-rate bakery around here; but of course she keeps forgetting. These cookies are just wonderful."

"Oh, now let me see. It could have been anything, for I often do try to bring a little something special if there is a meeting. I confess I do wonder sometimes whether it is appreciated, but it does improve the tone of our little gatherings."

"Oh, it could have been the last caucus, when that silly little man challenged dear Senator Ely for the endorsement. I believe I brought some of those nice little light lemon tarts. Yes, I imagine that was it."

She beamed with satisfaction at Martin and the twins, and there was a slight pause.

"Uh, Mrs. Crawley," Martin said, "Would you mind awfully saying where you got them? Mother would be so glad to know." He began to have the sinking feeling that in five more minutes he would be sounding just like his hostess.

"Where? Oh, oh, the bakery. No, dear, of course not. All the way down in Litchfield, Moore's on Main Street. I know it seems silly to go so far, but the places closer by simply are not satisfactory; and besides," she very nearly giggled, "it is such a good excuse to take Cousin Ella for a little spin."

"Cousin Ella?"

"The Porsche," mumbled Tom, through a mouthful of cooky.

"Of course," said Martin. "I forgot.

"Well, Mrs. Crawley, it's been a wonderful visit. I was thinking, you know, if some day you had nothing to do, maybe Mother could give you a call and you might like to come by. It's not far, and I know we'd all be happy to see you."

"Oh, my, Martin, I am sure you mean well; but I rather think your household would be a bit lively for me, don't you? Must you be going?"

They shuffled back into their boots and parkas, and made very awkward farewells and thanks. Mrs. Crawley was fading back into her shell, if indeed it had been she that came out of it, even as they left.

"She's so dippy she could do murder one day and not get around to remembering it the next," Tom proclaimed as they fled down the driveway to the road.

"Maybe," Mary said, "but I don't think so. I think we just hit her on a strange day, and when she realized she'd let on how bad she was feeling she got embarrassed. Did you catch that about calling Miss Peterson? She wasn't worried about Miss P., she was so lonesome she was ready to call somebody she didn't even like."

"Somebody or other," Martin said, "says people sometimes do loving things in unloving ways. Well, those were hospitable things in unhospitable ways."

"And the cocoa wasn't a patch on Joanie's," said Mary.

"All the same," Tom said reverently, "I call those cookies. Hey, Martin, what was all that stuff about the bakery and Mother and Daddy coming home, anyway? Mother never said any such thing, and you know it."

"I was trying to find out about the coffee cake in the library without having Mrs. Crawley know I was finding out," Martin said. "The people at the bakery will probably remember whether Mrs. Crawley bought one, now that we know where to ask, if we can ask them soon enough. And I wanted to see whether she would be interested in how long the parents were gone for. Once I found out she was maybe a little interested in how long they'd be away, I wanted her to think they were coming back almost immediately. No sense taking chances."

"Oooh," said Tom. "You're starting to think like a real detective and a real spy both at once. Wow."

"Not bad," Mary said judiciously. "But if Senator Ely asks her about your social studies project any time soon, you're sunk."

"I know, I know. Now let me think some more, all right?"

"Are we going to Mrs. Tonypandy's before lunch?" Mary persisted. "Unlike some people, I didn't put away two dozen butter cookies and a cup and a half of cocoa; and I am going to be hungry soon. Are you planning to get Mrs. Tonypandy to tell you about her cell in the Communist Party by asking her opinion on the space program?"

"I said, pipe down."

It was nearly noon when they reached our lane, and Martin decided to break for lunch, after all. He was also hoping that Agnes might be back from seeing Miss Peterson, so that he could settle the twins down with schoolwork, and visit Mrs. Tonypandy on his own. But the house was empty, except for Susie and Ribby; so they ate peanut butter sandwiches (in Tom's case, only a bite or two), and set back out for town.

The drug store was open, but empty, except for Mrs. Tonypandy, herself, hunched on the stool behind the high counter at the back. She was reading a magazine, and the isolation of the storm had not made her any more sociable than usual. She glanced up as Martin and the twins entered, and went right back to reading. Mary and Tom disposed themselves among the paperback books in the middle of the store, and Martin continued to the back. Mrs. Tonypandy must have heard his boots clumping, but she did not look up until he stopped in front of the counter.

Even then, she waited rather aggressively, Martin thought, for him to say the first word.

"Uh, good afternoon, Mrs. Tonypandy."

"Afternoon."

"Rotten weather, isn't it?"

"I don't mind it."

"I was wondering, Mrs. Tonypandy, if you would help me out with a project I've got for school."

"Maybe." She turned a page of her magazine.

"You see, we're supposed to find out, that is, it's about the McCarthy era, you know, when people were going around trying to find out who might be a Communist?"

"I heard of it."

"So, we're supposed to see what it would be like here, you know, I mean, if that happened here. We're supposed to ask about people who might be, uh, who might be suspected, you see. You see? To see how it might be if it happened here."

Martin knew he was floundering, but there was something awful, he told us later, about the way Mrs. Tonypandy was looking at him, or rather not looking at him. She focused on the empty space a couple of feet to the left of his head, so that he had the instinct that there was someone else there; and now and then she turned a page of her magazine.

"So?"

"So?"

"So, how would it be?"

"Uh, that's what we're supposed to find out, that is if you don't mind. I mean, we're supposed to ask people to think of people, uh, people in town, I mean, who might be, might be, uh, suspected, you see."

"I see."

"So would you help me?"

Then she closed her magazine, and leaned over the counter.

"'Would you help me,'" she mimicked. "No, I would not. Shall I tell you why not?

"I am up to here with you newcomers, that's why not. You think you can move into a town and take it over, and people who always lived here can just get out of the way. You, and that Crawley woman, and that library lady, you think we're backward and ignorant and you can do what you like and we'll say How high? Well, not me. We built this business, me and Fred Senior, and we worked for the party, and when Fred went I kept on working, the store and the party, too, and raised Freddie, too, and nobody's going to tell me now to shove on.

"You want to know how many votes I can still bring to a caucus? No, you got your snoot in the air and your head in the clouds, you're not thinking about votes at a caucus, but let me tell you, you got a surprise coming come primary time, and I don't even mind telling you now."

Martin began backing down the aisle, and tripped over Tom. "Oof, uh, I'm sorry, Mrs. Tonypandy. I shouldn't have bothered you."

"No bother," she said, and opened her magazine again.

They zipped their parkas and put on their gloves outside.

"What did I do?" Martin asked Mary and Tom.

"Holy cow," said Tom.

"Let's go talk to Mr. Wall," said Mary. "Look, he's just sitting inside his garage, watching the snow come down."

"I can't," Martin said. "Let's go home."

"It's for Miss Peterson and Agnes," Mary said reproachfully.

"Oh, for—all right, all right. Just give me a second to recover my dignity, will you?"

When Mr. Wall saw them coming, he knocked out his pipe on his shoe and set it on the desk in front of him. The desk stood at an angle, at the entrance of one of the bays of his garage, so that Mr. Wall could do his accounts and watch over the street at the same time.

"You guys been talking to Elva?" he said as they approached. "Not a good idea, in this weather. Old Fred met up with his bridge abutment on a day like this; it brings out the bear in Elva. Want some coffee?"

"No, thanks, Mr. Wall," said Martin. "Look, could I ask you about something?"

"Anything to do with a gunshot on a Saturday morning, or a couple of youngsters and a nun carting a librarian through the snow on a tractor?"

He smiled at the panic in their faces.

"Now, then, now, then, now, then, I reckon I can keep my counsel near as well as that old abbess up the road. I figured she wouldn't let one of her people out on a mission like that 'thouten there was some good cause. You pull up some chairs from the office.

"That's better. You change your mind about the coffee, it's on the stove upstairs from there.

"I also figured, seeing what we got for law enforcement around here, that people who are generally upright people may do things that seem a little strange without necessarily being on the wrong side of anything, if you get my meaning.

"So what were you up to with old Elva, and what do you want from me?"

He pulled a fresh pipe from an inner pocket of his quilted vest, and a can of tobacco from the desk, and set to work with them to let Martin collect his wits.

"Look, Mr. Wall, I can't tell you everything."

"People hardly ever can. I had a man in here last week, a stranger, Massachusetts plates on a nice Oldsmobile, not exactly new, but nice. Brand-new V-belt had wrapped itself around near everything in the engine compartment. Afore he thought what he was telling me, he told me he had somebody put it in not two days before; and then he clammed up; but I could read the rest of the story. Somebody he felt bound to had done a botch job, stripped a bolt on the generator mounting that keeps the tension proper on the belt; and he didn't want to give him away, not even to a stranger. Tried to fiddle a story to take the blame on himself, he did.

"I guess after twenty-three years of listening to people who ought to've taken better care of their cars, I can tell what kind of story I'm not hearing. So you just take your time, Martin, and tell me what you think proper."

Mr. Wall's fresh pipe was drawing now, and he stretched out his legs sideways from behind the desk.

Martin took a deep breath, and propped his elbows on his knees so he could fiddle with his gloves.

"Ok," he said. "Suppose I put it this way, and whatever—whatever inferences you draw are probably going to be correct, provided they're on the outlandish side."

"I figured that much," said Mr. Wall amiably.

Martin did the best job he could of telling half the story, and then fell silent. Mr. Wall puffed for a minute, so that Mary and Tom went to look at his new computer. "So your figuring," Mr. Wall said at last, "is that there's someone around here, maybe a resident and maybe a stranger, although where a stranger would hide is a question, someone who poisoned Miss Peterson some time during the day or two before last Tuesday, and took a shot at your mystery friend day before yesterday? And that this someone is working for the traitors, the what did you say? Moles? The moles in the CIA.

"Seems to me, now that Miss Peterson is safe in the abbey, you should all maybe sit tight until your friend handles it or calls in his superiors. Hmm?"

"Except that," Martin twisted his gloves some more, "Except that, I mean I hate to sound like a kid making up sensible reasons for having an adventure, but except that we have those food samples, and if they're important and spoil or something we're practically not doing our duty as citizens, are we? And what if Miss Peterson feels better tomorrow morning and decides to leave the abbey? Nobody could stop her, and so far our friend hasn't been able to get in touch with her, I mean his people, I mean—"

"Ho, a lady spy, is it?" observed Mr. Wall. "Now, don't feel bad, Martin, you've been doing fine. What about the little kids, though? You and Joanie are maybe borderline adults for some purposes, but nobody would want anything to happen to Mary and Tom; else what's your friend in this business for, or Miss Peterson either?"

"Believe me, I'm thinking about that," Martin said. "I don't think they've been in any real danger so far, barring the shooting, of course, and that nobody could've foreseen. I mean, that was pretty much the equivalent of a runaway garbage truck. And having our friend staying in the house with our parents away, well, the fact she's armed and competent sort of balances things out. I don't think anybody but you knows she's there, and, shoot, our parents left us alone when they went to Boston, and there's always the random chance of the violent burglar or the escaped convict, right? I mean, even the carefullest parents in the world can't protect their kids from absolutely everything; and Ag—and our friend is at least insurance against the ordinary burglar."

"Probably, although I wonder whether your parents would agree."

"Actually, I think they would, Mr. Wall. I mean, I know it's all very strange, but I think they'd say that a stranger who got hurt by trying to do good was entitled to shelter, or something like that."

"Mm, but they'd be a lot happier about it if they were there."

"Granted. So, do you have any advice?"

"Don't take anything to eat from Elva Tonypandy. Or any of your other suspects, either, I guess."

Martin sat up.

"Good Lord, I am an idiot. Mrs. Crawley's cookies!"

"Had a feed at Virginia Crawley's, did you?"

"Not so much me, and I feel OK, and Mary didn't eat much, either, but Tom, oh help."

"I wouldn't be too worried. She's a strange woman, and I wouldn't rule her out as a suspect, although I'd be real surprised if she would even handle a gun, let alone come within a block of hitting anything with it; a strange woman, and I wouldn't trust her not to be on the wrong side of something or other; but I don't see her poisoning children. Hmm?"

"And what about Joe Fredericks?"

"Joe, now. A tough, tough case. A tough life. I wouldn't want drink for my cross, from all I hear. Or Elva for my other one.

"Look, Martin, hardly anybody knows this, and you shouldn't spread it around; but it may be important, so I'll tell you. Joe Fredericks is Elva Tonypandy's nephew."

"*What?*"

"You heard me right. Not much devotion there on either side, I judge; in fact, if you're looking for combinations of people around here, you'd be as likely as not to find those two on opposite sides of any given thing, just for the sheer cussedness of it. But as I say, it may turn out to be a piece of your puzzle.

"It's a sad old story. Elva wanted Joe to be a doctor; Joe loved to cook. He washed out of three colleges, at considerable cost to Elva, before she washed her hands of him. The last was maybe ten years ago. Since then, as you know, Joe's drifted in and out of work in restaurants and back here again. I gave him the room over my old garage the last time but one. Not the steady tenant you might wish for, but I feel sorry for him.

"I'm not one to pry, but I did go in there the last time he went off for a job in New Haven. I just wanted to make sure everything was all right. Saddest thing I ever saw. Big, big bookshelf all full of medical texts, catalogues from medical schools, even an old microscope. Whether he was having hopes of becoming a doctor after all, or whether he was just torturing himself, the way I guess a drunk will, I couldn't guess.

"The other thing I don't know is whether Joe has any sympathy for Communism. But he is one of those disaffected-type people that those people sometimes use. His life is a wreck, so they get him to blame the system."

"Lord," said Martin. "Poor Joe."

"Mm. You can let him out of half of your little mystery, though—all of it, if you're assuming there's only one bad guy."

"Why?"

"He was standing right over there, talking to me, when I heard that gunshot Saturday morning."

"What? What did he say about it? What did you say about it?"

"Nothing."

"Nothing?"

Mr. Wall smiled.

"One other thing about Joe," he said. "He's stone deaf on his left side."

"And he was standing—"

"—with his left side toward the road, and his right toward that compressor. I'd closed up early on account of the weather, and I'd just come down to get some papers, and Joe came in to talk to me about the rent he owes. Here he comes."

Joe Fredericks lifted one hand in casual greeting as he came up the drive, and Martin half thought he would proceed past, to follow the alley back to his apartment. But Joe came to stand before Mr. Wall's desk, nodding to Martin and more vaguely in the direction of the twins. He tossed a dingy envelope on the desk.

"That's half the back rent I owe," he said. "I've been doing some extra jobs, and I ought to have the rest for you in a week or two."

Mr. Wall made no move to touch the envelope. Martin studied Joe, but found no signs of tragedy or of drunkenness. He looked as he had always looked, a tall, lean man, dark, with the face and bearing of someone in a shirt advertisement, someone who ought to have silly women chasing him, but perhaps hasn't.

"If you have some time tomorrow," Mr. Wall said, "you could knock off some of the rest of the rent splitting up the logs from that old maple out back."

"Think I'll be tied up tomorrow," Joe said easily. "Maybe Wednesday or Thursday."

"Don't leave it too long, or I'll get around to it, myself."

"Tomorrow afternoon, then, or Wednesday morning at the latest."

"Fine."

"See you, then. Martin."

"Take it easy, Joe."

"I always do."

Joe disappeared up the alley, and Mr. Wall looked questioningly at Martin.

Martin shrugged helplessly.

"What do I know?" he asked. "I'm not a detective, and I'm not an agent. Even if I were, how could I read that? Everyone else's personality just seems to—to bounce off him somehow, like the snow. I'm sure I've never seen him angry, which is odd, when you think about it. I mean, when my father or I do some kind of job, you know, fixing something or something, we nearly always get mad."

Mr. Wall chuckled. "Hmm. I throw something at something, myself, at least twice a day. More, if I'm working on a lot of new cars. Junk, they are. Too many fancy gadgets and not enough horse sense."

"Anyway, his having been with you at the time of the shooting pretty well clears him."

"Pretty well. When are your people coming home?"

"Probably not until Thursday or Friday, although I told Mrs. Crawley tonight or tomorrow."

"Really worried about her, are you?"

"I don't have any strong sense, one way or the other, for all she was in a very weird mood when we saw her. I was just being careful, you know, a—a sort of an exercise in tactics."

"It'll get dark early, with this weather. Better get those young-sters home. If I think of anything, I'll call you. Meanwhile, button up tight; and let me know if I can do anything."

Martin sighed. "Thanks a lot, Mr. Wall. It's been a relief just talking to you."

"No problem, Martin. Any time."

Martin collected the twins and headed home. It wasn't quite three o'clock, but it looked like dusk. The snow seemed to be coming down harder, too.

There were no footprints in our lane, and Susie and Ribby acted as if they had been abandoned for weeks. Martin began to worry about Agnes.

CHAPTER 8

An open marsh is the wildest place in all Christendom,
and in such an environment Nature has a way of
showing a man how fragile are his devices and
how weak are his noisy efforts.
—H.P. Sheldon, Dusking Ducks in the Money Hole

AS FOR me, I had stumbled down the field to the bridge well before the first glimmer of dawn, feeling lonely and very cold, in spite of all my winter clothes. In my knapsack I carried the food samples from our refrigerator, some cold chicken, a lightweight hot bottle of tea and some dried fruit. At the bottom of the knapsack was an emergency hot pack, the plastic kind you twist to activate the chemicals and make heat for sprains and things. There were also, upon the inspiration of utter paranoia, two highway flares.

Nick materialized from the darker dark behind a tree on our side of the bridge.

"Ack," I said.

"Sorry, old thing," he replied. "Trying to low-profile it from the point of view of the road, don't you know. Didn't mean to spike the blood pressure."

"You're out of sight of the road," I snapped. "Let's go."

He sighed, and tucked a shotgun under one arm, and a pair of waders under the other. We slithered across the bridge.

The lock of the gate worked easily, but getting to the fort was very slow work. The snow had drifted deep in unpredictable places, and there was plenty of ice both under it and elsewhere.

But when I found the mock orange and we turned onto the hidden path, the woods began to turn from black and loomy to pale grey and glimmery. We put the gun and the waders inside the sea chest.

"I suppose I should take the shells with me," Nick said. "Hold it half a minute."

"If you want to, you can hide them in the Clan Oak," I offered. "Nobody knows about it but us."

"The which?"

"I'll show you."

I took him around to the back of the fort, where stood an ancient tree, largely rotted, but with a few sound branches still.

"The O'Connor Clan Oak," I explained. By standing on a rock at its foot, I could just reach the hollow where a large limb had let go, many years before.

"It's quite dry and quite safe," I said. "We use it for secret messages and so forth. If you don't want to carry those things around with you, pass them up."

Nick deliberated for a second.

"Ok. I'm not sure, either way; but I can't imagine them coming to any harm there—or causing any."

We turned to go.

"Oops," I said, looking back at the tree.

"Which oops?"

"Footprints. I left footprints in the snow on the rock."

"Not to worry. There's more coming, plenty more, I should say, and soon. Can't you smell it?"

"I'm not that good. How did you learn to do that?"

"Hunting with Uncle Michael, I think. Can you do rain?"

"Sometimes, but that's easier."

"If you can do rain, you can do snow. You just need practice. Do you ever hunt?"

With a certain amount of scrambling and slithering we had reached the top of the ridge, and we turned to follow the edge of the trees along the perimeter of the abbey gardens. We could just see a few lights in the abbey itself, through the snow that sifted gently down through the still air.

"No. I don't have any aversion to hunting, and I've read about it in Mother's books; but I've never put together the motive and the opportunity. Is your uncle a good shot?"

He chuckled.

"Don't try to detect me, Joanie," he said. "Yes, Uncle Michael is an excellent shot, which is one very good reason I'd be inclined to exonerate him from our mystery, even if I didn't feel secure enough about his character to clear him on that alone."

"It is?"

"I mean that he is such a good shot, he is almost certainly not the fellow who shot Agnes."

"Oh, you mean he didn't—didn't kill her?"

"'Fraid so. Sorry if the reasoning seems cold blooded."

I sighed.

"Don't apologize, for goodness' sake. We keep saying we need cold-bloodedness around here if we're to solve the mystery."

"Talking of blood, I acquired one more datum yesterday, when I visited the abbey."

"Did you see Miss Peterson?"

"No. She was resting, and I wouldn't have disturbed her even if they would have let me. But I saw the infirmarian."

At the north end of the abbey gardens, a narrow track led back into the woods, toward the state forest. A sudden squall of snow made us glad to get back under cover.

"Is Miss Peterson going to be all right?"

"I think so, on balance. But it's the most curious thing. Do you know of Miss Peterson taking any trips to Africa lately?"

"Africa? She can't have. She's been around all the time. A couple of years ago she went to Rome, to do research for her book in the Vatican archives. That's all, though. What has Africa got to do with it?"

"Do you know anything about blackwater fever?"

I shuddered.

"'Men with blackwater die.'"

"*What?*"

"'Men with blackwater die.' It's a quotation. You're supposed to be literate."

"Sorry. From where?"

"*West with the Night.* Beryl Markham."

"The pilot?"

"Mm-Hmm, she met a man with blackwater fever, and it was very scary; but Miss Peterson can't have blackwater fever, can she? That's ridiculous."

"So are her red blood cells. When Sister Andrew got her blood under her microscope, there were hardly any left intact. Lysed, nearly all of them. You comprehend lysed?"

"I have taken high-school biology. Lysed, as in Lysol. Lysed means the—the walls of the cells dissolve, or get dissolved, broken down somehow, and the—the stuff inside mushes out. It's what disinfectant does to bacteria, lyses them. Miss Peterson's red blood cells were lysed?"

"Apparently. No wonder she had a hard time walking and talking. There was hardly anything left to carry oxygen anywhere for her. I don't know anything about poisons, except for the obvious public health ones like lead, so it doesn't mean anything that I don't happen to know of one that mimics blackwater fever. But Sister Andrew is pacing the cloister, because she's a—I guess I mean I gather she used to be some kind of serious doctor, and she can't figure it out."

"But how will she get better? Bone marrow makes blood cells, right? Will hers make more?"

"Probably. And meanwhile, several of the nuns have given blood so she can have transfusions."

"Whether it's blackwater fever, or poison, or some other disease, it sounds nasty."

"Oh, it's nasty enough. But the worst part of it, I mean from the point of view of making the mystery more mysterious—and even from the personal point of view, since solving the mystery is rather critical from the personal point of view—the worst part of it is that it doesn't make sense."

"None of this makes sense," I said rather flatly, for I was feeling overwhelmed and helpless all over again.

"I mean technically, not morally. Think for a second, Joanie. If you're a KGB agent, or a KGB mole in the CIA, and you're going to poison Miss Peterson, why go to the trouble with something that, if it's caught in time, is reversible? If you've figured out a way to slip her something, why not make it instantly lethal, or nearly so?"

"Watch it here. There's a little stream at the bottom of this hollow. It's probably frozen, but watch out, anyway. I guess you make it look like an illness if you don't want anyone to know it's poison. But don't they have stuff that looks like a stroke or a heart attack? I mean, a fatal stroke or a fatal heart attack?"

"Sure they have. Here's your stream. Frozen solid. A little slippery, but—" he stomped— "you're not going through. They have those things that they put on the tips of umbrellas, and somebody just has to have a little accident, a little random push and a little prick, hardly noticeable at the time, and voila. As you say, a heart attack.

"The only way I can see this thing making sense is if our culprit is somehow out of touch with his bosses—his or her bosses, I should perhaps say, to be in tune with the modern usages, and can't get hold of the advanced stuff."

"His or her? Are you thinking about Mrs. Tonypandy? Or Mrs. Crawley?"

We reached the barbed wire fence that divided the abbey land from the state forest. The top strand was nearly eight feet from the ground, doing double duty for trespassers and deer; and there were three more closer down. Nick held up the bottom strand for me to slither under; and then I held it up for him.

"Look," I said, "there's the path; it goes at an angle up this next ridge. With the trees bare it's easier to spot than it is in summer."

"Yes, I see. I don't think we can rule either of your ladies out, although I admit Mrs. Crawley has some heavy long-term cover for the gun business.

"The other thing, of course, is that one wishes to demonstrate conclusively that Miss Peterson was, in fact, poisoned by a conventional introduction of something or other into her food."

"Why on earth?"

"Don't you see? It practically exonerates Agnes."

"*It what?*"

"It seems pretty airtight that Agnes only arrived in town

Saturday morning. If Miss Peterson was poisoned, Agnes didn't do it; and since, given the apparent success of the poison, she probably isn't a second agent of the mole faction sent up to, uh, to account for Miss P., she probably is who she says she is."

"Look," I fumbled. "Agnes *has* to be who she says she is."

"Why?"

"Because she's—she's—"

"Because she's your friend?"

"Well, yes, although it sounds lame when you put it that way. Wait, wait. She didn't shoot herself. I heard the shot in the bushes."

"True. That's practically dispositive."

"Practically?"

"Miss Peterson's *real* friend could have shot her. Oh, I don't know. I'm trying to err on the side of caution, I suppose. I don't believe she's anything but what she says she is, either, really.

"Blast. I keep having an irrational conviction that instead of strolling through the woods with a pretty girl I ought to be on a bus to New Haven; I ought to be in the med school library, researching rare blood diseases."

I didn't answer, because nobody ever called me pretty, except for my father, and I always assumed that was friendly reassurance, keeping up the side. I let Nick think I was preoccupied with forensic medicine, and tried to run an objective inventory. Plain face: nothing actively ugly, but nothing remarkably good, either. Plain brown hair, plain figure. Pretty? Nah. Nick was keeping up the side, too.

We topped the first rise, opposite the abbey ridge, and looked back. The wind had quieted again, but the snow fell steadily, and the abbey was invisible behind a soft white curtain.

"Maybe a half a mile so far?" Nick guessed. "What did Martin say, eight to the highway? Is it all up and down?"

"No. One more ridge, I think, and then down into a fairly level valley. A lot of it's kind of a marsh, actually, but at this time of year we shouldn't have any problem. I was a little worried about keeping to the path this far, but once we hit the valley it doesn't much matter, as the stream in it crosses Route 7."

"Excelsior, then?"

"Something like that."

We kept an amiable silence for the next little while. I think we were both enjoying the relief of being out and doing something, rather than worrying and stewing.

Shortly after we reached the valley, we came around a spinney and surprised a doe and two almost-yearlings who were browsing in its sheltered undergrowth. We were all of us very surprised. The deer hardly seemed to touch the snowy ground as they flew away across the valley. Then, in a glade, large rabbit tracks crossed the trail.

"We must have just missed him," I said. "Here in the open, if he'd run by more than a couple of minutes ago the snow would've filled in the prints."

"Maybe on the way back," said Nick. "I've never seen a rabbit running in the snow."

"Neither have I."

We shoved snow off a log and sat down to drink some tea. I told Nick about the twins' groundhog, and he chuckled.

"I like the twins. I suppose they can be wearing, day in and day out; but to an outsider they are delightful."

"To us they're delightful just exactly often enough that we hold our hands the rest of the time." "Maybe that's the practical essence of healthy family life."

"We'd better get moving, before we stiffen up. What's the theoretical essence?"

"Oh, you know. Anybody can get himself damned all on his own, but nobody gets saved all by himself."

"There it is again."

"The rabbit?"

"No. It's a sickenish kind of mild jolt. A couple of times in the past couple of days I've had an awful, vague feeling that I'm missing something right in front of me. What you just said made me have it again."

"Joanie, you're a conscientious person. If you couldn't make a jigsaw puzzle work out, it wouldn't occur to you to count the pieces. You'd assume that it was your fault, that the solution was staring at you and you weren't seeing it, when maybe somebody else had swiped several key pieces."

"Thanks, I think, although you're the one who said you ought to be in the library. You mean you think we don't have enough pieces yet?"

"I mean I don't know whether we have or not. I think we ought to keep thinking up new pieces to look for, anyhow. Chasing our tails is just going to make us—"

"Dizzy."

"Dizzy."

"So you don't believe in detectives whose subconsciouses know the solution before they do?"

"Well, it seems kind of sneaky, when the author knows, and he can tell the fellow's subconscious as much as he pleases."

"Yeah, it's almost as bad as a confession. Could we get a confession, do you think?"

"I don't think we can afford to count on it. How many people have sudden conversions from movement communism?"

"You know, that almost makes it creepier than simple murder for money or passion or something."

"Why?"

"Well, I sometimes think it would be nice to have more money, so, even if I wouldn't kill someone to get it, it makes a kind of sense that somebody else would. And I guess I think—uh, love might be, uh, worthwhile, even if I wouldn't kill to get it. But communism?"

"I imagine it takes different people different ways, just as money and love do. There must be some who honestly think people are better off in a managed economy, for example."

"Somebody would try to kill Miss Peterson so that more people could live in managed economies?"

"Have a heart. I'm trying to figure it out as I go along. I fancy that—that perception, that conviction, could be the start of the involvement, or one of the convictions that start it. You know, along with capitalists being monsters and so on. After a while, though, personal and institutional loyalties would come into play."

"You mean that someone could feel about the moles Miss

Peterson could identify the way Agnes felt about her friend in the Lubyanka?"

"Her what?"

I told him, and he whistled softly.

"I don't think I'd like to be a spy," he said, "even for the good guys."

"Neither would I. But we don't have a Lubyanka to put the real bad guys in, do we?"

"No. Pretty easy time, would be my guess. Decent food, a good library; no real liberty, but those guys apparently don't value that."

"If I worked for the KGB, I'd almost let myself get caught. I'd think an American jail sounded pretty good."

"When we get back, you can do a travel brochure. Visit sunny Sing Sing."

"Yeah, maybe it can be a secret weapon in counterespionage. Sing Sing, Alcatraz—"

"Alcatraz is closed."

"For the right kind of tourists, we can re-open it. Modified American Plan. Nick, how can we make jokes about this stuff? Somebody tried to kill Miss Peterson, at least probably somebody did; somebody definitely tried to kill Agnes; and we're yukking it up out here in the woods."

"People try to lighten tension, Joanie. It's healthy. Doesn't your father, when he's working on a difficult case, or when there's an important political campaign? Uncle Michael does."

"Daddy does, too, you're right. I've never faced this kind of tension before."

"No more have I. Come on, we need a good marching song. I'll bet that line of trees up there is the highway. What's a good marching song?"

"Do you know 'Men of Harlech'?"

"What do you take me for? Of course I know 'Men of Harlech.'"

So we marched on to glory, or at least to Route 7. Nick had a nice, ordinary singing voice; and I forgot to feel self-conscious about my own, which is also ordinary, as I've mentioned. We scared away any wildlife we might otherwise have seen, but we picked up our pace and our spirits considerably.

The highway was deserted, and very snowy. The tire tracks that led up the northbound side were nearly obliterated; the southbound side was untouched.

"Everyone is waiting for the plows," I guessed. "I've been to Len Laurio's house only once, and it was a while ago; but I think the turn-off is about a half-mile up. Do you want to break for some more tea, or some dried apricots?"

"Not unless you do."

"No, let's just get there."

We didn't sing any more; maybe the road felt a little more public than the woods had, even though there was nobody else on it. The snow still fell with steady determination, and still there was no wind. We stomped along at the margin of the highway.

"How fast do you think it's coming down?" I wondered. "Do you think we'll have trouble getting back?"

"I don't think so," Nick said. "Think about our trip out. Even another twelve inches would only slow us down and make us a little tired—well, all right, a lot tired; and there isn't any way we're going to get that much in the next couple of hours. I wouldn't be surprised if we got all of that, and more, by the end of the day; but we ought to be in fine shape for getting back."

He checked his watch.

"It's just a little after ten. We'll have plenty of daylight, even if we slow down on the way back."

I couldn't imagine what might be wrong with this confident analysis, so I tried to banish my feeling of vague unease.

Len Laurio's mailbox was marked with his name. The trees along his lane bore large, hand-lettered signs: "Private land. No hunting or fishing if YOUR land is posted." His house stood backed into a circle of five huge maples, about fifty yards from the highway. It was a small affair of logs, with a large stone chimney whose smoke smelled very homey after a morning in the cold woods. A pointer and a retriever stood up in the low porch and began singing as we approached. They stayed in the shelter of the porch, though; and their master opened the door before we had to wonder about their intentions.

"All right, Murphy; quiet, Red. 'Morning, neighbors."

Len Laurio was in his middle sixties, short and fit, with a Marine brush haircut and a heavy plaid shirt tucked into heavy corduroy trousers. His face had deep seams, but also the bones at the brow and nose of a Florentine painting.

"Gotten lost looking for the state forest?"

His tone was entirely friendly, even cosmopolitan and conspiratorial. I thought he thought we were out for a lovers' ramble, and I felt myself blush.

"Mr. Laurio, it's Joan O'Connor. I was here with my father last year, when you were working on the Dinswater case."

"Oh, sure. Come on in. Never mind the dogs."

We knocked off as much snow as we could in the porch, and I made introductions.

"Michael Brown's nephew? Glad to meet you. Your uncle has a brain above room temperature, unusual in his line of work. Shuck your things over there, and sit by the fire. I was just going to make some fresh coffee, and I'll bet you won't turn down home-smoked trout."

"That sounds wonderful," Nick and I chorused.

There were dilapidated armchairs on either side of the big fire. Nick pulled a third from the front window, and we thawed and dried while Len Laurio ground coffee beans, sliced what looked like homemade bread, and unwrapped trout.

The room we were in took up most of the cabin. There was a rough kitchen at one end, with a bottle-gas stove and a kerosene refrigerator. It was all very plain, and very clean; and scarlet cushions on the chairs, and scarlet-trimmed white curtains at the front windows, made it cheerful. There was also a brown corduroy curtain across the other end of the room, presumably marking off the bedroom. Several guns leaned next to the kitchen side of the fireplace, along with the kind of cylindrical metal cases that protect good fishing rods. "Walked over through the forest, did you? See anything?"

We reported on the deer and the rabbit.

"Here you are." He brought us steaming mugs of fragrant coffee, and plates of toast and trout.

"Stay there and keep thawing while I get mine. The new ranger went completely overboard about stocking trout this past year; I did him a favor. Like it?"

"It's heaven, Mr. Laurio." I took a breath, and tried to sound grown-up and competent.

"We came to ask you something, though. Are you acquainted with Miss Estelle Peterson, at the North Salisbury library?"

"No, I'm sorry. I still do my librarying in Bridgeport, once a month or so. Habit dies hard. That stack of books, on that side of the fireplace, are the ones to be read; those over there are ready to go back. Why?"

"Well," I looked at Nick, and he waved me on.

"Well, maybe you're used to hearing odd stories, and I guess it'll be obvious that this is in strict confidence; but we found out a few days ago that Miss Peterson, uh, she's a very respectable library sort of person, scholarly, really; but we discovered more or less by accident that she sometimes used to do work, research work I guess, for, well, for the CIA."

I had been playing with my food, and now I looked up to see whether Len Laurio thought the story was already ridiculous. He raised one eyebrow in token of mild surprise, and nodded.

"Interesting. They farm out work more often than we might expect, the ones who have sense enough to value brains over careerism. Go on."

"Well, I gather, I really don't know but I gather, Miss Peterson used to be more actively involved. Anyhow, I had never heard of this before, but I guess I've been sheltered, do you know about the Church Committee hearings?"

Now his face closed a little; that is, he watched me more and showed me less.

"What about them?"

"Well, the story seems to be that some of the people inside the CIA fed other—other officers' and agents' identities to the Committee. Maybe some of the people who talked were, were moderates, if that's a sensible word to use, and apparently some others of them were, well, were working for someone else."

He nodded.

"Amazing, isn't it, the scummy behavior the human race can turn in? I said as much to your father, the last time I was trying to talk him out of his old Christianity. Not that I expected it to take with him."

"Sir?"

He smiled.

"I enjoy a philosophical bicker with your daddy now and then. He thinks the Church will save the West; I think it'll undermine it, sap its spirit. The argument can certainly be turned to the service of the bad guys; but the good guys cannot let it alone.

"So what has the Church Committee got to do with your librarian?"

"Well, it seems Miss Peterson knows enough to be able to identify the—the people who named names to the Committee, I mean the ones who used the Committee to expose our people."

"So you're concerned that she may be in some danger?"

"It's worse than that, actually. We think she's been poisoned."

"Oh-ho. And you haven't told your daddy because?"

"Because my parents are in Boston, because my uncle had a heart attack. And Dr. Michael is stuck in Norfolk with a broken axle. And we, I mean, my brother Martin and Nick collected samples of everything Miss Peterson's eaten, and we thought maybe you could—could. . . ."

"I see. And you haven't talked to the Resident State Trooper for reasons that are completely obvious to anyone who has ever so much as met the R.S.T., to say nothing of anyone who has had professional dealings with him. Hmm.

"What about just calling up the CIA or the FBI?"

Nick intervened.

"Just calling the CIA is no good, if part of the rot comes from there. And the FBI is a complete unknown. I mean, what business do we have, knowing maybe one-third of the story, to activate a totally different service? We might wreck everything. Right now, Miss Peterson's more or less stabilized; she's down at the Benedictine abbey, and there is a real doctor; and we have to assume that the normal authorities will be coming in to manage things as soon as the weather permits; but in the mean time—"

"In the mean time," I interjected, "we have these food samples. And it practically seems like it would be dereliction of duty if we didn't give them to someone."

Len Laurio deposited his empty plate and mug on the low table between the armchairs, tilted his chair back, and smiled.

"You mean, you'd like me to take them to the laboratory and get them checked, without starting a backward trail. When the—what did you say? When the normal authorities arrive you can turn over the lab results to them, and get some kind of citizen crime-buster award. No, I know you wouldn't care about that.

"And you mean there's at least one other thing you don't feel authorized to explain."

He was such a competent interrogator, I practically expected one of us to start talking about Agnes. But neither of us did.

Len Laurio tilted his chair farther back.

"You'll probably be forty," he said, "before you realize how frustrating it is to meet a brick wall in an otherwise intelligent being. I hope you are. I have been reading and reading and reading, trying to find something that might get your father's attention. Ridiculous, I call it, for a man of his evident abilities to be playing with the superstitious toys of old women."

He thumped his chair down, and leaned a little forward.

"Sure, I'll take your samples down, and I don't blame you for not calling in your Trooper Daniels. I'd gag and handcuff him, myself, if I were on a case in his district. My price is that you tell your father I'm waiting for him. I've been reading.

"Do you known it's remarkable what otherwise sane men will swallow? Lots of the pre-Socratic philosophers," he slapped the pile of books next to Nick's chair, "smart men in general, you should read about them, lots of the pre-Socratics, for example, would not eat beans. They actually seem to have believed that human souls migrated into beans. Human souls! Into beans! We're talking about bright men, the flower of a brightening civilization. Beans!"

Nick frowned distractedly.

"Beans," he said. "What does that make me think of? Ah,

probably just a random synapse misconnecting. Mr. Laurio, you say you'll you'll take those samples to a lab?"

"Oh, I'll take them," he said. "I was reserving the right to prolong a squabble, but I can see the point of the main job as well as the next fellow. If the plow doesn't come through in the next hour or so, I'll hitch up the four-wheel and make for Farmington. I can send a job through the lab without questions. What about beans?"

Nick put on his parka.

"Heaven knows. Could I come back and talk to you about trout fishing some day, Mr. Laurio?"

"Any time. Bring your uncle, if you can, even though he's another superstitious savage. Or come alone. Always welcome."

I handed over the food samples and their accompanying list from my detective notes to Len Laurio.

"Neat and tidy," he said. "Nice, professional work. I'll let you know when the lab knows anything. Maybe I can make shift to get by in a day or two, anyway, to see if you've learned anything. Once every couple of years I think it might be handy to have a telephone; but no. Red and Murphy would be yelping the whole time, and half-wits would be on the other end.

"Here, you have some room in your pack, now. Better put in a loaf of bread. With your mamma out of town, you might get started on that store-bought plastic."

We shook hands at the door.

"The trout and the coffee were outstanding," I said. "Thanks for dealing with the samples, Mr. Laurio. And thanks for the bread."

"Your daddy would tell you it's an old tradition that citizens are obliged to help solve crimes."

Nick looked stricken.

"By Jove," he said. "More Wimsey. We'd better be going, Joanie."

"Wimsey?" said Len Laurio. "Never could see the point of the fellow."

"I beg your pardon. Joan is right. Thank you so much for the marvelous provender. I shall try to bring Uncle Michael by."

Len Laurio went back to his comparative mythology, and Red and Murphy went back to cataloguing the shapes of snowflakes.

There were still plenty coming down. "Look," Nick said. "Still no new car tracks on the highway. The entire neighborhood appears to have settled in for the duration. Does it distress you to talk to an intelligent unbeliever?"

"Yes and no. Sometimes. When it's an adult it does, because I keep wanting to get to the bottom of it, and I don't want to be impertinent."

"Do you think it's pride, then?"

"That's hard." I tried to think. "I guess Len Laurio is proud of his mind, and why shouldn't he be? Daddy says he could easily have been police chief, if he hadn't taken early retirement. Or he could have taught at the state police academy, or even run it.

"And I guess he does sort of wave around his unbelief as a proof of his intelligence. But I don't see how that could be the cause. Does it bother you?"

"Only from the point of view of not wanting to see somebody I like unhappy, and I like Len Laurio very much, given our short acquaintance."

"Do you think he's unhappy? Peter Wimsey was an unbeliever, too."

Nick chuckled.

"And was Wimsey unhappy? I suppose not. He was definitely mostly grown-up, and I'm still not sure just what constitutes happiness for a grownup; but I think we have to take him as one of the more believably well-adjusted fellows in literature. Even when awful things happened, or threatened to happen, they didn't shake his—his inner self. He was, however, somewhat apologetic about his unbelief on the rare occasions that the matter arose."

"Are you sure you don't want to be a critic, too? It's not too late to change your mind, is it?"

"It kind of is. I think I like Wimsey because his motive is civic responsibility; and he's larkish about it because he enjoys the intellectual and personal challenges, and also so people won't suspect him of responsibility."

"And that's why you're larkish, too? And why you want to be a doctor? I'm sorry, that's none of my business. Please ignore the question."

"I think I will, if you don't mind. But I have two alternate career paths for you."

"What?"

"Shrink, or *eminence grise* behind the mighty and powerful."

I snapped a snowy bough just right so that it flipped its load all over him, which made us both feel better, I think. Anyway, we laughed, and turned into the state forest. We were glad to have been fortified by Len Laurio's brunch, for the deeper snow made walking difficult. I worried for a bit about finding the trail up from the valley, but we recognized the spinney where the deer had been, and shortly thereafter we were fairly certain we had reached the point where we had come down. We broke there for tea, just to have a reason to stop.

"Are you quite sure about the rest of this hike?" Nick asked. "This is the decision point, if it would be wiser to go back to Len Laurio's."

"I'll be OK. I feel like I've been doing hard work, but there's enough left of me to do the rest. And you?"

"Not so robust as I might like, nor so frail as I used to be, neither. Shall we?"

Getting up the first ridge was tough, because of its exposure on the valley side. The snow was hip-deep much of the time. At the top we stopped again.

"How is your nose?" I asked. "Is this going to keep up all week?"

"I don't think so, but mostly because it hardly ever snows for a week. I can't tell anything in the middle of it, sorry. The temperature doesn't seem to be changing, and if there's a wind I can't feel it. Your fireplace or Aunt Lou's is starting to look awfully good. Yours, I think, if you don't mind. I'm becoming very curious about what Martin's turned up."

"Of course you're very welcome, you know that. I'm wondering about Miss Peterson and Agnes, too."

We started down the other side of the ridge, and it turned out to be a lot easier than getting up had been.

"Indeed. Maybe we should stop by the abbey, in case they need more blood. Giving it's not my favorite activity, but I'm O-negative, so I'm used to it."

"I'm A-negative. Do you know what Miss Peterson is?"

"B-negative, Sister Andrew said. You're off the hook."

"I won't pretend I'm sorry, even though I'd be glad to have helped Miss Peterson when it was all over. I hate getting stuck like anything."

"Nobody likes it."

"You don't know the twins. They pestered Mother and Daddy no end to let them give in the last Red Cross drive."

"The Red Cross wouldn't have taken them."

"Oh, you have to understand the twins. They were seriously proposing that Mother lie about their age to get them in."

"Lord, be kind to mothers. Was I ever a child?"

"Sort of."

"Hey!"

"Sorry."

"Give me that knapsack. My turn, no arguments."

The last ridge before the abbey one was nearly impossible. We were practically swimming in snow, and of course the surface offered no clue at all about rocks and declivities. I began to ache from the wrenches of having my feet go down farther than they expected to, and stop sooner than they should. I pushed myself to just past half way, so that I could tell myself I had more than half finished, and then I simply turned around to face downhill, and sat down in the middle of it all. It came up to my chin, and I didn't care.

"I say, you can't stop here."

"I'm not. I mean, I'm stopping just for a minute. I have to. Sorry."

Nick sank down next to me.

"One minute is all you get. What about a chorus of 'My Knapsack on My Back'?"

"Sadist."

"How about 'Summer Is A-coming in'?"

"Never mind. I'll get up."

Somehow I did, and somehow we got to the top. We went a few steps down the other side, to where a tree had fallen and its branches had kept the trunk up high enough that we could actually see it, clear it off and sit on it. No doubt the snow was marginally warmer than the air, but we weren't particularly cold, just dog-tired. I know the vague stories, tribal memories, practically, about people sitting down in the snow and not bothering to get up, were circulating in my mind; and I imagine they were in Nick's, too. So we sat on the fallen tree and surveyed our surroundings. The track down to the foot of the abbey ridge was still identifiable, although everything looked just a little odd, whether because the snow was deep enough to hide a significant portion of each tree trunk, or because we were so tired. How well we might do at finding our way up the last incline, however, was a question. We couldn't see much of it from where we were. The daylight was just beginning to fade, and I was far from sure that I could do another up-hill like the last one.

"Did you say another twelve inches would make us feel a little tired?" I asked.

"Who's counting?" said Nick. "What about Plan B?"

"Which Plan B is that?"

"If we turn left at the bottom down there, and follow the base of the abbey ridge, musn't we eventually reach your land?"

"There will be the minor matter of the wall."

"We'll think of something. I'm not going up another one of these. We can always follow the wall to the gate."

"There isn't a path, but we ought to do OK. At least it'll be fairly level."

"Good egg."

So we slithered and plowed down, and set our faces for home.

When we got to the stone wall, we found the snow drifted against it invitingly. It looked as if we could simply climb up the drift and vault over the top. But the snow was too soft; we found ourselves wading deeper rather than gaining altitude.

We slogged along. Each time my foot hit an unexpected ditch or rock, the jolt seemed to bruise me all over. I was too tired to have any spring to my joints.

It was getting on for half past four, and well into dusk, when we reached the gate. Naturally the lock stuck, and Nick said complicated and unintelligible things as he fumbled with the key and a lighter.

"Excuse me," I murmured, when finally the key turned, "but the gun is going to stay at the fort?"

"Unless one of us is about to sprout wings, the gun is going to stay at the fort; and my shoulders are too cold and stiff."

"Just asking."

"And my disposition is too crabby."

"Aren't there crabby angels?"

"No blizzards in heaven. What's to be crabby about?"

At last we saw the kitchen lights from the house at the top of the field, and soon Susie was letting everyone know we were back. Martin met us at the door.

"Good Lord, I was about to call the Mounties. Agnes collapsed at the abbey with pneumonia, and Sister Andrew put her to bed. Your aunt called for the third time about ten minutes ago. She no more thinks you're out duck hunting than—words fail me. I guess you'd better have hot showers before we recriminate. I'll call Mrs. Brown."

God bless Martin, I thought, and stumbled upstairs.

CHAPTER 9

It's embarrassing to be taken seriously—as a person.
—D.L. Sayers, Busman's Honeymoon

AFTER A very hot shower I bundled up in the warmest clothes I could find, for little waves of shivers were still filtering up from my insides. I was glad to note that my very warmest old sweater was gone, though, for I missed Agnes, and it was a comfort to think she'd worn it on her trip out to the abbey. She'd shared my attic for only two nights, but it seemed a bit empty without her. Pneumonia: it was odd, after all our worrying about her legs. And had she been able to contact her people at the CIA before she left here, or after she got to the abbey? And if not, could we try to reach them? Should we?

I found Martin, Nick and the twins in the kitchen. Tom was standing on Mary's stool at the stove, stirring something. Mary sat at the table, drawing. Nick was just getting off the phone; he came to kibbitz over Mary's art. He wore a somewhat disreputable sweater that I recognized as Martin's, and trousers that the latter must have dug out of the bottom of Daddy's dresser. Martin's would have been several inches too short, but these had some extra pleats rather obviously being held up by a belt, and I giggled. Martin glared at me; Nick affected not to notice.

"Aunt Lou is definitely suspicious, but Uncle Michael is still not back, and she obviously doesn't feel she can do much about us with him gone. Rather a good cow, I should say, Mary. She has just the right sort of dumb, languid disdain for human events. I don't think she—Aunt Lou, I mean—thinks we're up to anything wrong or bad; I rather fancy she's more irritated at being left out of something than anything else. No dumb, languid disdain in Aunt Lou, not by a long shot."

"Have you heard from Mother and Daddy?" I asked Martin.

"Uncle Jerry had bypass surgery this morning, and he is doing fine. They're coming home tomorrow, if the roads are opened."

"If the roads are opened?"

"You know what Boston does in a blizzard."

"Not really."

"It closes. The police wander around arresting people who try to drive."

"Oh. And what's this about Agnes?"

"Sister Maura called here about half-past three. We'd only just gotten back; apparently she'd been trying to reach us for some time, figuring we'd be concerned. Agnes made it to the abbey about ten, asked to speak with Miss Peterson, and went out flat cold on the parlor floor. Or flat hot, rather, for she had a huge fever. She'll be fine, but I gather she tried to get up when she came to and Sister Andrew had to read her the riot act. I'd've liked to have been there."

"Me, too. How was your day?"

"So-so. Nick and I've filled each other in on the basics. Let's get some hot food into you guys, and then we'll talk. Got your notebook?"

"It's upstairs."

"I'll get it," said Mary. "You stay by the stove."

"Do I look that awful?" I shivered again. "Thanks. It's on my dresser."

Martin checked Tom's pot.

"That looks fine. You don't have to savage it, though. Just stir gently."

He put four loaves of French bread in front of me, speed-thawed and still warm from the oven.

"Break this up for a country Welsh rabbit, OK? I'm going to get in more wood for the fireplace. We can have our conference in the dining room."

So I broke the bread into chunks for easy dunking, and thought what a nice family I had, and how long it would be before I took another long hike in a blizzard. Mary brought down my notebook, and we set the dining-room table. There was a lovely blaze in the fireplace. Tom moved the Wise Men a few inches further west.

"That's too far," said Mary. "You'll have them in Bethlehem before Christmas, and they're not supposed to arrive until Epiphany."

"Aw, you never move 'em far enough," said Tom. "I'm just making up ground for your being so slow."

While they were at it, Martin cornered me at the other side of the fireplace from the living-room.

"This is probably nothing," he said. "But does Tom seem OK to you?"

"I guess so. Why?"

He looked embarrassed.

"He ate an awful lot of Mrs. Crawley's cookies."

"What? Oh. You don't really think she—"

"Of course I don't. I was just asking."

"She wouldn't have. She couldn't have. That's nuts."

"Well, Mary thinks *she's* nuts."

"She may well be, but there are nuts and there are nuts."

"That's what I think. So we just keep an eye on him, and don't worry about it?"

"You bet we don't worry about it. Nobody is that nuts."

"That's what I think."

Martin lit the first candle on the Advent wreath again, and handed the Bible to Nick.

The people that walked in darkness, have seen a great light: to them that dwelt in the region of the shadow of death, light is risen.

I rather wished one would. Most of the time, I like life the way it is now; but for just a moment, I had a strong subjective feel for the wish that the Lord would come back and settle things.

After a few bites of the crusty bread and hot cheese I finally stopped shivering.

Martin and the twins told us about their interviews, and Nick reported on what he had learned from the infirmarian.

"We sure have come up with a lot of stuff," Tom said.

"None of it proves anything at all," said Mary, "except that Joe

Fredericks didn't shoot Agnes and several people are mad at Miss Peterson. Some of them might be in the KGB, but we can't really tell."

"Some of them might be agents being run by the KGB," Martin corrected, "and we can't tell at all. So let's start, anyhow, from the basic operating theory. With the coffee cake being from a bakery, we know that Nick's idea might be right. The bag would've been open, not like the sealed package of a commercial cake. Mrs. Crawley could've left it at the front desk for a minute, and someone who just happened to be there could've put something in it. So, do we try to open the library tomorrow and see who comes in?"

"I've done enough odds and ends of volunteer work for Miss Peterson that I could probably get the key from Town Hall," I said. "Mrs. Redfern wouldn't think twice about it, probably—"

"Mrs. Redfern?"

"The Town Clerk. She'd probably give me the key, but I'm not really happy about it."

"Neither am I," said Martin. "Not that I don't think you'd do a bang-up job, for I'm sure you would. But it's a big exposure. Let's put that aside for a minute. What else can we follow up?"

"Miss Peterson's will," said Mary. "It must be in Daddy's office. I can go get it now."

"Hold it," said Nick. "It may be your own front yard, but you're being a good deal too intrepid. We'll put the will aside for now, too."

"But—" said Mary.

"Hold it," Martin affirmed. "What's going to be in the will, anyway? Leo Ely told us. We know about that already. What else have we got?"

"We've got Mrs. Tonypandy's personal war," said Nick. "Anybody know anything about that?"

"Daddy said there would be a war," said Tom.

"What?" said Nick.

"Over town committee," I explained. "Mrs. Tonypandy's run the candidates' subcommittee forever. They're supposed to recruit new people to run for office, but usually they recruit the same old people to sort-of run. So Miss Peterson said she wanted to try, at the last full town committee meeting. She said she'd like to take a turn at candidate recruitment."

"It's a turf thing," Martin explained. "I suppose I shouldn't have been so surprised at Mrs. Tonypandy's reaction this morning."

"Hardly sounds like a reason to do murder," Nick observed. "But when was that last meeting?"

"About two weeks ago," Mary said. "I'll check the calendar in the kitchen."

"And what about Joe Fredericks being her nephew?" Martin asked.

"It probably just means that we can expect unexpected reactions," Nick said. "Would Mrs. Tonypandy hold it *against* Miss Peterson that she'd helped Joe, gotten him jobs? I don't see it. Or would she feel inordinately grateful? Not according to what Mr. Wall said, and certainly Mrs. Tonypandy's behavior to me bears that out, considering that she appears to be lumping us in with Miss Peterson as the enemy class. It looks like a dead end to me."

"What about some kind of jealousy between Joe and Fred?" I asked.

I cannot see how it could affect Miss Peterson," Martin said.

"No more can I," said Nick.

Mary came back in.

"Three weeks ago tonight for the last town committee," she said. "I didn't think it'd been so long."

"Well before Miss Peterson got sick, then," Nick said. "Wasn't there one on for Saturday? Don't they always have them on the same night?"

"They keep trying to fix a day," Mary explained, "but enough people are too crabby about it that it keeps not working, and they have to schedule it from one meeting to the next."

"Contentious folks," Nick observed. "Let's try to cover the other thing about Mrs. Tonypandy."

"The Dilantin?" Martin asked. "We can't tell anything about that without the lab, can we?"

"I mean her disappearances," Nick said. "Can you people think back and pin down the past few times she's been away?"

The phone rang in the kitchen. Mary ran for it, and came right back.

"Nick, it's Sister Andrew, and she's asking for you."

The rest of us trailed out after him. Was Miss Peterson worse? I refused to let myself think the word, dead.

"Sister, it's Nick.

"—Oh, of course, a good thought.

"—Mm, Hmm.

"—a history of what? Never mind, I'm sorry. I heard you. Good heavens. But this—

"—No, that's what I was about to say.

"—Yes, of course. Well, that's good, in a way, isn't it?

"—Yes, yes, of course. I say, Sister, will you need more blood? I'm O-negative, so I'm rather used to it.

"—It will be a pleasure, honestly. I shall stop in in the morning, if that suits you.

"—Yes, all right. Thanks so much, Sister.

"—Good-bye."

He hung up, and looked around at us. His own face was puzzled and abstracted.

"Sister Andrew took the sensible precaution of calling Dr. Gerow in New Haven. His name was on the Dilantin bottles, you remember. Quite right to check in with him about his patient, after all; he might have known something about her present condition, or about something else we—I mean Sister Andrew—should be watching for.

"Well, he sort of did. Dr. Gerow was Miss Peterson's mother's physician, as well, you see; and Miss Peterson's mother suffered from chronic hypochromic anemia. Obviously there's more to what Miss Peterson's got now than just that; but it's a datum, isn't it?"

"What's hypochromic anemia?" Martin asked.

"Oh, you ought to be able to figure it out from the roots of the word," Nick said absently. "Hypo, meaning less or low; chromic, meaning color. Low color, low hemoglobin, actually; but the blood actually looks rather pale to the eye. Sometimes you can treat it with iron; sometimes you need transfusions; lots of different things cause it. . . .

"Blast it, anyway," he exclaimed. "There is something more here. I just know there is something more here. I want to know what Miss Peterson's mother died of, and I don't know why I want to know. I mean, I can't put together something she might have died of that would mean anything to what's going on now. What is the matter with my brain today, anyway?"

He spun away from us, and went to stare out the window.

"What's hemoglobin?" Tom asked.

"It's what carries oxygen around in your blood," Mary said. "It's what you need iron for, dummy; it's why you have to eat liver and spinach."

"I knew it sounded nasty," Tom said, and she kicked him in the shin, for we were all still watching Nick.

"I'm sorry," the latter said, turning finally. "I can practically point to the place in my head where it's supposed to be, but it isn't there now. I told Sister Andrew I'd give some blood tomorrow for Miss Peterson's transfusions; maybe that'll help. You know, like leeches in the Middle Ages. I'll eat liver for a week to catch up. Let's get back to detecting."

We trailed back into the dining room. I stirred up the fire and put on another log.

"Nick?"

"Yes, Joan?"

"Does this mean maybe Miss Peterson wasn't poisoned after all? Maybe she just has a bad case of whatever her mother had?"

"Maybe. We've never been positive about poison, remember. This does tend to make it less probable, but it doesn't eliminate it, I don't think. There are other things going on in her blood, weird things, not just plain old anemia."

"Hey, Nick!" said Tom.

"Yes, Tom," said Nick, a little tiredly, a little patiently.

"Wouldn't it help if you could look at some medical books?"

Nick sighed.

"It might. I've been wondering whether I ought to try to get down to the med school library." He glanced at me. "Uncle Michael doesn't have anything at all at his house. His stuff is all at his office in Norfolk; it might as well be on Mars."

"I know where you can get some medical books."

We all looked at Tom.

"Oh, no," said Martin. "You can't go breaking into Joe Fredericks' apartment; and you can't ask him for his books, either. Apart from setting off an alarm, in case Joe is a bad guy, after all, or more likely in case he might talk to a bad guy, it'd violate Mr. Wall's confidence. Joe doesn't know Mr. Wall's been in there."

"Mr. Wall could let us in," said Mary, "and one of us could keep watch in case Joe came back."

"Are you out of your mind?" Martin said. "Having a spy in the house has gone to your head."

"Wait," I said. Martin glared at me. "No, listen. Nick, do you remember what Len Laurio said? About citizens having a responsibility to help apprehend criminals?"

"I don't think that extends to warrantless searches," Martin said.

"This isn't a search," I persisted. "We're not looking for evidence against Joe. He's in the clear, remember? Mr. Wall said Joe was standing in the garage with him when he heard the shot Saturday morning. We just need some information, and Joe just— just happens to have some books."

"If it isn't a warrantless search," Martin said, "it's breaking and entering."

"Not if the landlord lets us in," Mary said.

"You don't know landlord-tenant law," said Martin. "We're not lawyers any more than we're doctors. The law probably says the landlord can go in if he has a real reason to think there's a safety hazard, or something."

"I'll bet it also says something about if the tenant is behind in the rent," Mary retorted. "And maybe there is a safety hazard, too."

"Oh, sure," said Martin. "Joe hasn't cleaned his hamster cage in a month."

Mary looked reproachfully at him.

"Look," said Nick, still looking fuddled, and now looking torn, too. "Look, let's put that one on the table, too, OK? Along with the other things we're going to talk more about, or look into."

"They're piling up," I said, looking at my notebook.

"Let 'em pile," Martin said. "Difficult as it may be to remember at the moment, Mother and Dad did say something about staying out of trouble."

"Maybe Leo Ely could get a warrant," Mary said.

"Be serious," said Martin, more gently. "For starters, can you imagine what Agnes would say if we told one more person? And to go on with, we don't even know for sure that Leo Ely's clean in this. And furthermore, no judge is going to issue a warrant that would allow a bunch of kids to search, yes, I said search because that's the only kind of warrant would apply, to search somebody's premises; and much moreover, there aren't any judges within walking distance, and the only person we know with a four-wheel drive is Len Laurio, and he doesn't have a phone.

"Now, I'm sorry I was nasty before, but will you can it, Mary?"

"With reservations," she said calmly.

"Phooey," said Martin. "You should be in bed. Where the devil were we?"

"Well," said Nick, "talking of the authorities, what about Agnes's friends in Virginia?"

"In where?" asked Martin.

"Langley, Virginia. The CIA. Can we assume she reached them this morning before she left for the abbey? I think not. She may have, but we have to assume the worst. Supposing she didn't, should we try?"

"We've been part way through this before," I said. "At least, Martin and I have.

"Look, we can't just call the CIA and tell our story. If what Agnes said is true, we might tell it to exactly the wrong person. We might tell it to a—to a bad guy. And to anybody else we would probably sound like a bunch of imaginative kids. Or pranksters."

"What about Miss Peterson's code?" asked Mary.

"Her code?" Martin repeated. "Oh, you mean the saint. Saint—who was it?"

"St. Eligius," said Tom. "That's right. We can call the CIA and say we have some important information about St. Eligius. Then they'd know we were serious, and they'd let us talk to the right person."

"There's something wrong with that," I said. "Yes. Here, look. Do you remember what Miss Peterson said? She thought first what day it was, right? 'December 1, Eligius,' that's what she said. I'll bet the code changes with the calendar. Where's the calendar?"

Mary flew to the kitchen this time, but she came back drooping.

"There's nothing on it for today or tomorrow," she said.

Nick chuckled.

"Newfangled calendar," he said. "Not enough saints. You need an old one, or a *Lives of the Saints.*"

"*Lives of the Saints,*" I whispered. "Miss Peterson's book."

Mary ran a few steps toward the living room, where most of the books are, and stopped.

"It's in Daddy's office," she said. "I'll bet you anything. Remember? Mother said something had to go, and the older religion books matched best with the law books."

We looked at each other.

"What do we do, vote?" asked Martin. "I'm not happy, but if you guys agree, I guess we find out tomorrow's saint and call."

"Absolutely," said Tom.

"You're too young to vote," said Martin. "Nick?"

"Abstain. Sorry. I just can't come up with a clear idea of what's wrong with the idea, or of what's right with it, either. Joanie?"

"Thanks a whole lot. What good is my judgment? All right, yes. Miss Peterson didn't think the bad guys knew the code, and Agnes didn't, either. I have to trust their judgment. I say we call."

We all felt a little better, I think, for having a definite plan. It gave us a taste for more.

"What do we tell them?" I asked.

"About Miss Peterson and Agnes," said Tom.

"And what about our suspects?" asked Martin.

"Hmm," said Nick. "Agnes was talking of having her people run checks on them. We could do the same, or at least we could ask."

"Well, OK," said Martin. "But who?"

"Mrs. Crawley," said Mary, quite firmly.

"Nobody does murder over a car," said Martin.

"I told you before, she's nuts. And there's the regular jealousy over the library, too. And besides, it might not be personal. It might be political. It might be because of the KGB stuff. That's the only reason the CIA'd be any good, anyway."

"Well, Senator Ely, too, then," said Tom. "You never know. There might have been something he didn't like about that change in the will."

"And Mrs. Tonypandy," said Mary. "She was much more crabby than the situation called for."

"And Joe Fredericks," said Nick.

"Joe is in the clear," said Tom.

"Probably," said Mary. "Why not definitely?"

"We have only Mr. Wall's word that Joe didn't shoot Agnes—"

"Oh, come on."

"—and I still remember what Miss Peterson sounded like when she told us not to get Joe to help. And she didn't want him to come in, when we first knocked at her door and she thought it was Joe."

"Anyone else?" I asked, finishing off the list in my notebook. Nobody answered.

"What else have we got?" Martin asked.

I reviewed my notes.

"Miscellaneous things that don't seem to point anywhere. The asperula, by person or persons unknown. Miss Peterson's telephone being cut, maybe by the wind and maybe not."

"What about opening the library?" asked Nick. "Joan?"

"I have to live in this town, you know, when all the fun is over."

"And what does she do with him if she bags him?" asked Martin.

"Hmm," said Nick. "If we receive reinforcements from Langley, she could just finger him quietly."

"Finger him?" Mary asked.

"I-den-ti-fy him, dummy," said Tom.

"And if they don't get here?" I asked.

"Let's make that a contingent plan, then," said Nick. "If the reinforcements say they'll be here, Joan gets the key from Town Hall and opens the library. How's that?"

He looked at me.

"I guess so. I don't like it, but I can't tell whether I don't like it because it's dumb, or because I don't like putting myself forward."

"So if you always knew why you feel the way you feel," said Nick, "you'd be abnormal."

"Baloney."

"OK, so chase your own tail and be miserable, if that makes you feel better. Oh, Lord, I'm sorry, Joanie. Please forgive me. I didn't actually mean that. I was just tired, and it kind of fell out of my mouth."

"It's OK." I turned away. "I'll do it."

"Harumph," said Martin, "or something to that effect. What's next, people? First thing tomorrow, we need Miss Peterson's will and the *Lives of the Saints* from down in Dad's office. What else?"

"The file on Dr. Michael's house," I said. "You want to play it out, we'll play it out. And I vote we also check Daddy's computer for anybody else we're interested in. He may have done some other work for one of them, something we don't know about if it's long enough ago. There might be a clue. Probably not, but there might be."

"Good thinking," said Nick, dead even. "What about Joe Frederick's books?"

"No," said Martin.

"You're straining at gnats," I told him.

He stared at me. "You actually think we should break into somebody's apartment—somebody's house, I may as well say, for it comes to the same thing. How would you feel if somebody broke in here?"

I thought about Agnes at my attic window two nights before, and what I had felt about the twins, sleeping peacefully, and the threat of someone maybe coming.

"That's not fair. That's—that's what Daddy calls a false equivalence. You know, like when some liberal says the United States and the Soviet Union should stop being nasty to each other. Property rights are very important, but you can—can abrogate them, is that the word? You can abrogate them for a good reason, if it is a good enough reason. Like if you're rescuing somebody from a burning building, that's not trespassing."

"And like a mutiny when the captain's cuckoo," said Tom. Martin glared at him.

"If you start saying everything's OK in a good enough cause," said Martin, "you end up with no law at all. You end up saying you can suspend the rules just because you feel like it."

"It isn't just because I feel like it, and I promise you I don't feel like it, not one bit. It's because there may very well be information there that can help save Miss Peterson's life, and maybe Agnes's, too, if it leads to a killer who might otherwise get her. She's not going to stay safe in the abbey for long, you know."

"Oh, so you're going to protect a CIA officer."

"Maybe I am. It's sort of an accident, like the weather is an accident. If it weren't for the weather, Dr. Michael would be here now, and we could count on Mother and Daddy being here tomorrow. If it weren't for the weather, Agnes wouldn't have sprained her ankle, and she might also be here.

"Come to think of it, Trooper Daniels being who he is is like the weather, too. A different Resident State Trooper would be somebody we'd have gone to Saturday afternoon, and all of this would be out of our hands.

"But it isn't out of our hands, is it? You just got finished saying I ought to go open the library tomorrow, and you didn't happen to mention that that's going to involve lying to the people at Town Hall, at least by implication, about Miss Peterson's wanting me to have the key. If you look at it in a vacuum, I don't have any business opening the library; and we don't have any business going through Joe's books. But it isn't in a vacuum, is it?"

Martin was angry.

"You're talking situational ethics," he said.

"Don't swear at me. I'm not, and you know it. I am saying that for a good enough reason, it's sometimes right to break a rule—or to say the rule doesn't apply."

"Sister, you'd better be pretty sure you know when the reason is good enough."

"Mostly I don't, or rather, mostly it isn't; and so I follow the rules, or at least I—"

"At least she affirms that she ought to follow them," said Nick. "Joan is right, Martin. This is a pretty sophisticated problem, and Joan is right. Look, think backwards to the reasons for the rules. Why are we not supposed to go into other people's houses? Because property rights are one of the things that keep us free to live our lives. Only policemen with warrants are supposed to break in. Well, do you think Agnes gets a warrant when she has to go into someone's house? And is that wrong? When she does it, it's at least potentially a matter of life and death. And when does a judge issue a warrant? When it's a matter of life and death, or at least of a serious crime, so serious that it justifies overriding property rights.

"Besides," he made a funny face at Martin. "I wouldn't mind if Agnes broke into my apartment. Oh, all right. I'm sorry. But, you know, according to what you said that Mr. Wall said, Fredericks is behind in his rent."

Martin sighed.

"That may be the saving grace in the situation," he said. "But it seems like a pretty weak reed to lean on. Do you really think that looking at those books could make a difference?"

"Ach," said Nick. "I don't know. Sister Andrew is beating her head against the wall; I'm beating my head against the wall. It's this awful feeling that there's something there, something we're not seeing—"

"All of the pieces are there," I murmured.

"All right, fair enough, yes. All of the pieces are there, and I'm just not looking at one of them right. If I can just look through some haematology—"

"Some what?" asked Tom.

"Good grief, what time is it?" asked Martin. "Nine thirty-five! You guys, upstairs. Move it."

"But—"

"Let me say it just one more time. You give me just one little bit of trouble, buster, and I promise you the next time Mother and Dad go out of town—"

"Oh, all right."

Tom started up the stairs.

"I'll be up to hear prayers," I called after him. He grumped something unintelligible. Mary stood in front of me.

"Is it really right that sometimes you're supposed to break rules?"

"Oh, Lord, sweetheart. I think it's more that sometimes a rule doesn't apply. But you have to be awfully careful. You have to know, *to know*, that the—the rule you're following is more important than the one you're breaking, or is the one that—that more applies."

"You mean what Mr. Laurio said? That we're supposed to help catch criminals?"

"Mary, listen. Most of the time, there are proper police and things to catch criminals; and the most everybody else gets to do is just tell the police things. This is a very unusual situation. None of us will probably ever see anything like this happen again. OK?"

"OK, Joanie. We'll be ready for prayers in a minute."

"OK, sweetheart."

She went upstairs, too; and I looked at Martin and Nick.

"If we hadn't already decided to call the CIA, that would do it."

"You did fine, Joanie," said Martin. "Look, normal kids their age play cop all the time."

"Yeah, but suppose there's a robbery in town next month."

"We'll lock up the twins until the ordinary authorities have finished the job."

Nick rose.

"I'd better go make peace with Aunt Lou," he said, "and get some sleep before parting with a pint of the best in the morning. I'll be back right after that. I imagine Sister Andrew keeps early hours."

"We're going to have to retrieve your uncle's gun," I reminded him.

"If the weather's fit, I'll get it on the way back here," he said.

Martin began to cart dishes out to the kitchen, and I saw Nick to the front door, which was the more direct to the Browns' house. He put on his coat, and paused.

"Joanie, would you allow me to apologize again for my stupid remark?"

I froze.

"Oh, it's all right. Forget it."

"It isn't, and I can't. Look, you've done splendidly. What I said was—please let me explain. You're too sensible to have your head turned, even supposing my ego were inflated enough to suppose I might turn it. How can I say this? Look, I'll probably never fall in love with you; I may well never fall in love with anybody; but if ever I do fall in love with anybody, she'll have to be as good as you've been the past couple of days. I mean it. What did Richard Hannay say about his wife? 'She didn't scare, and she didn't soil.' Really, Joanie, you've been outstanding. I just wanted you to stop giving yourself a hard time; and that was not really a reasonable wish, given who you are. OK?"

"Well, think it over. I meant what I said—I mean, what I just now said. Good night."

"Good night," I said noncommittally, and locked the door behind him.

I'm sorry I was crabby. I didn't say it out loud. Maybe because it might have been just a polite noise in return for the compliment? Maybe because the compliment made me feel thorny and crabby all over again.

But it was a decent compliment. I didn't mind thinking it over when I went up to hear the twins' prayers, or when I came back down to help Martin with the washing up.

CHAPTER 10

There's only you and I that can do anything.
—John Buchan, Castle Gay

A SENSIBLE person who had spent most of the day hiking and
climbing through a blizzard would have slept soundly that night.
I awoke just after one o'clock, imagining that I saw Agnes standing by the window, peering out past the edge of the curtain. After
that I tried telling myself that I would need the best judgment and
most grown-up demeanor I could muster on the morrow; and I
tried reciting The Lord is my shepherd, which usually helps me
settle down; and neither worked. I fell asleep a few times, but each
time the dreams got sillier.

—I was following Nick down a row of library stacks, and he
was pulling book after book from the shelves, and throwing them
on the floor. He hardly seemed to read a page before he cast aside
one volume and pulled out the next. I was sure the librarian would
be coming any second to yell at us; and I was picking up books
after him and trying to shelve them; but I couldn't read their titles
or the call letters inked on their spines. Footsteps approached, and
I turned to see a tall man, a stranger, the librarian or someone
worse. I could make nothing of his features: his face was just a
blur. I tried to warn Nick, and found that I couldn't speak. I woke
up and tried to laugh at myself. The old futility dream. Truly sea-
soned detectives knew how to ignore that one.

—I was shoveling snow from the path up the abbey ridge
toward the fort, and it was falling faster than I could shovel. I
could not make any headway up the rocky slope. Near the top,
next to the turning, sat Agnes in one of our kitchen chairs. She

162

was tied to it, and gagged. Ribby sat in her lap, fast asleep. I thought that if I could wake Ribby, she could chew and claw through the ropes and free Agnes. I tried to call to the cat, but I found that I could not speak.

I sat up in bed.

"This is utterly ridiculous. Next thing I know, Susie will be on the phone to the CIA."

The ghosts vanished, at least. It was nearly five o'clock. I headed for the shower.

By six-thirty I had some sweet rolls in the oven, and the coal stove was going full blast. I was operating through a cloud of fatigue, but operating any old how felt better than being a dummy in bed. A little hint of dawn should have been coming up in the East, but it wasn't. Susie began to fuss at the kitchen door, so I opened it.

Someone was walking up the driveway. He was about twenty yards from the house. My ears roared with adrenaline, and I nearly closed the door on Susie's hindquarters.

"Joanie."

It was Nick.

"Of all the—"

"This must be our fated hour."

"Lunatic. You can help yourself to coffee, while I decide whether or not I've had a heart attack."

He did.

"I saw the lights as I was walking to the abbey, and thought I'd stop for a second. Mm, coffee for all the angels and saints. Couldn't you sleep, either?"

"Not much," I admitted.

"There's a faint breeze, almost warm. Something funny's going to happen."

"I am not ready for something funny."

"Take heart. Maybe the bad guys aren't either."

Susie whined at the door, and I let her in. I could almost smell what Nick meant. The air was still dead cold, and dead black when it should have been softening to grey; but there was a something lurking just under the threshold of noticeableness. I shook my head and closed the door.

"I'd almost prefer a blizzard."

"We'll see. The meteorology is the Lord's, and the fulness thereof. I must be off. England and Sister Andrew's blood bank expect every man to do his duty, what? I shall be back as soon as I can."

"Watch out for whatever it is that hangs out in strange mornings."

"Not to worry."

I shut the door again, and shivered. There was almost a dampness to the air now, which was impossible in the cold. Susie whined again, and pressed down into her bed. Ribby appeared from nowhere, and joined her; and Mary followed soon after.

And sneezed, hard.

"Good morning, I think"

"That sounds terrible."

"'Sdothing." She sneezed again.

"Says you. Sounds like a rhinovirus nothing to me."

"If I go back up for some Vicks, will you quit clucking?"

"Maybe."

I put on a pot for oatmeal, and Mary came back, smelling like a camphor factory.

"Why isn't it getting light faster? It's nearly seven."

I pressed my nose to the window, and got no wiser. Susie scrambled up and walked to the door—a matter of duty, apparently, rather than desire. I opened it, and understood. There was finally enough light to show the white bank that lay at the bottom of the field, down by the stream and the abbey fence, much higher than the snow could be.

"Fog."

"You're kidding."

Mary came to look out, too. There was a haze over the road, also, thinner and higher than the one over the stream. We could almost taste it in the air, dank and nearly still, with just a tiny, wandery motion. It was definitely growing warmer. I shut the door, and shivered some more.

"Do you want some cocoa?"

"No, thanks. I'll make some tea. I'm not hungry."

"Uh-oh."

"You said you'd stop clucking."

Martin and Tom came down, then, so subdued that they did not even bother to check on my report of the weather. We were just finishing breakfast when Susie barked, and I let Nick in. The mist from the road had reached the house, and thickened. I could hardly tell the difference between the top of the snow and the bottom of the fog. The whole world was palest grey, with a dim glow that came from nowhere and illuminated nothing. I stood at the door for a moment, and heard the occasional drip and sigh that told of snow melting on trees.

"Whew," said Nick. "It's getting thicker by the minute. If I hadn't had it 'graved on my childhood consciousness I should have missed the turning for your house. Ah, I thought you were baking," and he pounced on the remaining sweet rolls. His consciousness and his appetite were apparently unaffected by the peculiar weather.

"Did you see Miss Peterson?" I asked. "And Agnes? How are they?"

"No, they were still asleep, but Miss P. had given a message to Sister Andrew."

He looked at me neutrally, appraisingly.

"She said perhaps it would be a good idea for you to open the library today. The abbess, whom I also did not see, said to tell you that Miss P. seemed to regard this as a matter of local civic duty only, and that she herself voted neither yea nor nay. I cannot tell whether that is in code, but it appears to be in your lap."

I nodded noncommittally, and turned away to try to think.

"Sister Andrew said Agnes was restless and feverish for hours," he continued, "but finally sleeping quietly. Miss P. had a good night. Apparently the transfusions are helping, although we won't know for certain until Sister can get some more of her blood under the microscope."

He flexed his left arm.

"Did it hurt?" Tom asked.

"A little, not enough to write home about. You guys are rough and tough; you won't mind a bit when you're big enough."

"We're big enough now, only Mother won't give us permission."

"I always did say your mother was a sensible person."

"Aw, you're starting to sound like a grown-up."

Martin drained his coffee.

"It's high time somebody did," he said. "Now, if nobody has any wisdom to add to what we worked out last night, the first order of business is Miss Peterson's will, and I suppose the *Lives of the Saints*. Nick and I will go down to the barn and find them."

"But," said Mary.

"Never mind But. My all-purpose threat still holds good. In case everybody else has forgotten it, there may be dangerous people out there. I only wish Nick still had Agnes's gun."

"It is in my inner pocket, as a matter of fact, although I don't honestly know whether I am happy about it or not."

"What?"

Nick wrinkled his nose.

"Sister Mark gave it to me this morning. Read me a lecture on firearms safety, she did; and made me show her my permit." He grimaced again. "What a good thing it was my fingernails were clean."

He stood.

"Ready when you are, old thing."

They didn't even need their parkas, it was getting so warm; but it was very nearly a case of needing a compass, the fog was getting so thick. They were out of sight in six paces, although I could hear their boots in the slushy snow long after. I wondered for a second whether the groundhog would take a false alarm, and awaken before his time; then I bolted the door.

The damp crept in everywhere. Daddy and Martin have made our house fairly snug as to wind and drafts, tightening up window frames and stuffing in insulation; but when cold damp decides to march in, nothing can stop it. Tom and I made up the fire in the dining room, and Mary brought down an old quilt in which to huddle before it.

I gave the twins a new *Life of St. Ignatius of Loyola* to read, with pictures to color. It was maybe too lively for the circumstances; but it was what lay on top of Mother's stack of new materials.

Mother called to report that Boston was expecting to come out from under siege by noon. They should be home for a late supper, she said; but we were not to wait dinner. I had just hung up when the intercom line buzzed.

"Hello?"

"'Sme," Martin said from the office telephone. "We have Miss P's will, and Dr. Michael's closing file, and the *Lives of the Saints.* Do you still think we ought to look up the other folks?"

I shivered.

"Heck, no. Just get back up here."

"Shall do."

He and Nick came in dripping. They kicked off their boots, and stood shoulder to shoulder in front of the fire.

"Of course it isn't really cold any more," said Martin, "but brother, that damp has eaten into my bones. Here are the files."

Nobody else moved toward them, so I opened the top one and began to read aloud.

"The Last Will and Testament of
Estelle Francesca Peterson

"Know all ye men by these presents that I, Estelle Francesca Peterson, presently of the Town of North Salisbury, County of Litchfield and State of Connecticut, being of lawful age and of sound and disposing mind, memory and judgment—"

"I am not going to enjoy this," Nick said. "Could you get to the bit about the nieces and nephews?"

"What's wrong?" I asked him.

"Sorry, it just feels like she's dead and we're the greedy relations."

"Well, she isn't, and we're not. Let's see. . . ."

"Here. She directs that all her debts be disposed of, and whatnot; and she requests a funeral Mass at the abbey, which I suppose is mildly interesting. Then we have this:

"Article Four. I hereby give, bequeath and devise all the rest, residue and remainder of my estate of whatsoever nature and wheresoever situated in six equal shares, one share each, *per stirpes*, to my beloved nephews and nieces: . . ."

"What's *per stirpes?*" asked Mary.

"If one of them died before Miss P. did," Martin said, "and that one had children, his share would pass to his children rather than passing sideways, so to speak, to be added to the shares of his siblings and cousins. If it passed sideways, it would be *per capita.*"

"See how educational this is?" asked Tom. "Hemoglobin, *per stirpes—*"

"Belay that," said Mary.

"Ahem. . . . nephews and nieces: Anthony Harald Oliviera, presently of the City and County of New Haven, Connecticut; Francesca Elizabeth Oliviera, presently of the City and County of New Haven, Connecticut; Joseph Hugh Rossi, presently of the City and County of New Haven, Connecticut; Rosa Anne Rossi, presently of the City and County of New Haven, Connecticut; John Edward Rossi, presently of the City and County of New Haven, Connecticut; and Mary Alexandra Rossi, presently of the City and County of New Haven, Connecticut.

"If, as a result of the foregoing distribution, any share of my estate should be payable to any beneficiary of mine who has not yet attained the age of twenty-five years, I then give, bequeath and devise any such share to Anthony della Rucco, Esquire, presently of the City and County of New Haven, Connecticut, as trustee, to have and hold such share in a separate trust and accumulate therein the net income attributable to such share; such share and its net income to be paid to such beneficiary upon his attainment of twenty-five years of age."

I looked up at Martin and Nick.

"Anything strike you as odd about that?"

"A little," said Martin. "But let's hear the codicil, first."

I flipped through the rest of the will without admitting that the business about funeral arrangements made me uncomfortable, too.

"Here.

"I, Estelle Francesca Peterson, presently residing in the Town of North Salisbury, County of Litchfield, and State of Connecticut, do hereby make, publish and declare this to be a first codicil to my Will dated the 21st day of January, 1965.

"First: I revoke and delete Article Four of my Will and I substitute and insert in lieu thereof the following:

"My nephews and nieces, Anthony Harald Oliviera, presently of the City and County of New Haven, Connecticut; Francesca Elizabeth Oliviera, presently of the City and County of New Haven, Connecticut; Joseph Hugh Rossi, presently of the City and County of New Haven, Connecticut; Rosa Anne Rossi, presently of the City and County of New Haven, Connecticut; John Edward Rossi, presently of the City and County of New Haven, Connecticut; and Mary Alexandra Rossi, presently of the City and County of New Haven, Connecticut, having attained both a reasonable level of material comfort and security in the world and a reasonable level of competence in dealing with it, I bequeath to each of them the sum of two hundred dollars, along with the wish that they employ it in some reasonably wholesome fashion.

"The rest and residuum of my estate I bequeath to Edmund Thomas Adams, presently of the Town of Deale, County of Anne Arundel, and State of Maryland, as trustee, such funds to be administered in his entire discretion, principal and interest, for the benefit of the widows and orphans of United States intelligence officers deceased in the line of duty. The said trustee is to serve without bond. . . . Shall I go on?"

"Does it say anywhere how much she has?" Martin asked.

"Ghoul," said I. "Of course it doesn't. You know better than that. It could be anything. What does it matter?

"Second: Except as changed by this first codicil, I ratify and confirm my Will in all respects. . . ."

The twins had gone back to St. Ignatius.

"It doesn't tell us much," said Martin.

"It tells us a few things," said Nick, looking worried.

They pulled out chairs, finally, and sat at the table, assuming similar attitudes of elbows and chins.

"All of the nieces and nephews have Italian names," said Martin, looking at the table. "And Anglo-Saxon middle names," said Nick.

"Has Miss Peterson ever struck you as a closet Italian?" asked Martin.

"Miss Peterson has never struck me as a closet anything," I said. "She's always been what she is. What does it matter?"

"It matters," Nick murmured, also still looking at the table. "I don't know why, and I don't know why I don't know why, but it matters."

"Why do we feel defensive about it?" Martin asked. "We're starting to sound like Mrs. Tonypandy. Oh." He looked up, finally.

"Yes," said Nick. "It's something along Mrs. Tonypandy's lines; but I'm still not getting it. What is it going to take to kick my brain into gear?"

He stood up.

"There is more to this than our not sharing the swamp yankee's prejudice against the Italian. Martin, I want to see those books."

Martin sighed.

"I give up. No, wait. We still have to call the CIA."

We looked at each other. Now that it came to it, we were all a bit shy.

"We can't just call the CIA," Tom said, wandering back from his book. "I mean, can we?"

"Of course we can," Mary said. "Where are the saints?"

"Where are the what?" asked Martin. "Oh, the *Lives of the Saints*. Here."

I turned the pages.

"December 4. Well, we have St. Peter Chrysologus, St. Barbara, St. Clement of Alexandria, St. Maruthas, St. Anno, St. Somund and St. Bernard. How do we choose?"

"Was St. Eligius listed first for December 1st?" Mary asked. I flipped back in the book.

"Nope. One, two, three, fourth. Now what?"

"Let me see," said Mary.

"Look," she said. "St. Peter Chrysologus is OK; I mean, he's a Doctor of the Church, that means he was very smart, right? But St. Barbara! Look. St. Barbara is the patroness of gunners."

Nick smiled at last, lightheartedly.

"How can you turn it down?" he asked, and went toward the kitchen.

"Where are you going?" Martin demanded.

"I am going to call the CIA, and ask to speak to whoever is in charge of research into St. Barbara."

"You can't."

"Watch me."

So we followed him out, and watched him dial. I realized that I hadn't believed until then that we could just pick up the phone and call the CIA.

"Good morning, operator. I should like a number for Langley, Virginia, if you please. . . ."

We looked at each other while he waited for the number, and then for the connection. Tom was practically climbing up Nick's back, until Martin pulled him away. Even Susie and Ribby realized something was up, and circled around.

"Yes, good morning, sir," Nick finally said. "I should like to speak to someone about research on St. Barbara, if you please."

"—That's right, St. Barbara."

He made it sound normal, somehow. There was a long pause, during which Nick surveyed the rest of us with every appearance of aplomb and confidence.

"Yes? Oh, hello. I am calling with some data about St. Barbara, if you please. Is there someone there who is interested in research about St. Barbara?

"—Me? Oh, my name is Nicholas Brown. No, oh-double-yew-enn. Yes. And to whom am I speaking, please?

"—Mr. Adams. Mr. Adams? Oh, Lord, are you Mr. Edmund Adams?

"—No, no, please forgive me. I just—well, my job just got easier, sir. To start the wrong way around, you see, I was just looking at—oh. I shouldn't—I suppose this is silly, sir, but is this a secure line?

"—Quite right. No, of course we don't—I don't mind. It is a rather unusual situation, but of course we—I want to—to do things the right way, if at all possible. Joanie! Your number is not printed on your telephone."

"Sorry," said I. "203, of course—"

"203," said Nick.

"555-4736."

"555-4736. Yes, sir. Yes, it is a private residence. Yes, as far as we know the building is secure, yes sir.

"Of course, sir. Yes. Good-bye."

He hung up, and looked at us.

"I think it worked. He's going to call us back on a secure line."

"Great heavens," said Martin.

"Of course it worked," scoffed Mary. "I told you. St. Barbara."

The telephone rang. We could see Nick gather his seriousness.

"Hello.

"—Yes sir.

"—Well, I guess you would say we are civilians, sir. . . ."

At this point Martin caught my eye; we nodded in unison; he grabbed Tom and I grabbed Mary; and we frog-marched them into the dining room. They had just enough sense to wait to complain until the door swung shut behind us.

Nick was on the phone nearly ten minutes. I could see that Martin wanted to eavesdrop as much as I did; but I was betting Nick would be better off without an audience; and it was completely obvious he didn't need the twins breathing down his neck while he tried to sound like a coherent adult. So we waited. Eventually the twins lay on their tummies, puffing bits of ash into the fireplace; we all scrambled up when Nick came back in.

He looked around at us. "I persuaded him," he said, and let out a long breath, and leaned against the doorjamb.

"What did you say?" demanded Tom.

"What did he say?" demanded Mary.

"I told him everything I knew, and some of the things I guessed;

and I told him our local suspects. He said we should sit tight and not do anything, and he'd get someone here as soon as he could." I felt deflated.

"That isn't very specific, or very consoling," Martin said.

"No."

We drifted back to the table.

"What about Mrs. Crawley?" Mary persisted.

"What about Joe Fredericks?" asked Tom.

Nick shrugged.

"I told you, I told him everything I knew." He rested his forearms on the table, and his chin on top.

Martin regarded him for a moment.

"Do we do it?" he finally asked, rather gently.

"Do what?" demanded Tom.

"Do what he said, Mr. Adabs," said Mary, impatiently. "Do we sit aroud and do dothing while a KGB agedt codtidues od his course of bayheb add a poisoder baybe poisods sobebody else?"

Her expression was hampered a bit by her cold, which had been developing rapidly; but the frustration came through clearly enough.

Nick looked at her strangely.

"They're supposed to be the same person, remember?"

"Whatever," she shrugged, and blew her nose. "Excuse me. Do we sit on our hands while they—excuse me, while he does whatever he wants," she sneezed, "and just hope the government gets around to shipping somebody up here before March? This *is* the government we're talking about, remember?"

"It's the CIA," said Tom, outraged at the insult to Our Spies.

"The CIA is part of the government," said Mary, with full contempt. She looked at Nick and Martin and me, and sneezed again. "Well?"

Martin turned back to Nick.

"What's your guess?" he asked. "Will your Mr. Adams get someone up here fast? You said he believed you."

Nick drew a slow spiral on the table with his finger. "If I had to guess, I should say yes. But I am far from certain. I spoke to the fellow for all of ten minutes, you know. He sounded sharp, but how can I guess how many divisions he has?"

Martin nodded.

"Then I vote no," he said, "or yes, according to Mary's phrasing. I vote we stay put, and wait for reinforcements. Agnes and Miss Peterson are adults; they got into this of their own free will; we have gotten them to a pretty safe place; we have no particular reason to suppose that anyone else is in danger. We have a couple of minors under our care. Shut up," he said, as Mary moved to protest. "Technically, in point of fact, we are all of us minors except for Nick. I say we tend to the orders of the day; and at the moment Mr. Adams is the closest thing we have to the officer of the day.

"Nick?"

Nick nodded briefly, and I held my breath. If he sided with Martin, would I have the gumption to do what I had to do on my own? Much more difficult, would I be able to think of a *way* to do it on my own?

But Nick pushed back in his chair, and shook his head.

"I cannot agree. With all due respect, Martin, and I give you rather a lot, for whatever it's worth; I cannot agree. We are uniquely situated to do a couple of things that nobody else could do, and for which no other time is likely to serve.

"Above all, there *are* others involved, although we do not know who they are. There are the other intelligence officers and agents whom this mole might betray in the future; and there are quite likely other people like Miss Peterson who are in danger because they are able to identify him and his confreres. If we sit still, we improve his odds of escape. We have a couple of paths open to us, low risk from our point of view, and from the point of view of alarming him. So, with the proviso that we secure the twins at my aunt's house—sorry, you guys—I vote we carry on, according to plan."

He smiled faintly.

"Mr. Adams is likely to be a bit annoyed; but we can always quote Mr. Laurio on the responsibility of the citizen."

Martin leaned back, likewise.

"Joanie, are you going to listen to sense?"

"Nope. Sorry, Martin. I honestly think Nick is right; and I don't think I'm being swayed by a desire for action and adventure. I've really had plenty of both. It's nearly nine o'clock. I have to stop at the abbey first, because I promised the Abbess I'd see her this morning; and then I'm going down to Town Hall to get the key to the library."

"Hold it, Britomart," said Nick, with affectionate amusement. "What are you going to do if the bad guy comes in?"

"I was just getting to that. If it looks like I can hold him there for a while, talking or whatever, I'll call and say that the other volunteer hasn't turned up, so I'll be late coming home. Then you guys, or whoever's here, can call in Trooper Daniels. He may not be good for much, but he'll arrest a stranger on our say-so, and hold on to him long enough for Mr. Adams's reinforcements to get here. OK?"

"That seems sound," Nick said. "What if you can't keep him?"

"The only thing I've been able to think of, and I promise you I'll welcome any suggestions, is to take him here the slow way, which ought to give you time to get Trooper Daniels. In that case, I'll call and ask if there's anything I should pick up on my way home. If necessary, I'll tell him that my family expect me to call."

"I think I can improve on that a little," Nick said. "I am going to try to get into Joe Fredericks' apartment. Assuming he'll be out most of the day, I shall be in there for a few hours, unless I find what I am looking for quickly. If you are going to have to move out with your—your subject, I guess is the word, call Mr. Wall. You can pretend you're calling home. I'll tell him to get me out, pronto, if you do; and he can call Trooper Daniels, too. How's that?"

"Shaky," said Martin. He thought for a second.

"OK," he said. "I'll go along with this, if you absolutely promise me, Joanie, that if you don't get reassurance from Mr. Wall, you won't budge from the library. If you have to let the bad guy go, let him go, do you understand?"

I nodded, and he turned to Nick.

"I can't see just how this is going to play out, and I don't like that. As far as I can see, the only person who might be getting into an actual dangerous situation is my sister, and I plenty don't like that. You have to promise to work it out with Mr. Wall that if it comes down to it, you and he will both shadow Joanie and the bad guy, and you will not make one single dangerous move until and unless she is absolutely guaranteed out of the way. Have you got that?"

Nick looked at him steadily.

"If I weren't chalking that up to your concern for your sister rather than to your low opinion of my concern for your sister, I should be furious. As it is, yes, I understand; and I agree. As a matter of fact, I can innocently extricate Joanie if it seems advisable. Darling!" He mock-swooned at me. "Where have you been?"

I scowled.

Martin grumbled, "I imagine I'm over-imagining the danger. Even KGB agents, or probably especially KGB agents, don't want to be responsible for anything happening to a civilian. And Mr. Adams will probably get his troops here; and the bad guy will probably not turn up at the library, or if he does he'll be indistinguishable from everybody else. All right. I don't like it at all, but I suppose it is all right. Am I supposed to do anything, incidentally?"

"Well, somebody who knows the ground has to wait for Mr. Adams," said Nick. "No, I am not casting you as a coward. We all know better than that. Somebody simply has to; and only I can look at the blasted medical books; and only Joanie can run the library. They also serve who watch and wait, you know."

"Oh, sure. You wait and see who watches and waits if we ever have another adventure around here, which God forbid."

"Amen."

The twins had been conferring in undertones, which we ought to have taken for a danger sign.

"Look," said Mary, in her most reasonable voice. "I give up, all right? I mean, I feel awful; and I give up. I'll go over to Mrs. Brown's house, and lie around and drink lemon tea all day. But Nick really is going to need someone as a look-out, and Tom's the only one left. You ought to let him go along."

We all felt deeply moved by what it must have cost Mary, cold and all, to give up on a piece of the action.

"I'll be responsible, truly," said Tom. "I'll do just what Nick says. I'll stay out of the way. But you do need a look-out. You don't want Joe finding you in his apartment."

"Mr. Wall can be the look-out," said Martin.

"Not all day," Mary said. "He has his own work to do."

"Joanie?" said Martin.

I shrugged.

"Mary with a cold'll be a lot easier on Mrs. Brown than Mary with a cold and Tom without one. And if Tom really stays on good behavior—" I tried to look fiercely at him, and he tried to look angelically at me.

"Oh, I guess. If Nick can stand it."

"I think it makes sense," said Nick. "But you have to remember," he said quite sternly to Tom, "No independent action. That means none."

"I promise," said Tom, looking so upright that I began to worry.

"Troops out, then?" asked Nick.

"Let's run through Joanie's codes once more," said Martin. So we did; and then we organized and went our ways.

CHAPTER 11

What is a weapon? People have been murdered with
the mildest domestic comforts; certainly with
tea-kettles; probably with tea-cosies.
—G.K. *Chesterton, The Fairy Tale of Father Brown*

NICK AND TOM and I were to walk as far as the abbey together, but first we accompanied Mary across the upper field, and waited in the Browns' lane until she was inside their house. The fog was a bit thinner up on the rise. Mrs. Brown shot us a distracted wave from her kitchen door.

"She's going to let you have it but good," I reminded Nick, "when she finds out that she's been missing the adventure of the decade."

"Don't I know it. If today isn't the day all the grownups in the world come into it, tomorrow surely will be. I've been half wishing they already had, and the other half wishing they never would."

"What do we need them for?" asked Tom. "You're practically grown up, and we're doing fine."

"Grownups run the CIA," I said.

"And the prisons," Nick added, "which is where somebody out there belongs." He waved at the mist.

"And the courts that will send him there," I concluded. It was comforting to invoke the apparatus of law and order just then, for the fog thickened once more as we descended the Browns' lane. From the right-hand margin of the state road, where we turned toward the abbey and the village, we could not see the other side. The remaining snow, now gone to soft mush, muffled our footsteps. We could hear an occasional drip from a branch, and nothing else. Even Tom was quiet. The whole world seemed to have suspended its business so that we could play out our story—or even to have gone away altogether, for there was very little of it to be seen.

A dense fog in the day time is much stranger than one at night, for one keeps thinking one ought to be able to see things; there is light, after a fashion, but it illuminates only the fog. The fog begins to feel like a thing, an obstacle; after a while one dodges a little, and winces as at a blow, on encountering a thicker patch.

"Limited sight distance," said the sign at the last curve north of the abbey. Nick practically walked into it in the chilly, cottony murk; and Tom laughed nervously.

"I suppose you would take it ill," said Nick, "if I suggested that you exercise caution."

"I certainly would. You be careful, too. And Tom—"

"I know. Don't worry. You wouldn't recognize me."

"Ciao, then," said Nick.

"Ciao."

I made my way up the abbey drive by keeping to its edge; I could see only a step or two in front of my feet. But the light at the entry seemed to push back the mist.

"Deo gratias," said Sister Maura to me, and shook her head at the fog. "A bit too romantic for my taste," she said; and it sounded as if she were criticizing someone's clothing, so that I almost expected the fog to apologize and melt away.

"Come and get warm, Joanie. It's not as cold as it was, of course, but it feels colder to me. The Abbess is expecting you. I'll let her know."

I sat in one of the comfortable chairs by the grille, and reviewed my essay for only a couple of minutes. It was not august; it was not even incisive. I had spun out my original idea at least as far as I felt it could legitimately go; and I had found nothing else to set it in.

The Abbess was more brief than she had been on Sunday. I slid the essay through the grille; and she read it quickly and quietly. At the end she pursed her lips, and nodded, and looked up at me.

"It is very good, Joan," she said. "It suffers only from your very evident wish that it were more broad, or more profound. It is a good, solid note; you can make it better simply by excising the evidence of that wish. See? Here, and here. Spare us the 'It would seem that' and the 'It might be said that.' Just tell us what you think."

She handed it back through the bars, and tilted her head at me. "You are dissatisfied because you cannot do a round of six-foot fences in three minutes? But you have done a solid job at two-foot-six, with even a little interesting personality thrown in. You are too sensible to expect to be a star right away. But you have a gift for interpretation."

"Do you mean I could be a good critic?"

"If you work, yes. Now, tell me about your mystery. I have seen your friend Miss Breslin, but I have not wanted to tax her with many questions. Not yet." She smiled slightly.

"It's a muddle," I said. "Now that Joe Fredericks is in the clear, I realize I was sort of counting on him to be—to be the bad guy."

"Why is he in the clear?"

"He was standing next to Mr. Wall, at the garage in town, when Mr. Wall heard the shot Saturday morning, the shot that hit Agnes."

"This clears him also of attempting to poison Miss Peterson?"

"Mother, how likely is it that two different people would want to hurt Miss Peterson?"

"According to what your friend Nicholas told Sister Andrew, several other people are carrying grudges, if nothing worse, against that apparently harmless lady."

"I know. It seems so strange. Of all people to have so many people mad at her; I mean even apart from the KGB."

"Why of all people?"

"Well, because Miss Peterson is kind, I suppose, and—and competent and responsible, and—and rational. Why would a rational person attract all this—this unreasonableness?"

"Hmm. Perhaps it is common for people not to like reasonableness, or competence, or even kindness?"

I shook my head, feeling as if some fluff had gotten in my ears.

"Perhaps reason is a magnet for unreason," she said, "unreason being furious at reason's mere existence? Perhaps kindness is a magnet for malice."

"But I thought if we were good and kind other people would be, too. I'm putting it in a baby way, but you know what I mean."

"Sometimes that works, and sometimes it doesn't. People get angry at goodness, and duty, and kindness, too."

"If they don't want to be good and dutiful and kind, you mean?"

"I am afraid so, and I am sorry to give you a sad thought to work on."

I did sigh, but I shook myself.

"I'd still rather know what's true, Mother. You would, too, wouldn't you?"

"Oh, yes. I am quite looking forward to interviewing your friends, when they are feeling better."

She rose, leaning heavily on her cane.

"Sister Andrew or Sister Maura will let you know when you can visit them. And you will bring me your next essay."

"If you don't mind the bother."

"I stopped minding much worse bothers a long time ago. Good-bye, Joan."

"Good-bye. Thank you."

I let myself out into the fog, and walked to the village.

The streetlights in the square made little luminous clouds, without illuminating much of anything under them. I had only a general sense of the shapes of the shops at the top of the street; the ones at the southern end, and the Town Hall, might have vanished for all I could tell.

I set my teeth to pass the spot where Agnes had been shot. *St. Michael the Archangel, defend us in battle.*

The Town Hall materialized at last, looking like its own ghost on the outside, but it was its own prosaic self on the inside. Off the little white entrance hall, the town clerk's room stood empty, its file cabinets and shelves of bound land records in serried ranks assembled. The typewriter on Mrs. Redfern's desk hummed peaceably, so I thought she could not be far away. I turned back into the entry to call, and heard her voice and someone else's—

Joe Fredericks'. They were in the meeting room on the other side of the hall.

"But you couldn't do it all today, Joe?"

"Nah, I got some wood to cut back home this afternoon. But I can get a good start on the floor and front of the stage this morning, and finish the rest down here tomorrow."

"All, right, then."

I felt reluctant to see Joe, so I waited for Mrs. Redfern to come out. As she did, the sounds of furniture being moved in the meeting room reminded me suddenly of Miss Peterson's barricade on Saturday morning, and put me off my stride.

"Oh, can I help you?" Mrs. Redfern began.

"—Oh, Joanie, hello, sorry. How are you?"

"Fine, Mrs. Redfern, thanks. And you?"

She shook her head at the meeting room door, and sighed.

"Come on in. Want some coffee?"

"No, thanks." I followed her back into her office. Mrs. Redfern is almost as stout as Mrs. Tonypandy, but in her case it is all the more of her to be tidy with. System and order follow her around the way the cloud of dirt follows Pigpen in Peanuts.

"Miss Peterson's not feeling well," I plunged, "and she wants me to open the library this morning. Could I have the key, please?"

"Of course. You won't get many customers, but it's nice that school's still closed and you can do it."

She didn't ask me why I couldn't get Miss Peterson's own key from her. She opened the bottom drawer of her desk, and flipped through the files hanging from their steel rods.

"Here you are."

The key was in a little envelope taped to the inside of a file called, "Library." She handed it over.

"Will you stay open all day? Is Ginnie Crawley coming in?"

"I don't know, Mrs. Redfern, I'm sorry. I'll bring it back before I go home."

"That's fine, dear. Sure you don't want some coffee?"

"I'm sure, thanks."

"Have a nice time."

"Thanks, Mrs. Redfern."

The ghostly street seemed even stranger after Mrs. Redfern's ordinariness. I hunched up my shoulders and tried to keep from running, and from wondering whether anyone was watching from behind the hedge. I thought perhaps it would be pleasant to be a town clerk, far pleasanter than a literary critic, or a spy.

The library was very dark, and the mad moment in which I had to decide whether to turn on the light first, or close the door behind me first, seemed to stretch far too long. Self-consciousness won over general nerves, and I closed the door. My hand knew where the switch was then, and the fluorescent fixtures blinked on in succession over the reading tables in front.

Be our protection against the wickedness and snares of the Devil. I put my parka and boots in the closet, and picked up the books that people had returned through the tipping drawer in the outside wall. I could check them in and shelve them, I thought, along with the others that had accumulated on the cart.

~ ~ ~

Nick and Tom found Mr. Wall under his own tow truck in the first bay of the garage.

"Morning," he said. "Mechanics' own vehicles are like the shoemakers' own children: no bearings, no shoes. What can I do for you? Any word on Estelle Peterson?"

Nick gave a brief medical report, and explained their errand.

"We thought Tom could watch from the window," he concluded, "in case Joe came back; but with this weather I don't think he'd see him in time. Maybe I should just take the chance. It's kind of worth it, except for making trouble for you."

Mr. Wall came out from under the lift, and re-lit his pipe.

"Well, now, let me see. Ordinarily I'd be inclined to protect Joe's privacy, behind on his rent though he is. But I—let's just say maybe there are other concerns, concerns that you don't need to know about, any more than I need to know the parts of *your* story that *you're* not telling *me*."

He smiled faintly at Nick.

"I've never been an accessory to trespass before, but I guess it's just a misdemeanor, since you're not planning to burgle anything."

"Actually," Tom said helpfully, "this is probably a conspiracy, and in lots of states that's a felony even if it's just a conspiracy to commit a misdemeanor."

"You're kidding," said Nick.

"You can look it up," said Tom earnestly. "If you conspire to commit a misdemeanor, it's a felony." Mr. Wall laughed, and walked to his desk. He pulled a key from the top drawer.

"We'll look it up later," he said. "Joe just went down to Town Hall a few minutes ago. He said he'd be back to cut up an old tree for me by early afternoon, to make up some of his back rent. You stay and help me, Tom. If Joe comes back early I'll keep him here while you run and warn Nick; but he won't. Joe hates cutting wood, and he likes making cash money, which is what he'll be doing at Town Hall.

"I don't have to tell you not to touch anything but the books, do I?"

"No sir," said Nick, and took the key.

Tom was sensible enough to realize that he would have much more fun covering himself in grease and automotive terminology than standing at Joe's window while Nick read textbooks, so he proceeded to cooperate.

Nick slipped quietly up the alley to the old garage, and let himself in the little door at the side. He held his big flashlight low, but he could see an enormous old hay wagon that took up most of both bays; and he could see the steps that climbed the near wall to the apartment above.

There was a tiny landing at the top; the two-by-four railing of the stairs followed its edge to the upper wall that hung out over the bays. Nick found that the same key worked in the door there, and let himself in.

The apartment was very dark, its air as still and cold as in the garage below. Nick moved the beam of his flashlight around very cautiously, and saw that the two windows on the side wall were heavily curtained; closer inspection showed insulated shades behind the curtains, so he made bold to light the plain kerosene lamp that stood on the rough table.

"That was the only moment I felt any compunction," he said later. "At that moment it seemed wrong to use Joe's kerosene without asking. Silly, what?"

The narrow bed held two quilted blankets of the kind that moving men use to protect furniture, neatly folded at the foot, and a misshapen pillow. That part of the view was unavoidable, but Nick had not come with the intention of general spying, so he avoided looking toward the kitchenette end of the apartment, receiving only a vague impression of moderate, ordinary disorder.

Books were stacked high on the table that stood nearer the door, in four piles around an apparent work area; there was also a wide case of them, of the nicer kind that one can get in a budget-conscious department store. They were all medical texts. At the work area, where the single, elderly chair stood, there were also a tall dirty glass and a large bottle of bourbon, one-third full. Nick did not even consider them, and set to work about the books.

And got nowhere. Ninety minutes later he began to pace the apartment, wishing he had brought coffee with him.

There was no personal mark anywhere in the room: not even a cheap print, such as the youngest and least imaginative college student will hang upon his dormitory wall. The curtains were pure utility; the bed was as embarrassing to behold as at first. But there was a corner of paper showing from under the moving blankets. The blankets were folded high enough to block it from the viewpoint of the door; it was visible only from the kitchenette end. Nick hesitated, and then pulled the paper out, noting its angle so that he could replace it.

It was a computer printout. Originally it had consisted of four pages, but all of the first had been torn off, except for a corner around the staple. Most of the second page was also missing; only the first sentence remained.

The peripheral blood smear is bizarre, showing nucleated cells, target cells, hypochromia. . . .

"So it is," murmured Nick.

Only the blank upper margin remained of the third page; the fourth was intact, although it began in mid-sentence.

. . . enzymes were found in all subjects examined both with pos-

itive and negative histories of haemolytic crises after fava bean or drug ingestion. In contrast, high levels of catalase and GSH-Px were found in a small group of G-6-PD deficient subjects (hemizygous and heterozygous) with beta-thalassemia trait, probably by reason of the chronically enhanced oxidant stress which is present in beta-thalassemia. Author-abstract.
END OF DOCUMENTS IN LIST

"By heaven, that is it. Pre-socratic superstitions, my left foot. But why? Why? Why?"

Nick lifted the blankets to replace the printout. There was another paper there: a letter dated the previous February. It bore no letterhead, but the paper was of good quality.

Dear Joe,

We both know that you are intelligent enough to be a physician, and we both know that you are otherwise not qualified to be one. I shall spare us both the pain of specifying. I cannot in good conscience recommend you for admission to the medical school in Grenada, or to any other. Your asking me again will only grieve us both, for the answer must remain no. It is quite true that once I thought you would make a fine doctor, and encouraged you in that ambition; but you will be a happier man if you give up that hope.

Yours sincerely,

John Gerow.

Nick replaced both papers, blew out the lamp, and let himself out as quickly and as quietly as he could.

Nearly two hours after leaving Tom and Mr. Wall, he rejoined them. They were having a happy time under the pickup; Tom was as well greased as any boy could wish to be. But Mr. Wall called off operations when he saw Nick's face.

"What did you find?"

Tom began to object, and then repeated, "What did you find?"

"I am a Bear of No Brain At All," said Nick. "*Beta thalassemia.*"

"*Beta* who?" said Tom.

"Let's sit down," said Mr. Wall, and did, and began to fill a fresh pipe.

Nick didn't see the chair Mr. Wall offered; he paced, and talked.

"*Beta thalassemia* is an anemia largely confined to people of African and Mediterranean ancestry," he said. "It has several forms, both chronic and acute. That means," he explained, "some people just get a little anemic all or most of the time, and some people get so anemic they die, or nearly die.

"Uh, there's a form of *beta thalassemia* that, heaven help me for a chronic idiot, medical students get told about all the time, because it is a classic case of a genetic predisposition, something you're born with, meeting an environmental trigger, something that happens along to make you sick just because you happen to have this—this thing in your heredity, just because you happen to be susceptible.

"People with this predisposition can go through their whole lives and never know it, unless they happen to meet the trigger. In this case, the trigger is fava beans. It's one of those ghastly little regional ironies that northern Europeans, who tend to lack the predisposition for thalassemia, also don't eat the blasted things. But Mediterranean and African people do; and they're also the ones who sometimes carry the gene for beta thalassemia. Uh, and the fava beans trigger the disease. They're sort of like great, big lima beans in coarse pods—"

"Ick," said Tom.

"Ick doesn't begin to describe it," said Nick. "If you've got the genetic predisposition, and you eat them, your liver begins to lyse your red blood cells—"

"Lyse," said Tom. "That's what Joanie said. Miss Peterson's blood is lysing."

"Her red blood cells were being lysed," Nick said. "Did I tell you about what Sister Andrew said? There were all kinds of crazy things—target cells, uh, they're also called Mexican hat cells, those are red blood cells that have been partly processed by the person's own liver; they look deformed and weird under the microscope; nucleated cells, those are red blood cells that have been released prematurely by the bone marrow, to make up for the ones that are missing in action. Ordinarily, red blood cells have lost their nuclei before they make it into the blood. When you see a lot of them with nuclei, you know they're being let out too soon. Miss Peterson's blood looked wack-oh under Sister Andrew's microscope. Well, listen to this."

He fetched a scribble from his parka pocket.

"The peripheral blood smear is bizarre, showing nucleated cells, target cells, hypochromia. . . ."

He looked up.

"Sister didn't get it because she went to medical school twenty-five years ago. I have no excuse. And—"

He looked at Mr. Wall, who had been studying him.

"And under the blanket on Joe Fredericks' bed there is a letter from a Dr. Gerow in New Haven, declining rather emotionally to recommend Joe for the medical school in Grenada. Dr. Gerow just happens to be Miss Peterson's physician. He also just happens to have been Miss Peterson's mother's physician. He's got to be pretty old. He'd have some kind of decent excuse for not knowing about unusual forms of thalassemia, or genetic predispositions and environmental triggers. But Miss P's mother happens to have suffered from chronic anemia; and Dr. Gerow could quite easily have mentioned that fact to someone who happened to come from the same town, and who happened by some perverse chance to be doing odd jobs for him.

"Uh, Mr. Wall, did Martin mention the minestrone Joe made for Miss Peterson?"

Mr. Wall puffed on his pipe for a moment.

"What reason might Joe Fredericks have to suppose that Estelle Peterson had African or Mediterranean ancestry?" he asked.

Nick shook his head.

"If he were doing odd jobs for this Dr. Gerow, or happened to be acquainted with him some other way, he might have learned about Miss Peterson's family."

"The will," said Tom. "The Italians in the will. Italy is in the Mediterranean."

Nick nodded.

"And her mother," he said. "I still feel dazed. I wanted to know how her mother died, do you remember, Tom? And Senator Ely said Miss Peterson couldn't drink a gin and tonic. It was the quinine in the tonic water; quinine can trigger a *beta thalassemia* episode."

Tom's whole face was wrinkled up in puzzlement.

"But why?" he asked. "Why would Joe want to hurt Miss Peterson? She helped him; she was kind to him. She got jobs for him in those restaurants, and he wanted to be a chef. That was what he wanted, right? He didn't want to be a doctor. He wanted to be a chef. Joe wouldn't hurt her. Why would he?"

Nick slumped into the remaining chair.

"I don't know," he said. "But I know I'm right. I don't know why any more than you do, Tom. But at last, finally, I know I'm right.

"When you know How, you know Who, remember? We now know both, and it simply does not matter that we don't know Why.

"All right, it bothers the living daylights out of me that I don't know Why. But it doesn't matter.

"Joe Fredericks made a minestrone for Miss Peterson, and he put fava beans in it because somehow he knew that her mother had suffered from chronic *beta thalassemia*, and there was a good chance she was predisposed for an acute attack. It was the perfect poison, because unless a person happened to have the predisposition, it wasn't a poison at all. It wouldn't show up in a test, it wouldn't even taste funny. The victim would look just plain sick, just as the victims of those KGB umbrellas look like strokes or heart attacks. It was poison, all the same."

"But why?" Tom repeated. "What kind of person would— would poison, not just someone who never hurt him, but someone who had helped him? Helped him a lot?"

"I suppose Joe must be somehow connected to the moles in the CIA," Nick said, "the people who are afraid Miss Peterson can identify them. I suppose he must, but it doesn't account for him, somehow."

"No."

Mr. Wall sat up.

"It's purely personal with Joe," he said. "Politics and espionage don't enter into it. Miss Peterson did him the greatest injury of all. Of course you don't see it, for you have not seen much yet, either of you, of how twisted people can become. You could never guess the great, unforgivable injury Miss Peterson did to Joe."

Nick and Tom stared at him. He shook his head, and smiled bitterly.

"You have already said it," he said. "She helped him."

And Mr. Wall knocked out his pipe, and set it on his desk.

"What?" asked Nick. "Helping him injured him? You don't mean that getting jobs in restaurants kept him from his medical studies? He didn't want to be a doctor. He wanted to be a chef."

"You are still thinking like a healthy-minded person," said Mr. Wall. He pulled the tobacco can and a fresh pipe toward himself, and began to operate upon them. "When a man has been twisted hard enough and long enough," he said, "and indulged little weaknesses, and believed little lies, he is very unusual if he escapes the greatest lie, the oldest sin."

They looked blankly at him.

"Pride," he said softly. "Pride. A person who helps us points up our need of help. Assistance is a demonstration that we need assistance. Ingratitude is not always just carelessness; it can also be resentment, because we have been shown that we have something to be grateful for."

He looked at Tom.

"I am sorry, a bit," he said, "because this is a nasty thing for you to hear, nastier than all the bad words you may hear when you go out from your good mother's home and go to our godforsaken schools. But you are horrified, and so you will know to guard against this terrible evil.

"It is fairly common in the world, although it doesn't usually go to the lengths of poison. People resent the people who help them. They resent them deeply. I think you will never fall into that error, Tom."

He lit his pipe, and waited for the other penny to drop.

Nick rose again, and looked at him.

"You are saying that Joe is an independent operator."

Mr. Wall nodded.

"He has nothing to do with the moles in the CIA."

Mr. Wall nodded.

"We have been working from a false assumption. There is someone else to worry about. There were two people trying to kill Miss Peterson."

Mr. Wall nodded.

"That's what I figure. And I advise you to hold off blaming yourself while others are at risk."

CHAPTER 12

Measured by the standards of the New England community
where he lived and drank and died, Jim failed to earn
so much as an average merit mark.
—H.P. Sheldon, Ol' Sassify Does Her Stuff.

I CHECKED in the books that had been returned, and began to shelve them, wheeling the little cart around the narrow stacks with me. Except for the beautiful old reading tables in the front, our library is a very crowded place, for Miss Peterson pursued over many years the opposite of the normal pattern of small-town libraries. She visited the clearing-out sales all the other ones had every spring, and bought up old books for fifty cents. This practice makes life difficult when it comes time to dust, and the vacuum cleaner does not fit very well in the stacks; but it is helpful when one wishes to find an actual book, as opposed to a pretty room, which is what most suburban libraries are.

The cart was quite full, and I stopped after half an hour or so to start the kettle in the kitchenette and put a Haydn tape into the player. I was beginning to feel quite at home; the work was a pleasant change from the previous few days' activities.

I was well toward the far end of Biography when the kettle whistled and the door opened. I tossed a hasty "Good morning" in the direction of the latter as I ran for the former; but I was able to look at the visitor from the door of the back office as I started some tea brewing.

He was not looking in my direction. He was surveying the science and history projects that the elementary school had posted on the wide community board that stood like an over-sized easel between the reading tables. *Geology of North Salisbury; North Salisbury in the 18th Century; Watersheds and Aquifers in the North Salisbury Region.*

He was of middle height and middle weight, and in his middle forties, I guessed; and conservatively dressed—perhaps a little too dressy for a nasty day, but only a little. His nondescript light brown hair was thinning in front, and cut short in back; he had shed a camel-colored overcoat, so that I could see a plainish tweed jacket and flannel trousers; and he was carrying the coat and a large, black umbrella under his left arm.

His face, at a distance, was reasonably amiable and reasonably intelligent. He might have been shopping for real estate in the neighborhood, and have stopped in at the library for local color; many such people did. He might be someone I simply hadn't happened ever to meet; there weren't many in town, but there were some. I wondered about the umbrella, however. I also wondered, fleetingly, whether Mrs. Crawley might turn up soon. Then I decided I had been out of sight long enough.

"Can I help you with anything, sir?"

He turned and smiled.

"You can't be the librarian?"

"I'm a volunteer, but I might be able to help you."

"Is the library ordinarily closed on Mondays? I came by yesterday, and there was no sign of life."

I actually managed to preserve my cool. There is something about even a semi-official position that is a wonderful aid to poise.

"Not ordinarily, but it's a small town; you know how it is."

"Of course. I've been staying with a friend in the area, looking at a couple of the little farms as possible summer homes, and I find that an old friend is actually the librarian here Estelle Peterson. Is she in today?"

"No, sir; I'm sorry. Uh, would you like to leave a note for her?"

I offered him a pencil and paper. He smiled.

"No, thanks. I was hoping to surprise her. I'll come back another day. Do you have a local-interest section?"

"Over here." I pointed to the shelves just past the desk.

"Thank you."

I tried to think. Coincidence? He could, in fact, be an old friend of Miss Peterson's.

No.

This time, I had to get it right. This man had shot Agnes. He, or one of his friends, had killed Miss Peterson's friend. I had to hold on to him long enough for Mr. Wall to get help; I couldn't let him go.

"Sir?"

"Yes?"

"If you really want to surprise Miss Peterson, and you don't mind a bit of a hike, I have an idea."

He turned and smiled. I prayed my voice wouldn't shake.

"She's spending the morning at our family fort in the woods, communing with nature. I could take you there. I could close the library; no one's coming in."

He started to put on his coat.

"My car's around the corner, on the side street."

"Uh, please don't be insulted, but I'm not allowed to get into strangers' cars."

"A reasonable rule. How long a walk is it?"

"Around twenty minutes."

"That's great! Thanks very much!"

I wanted to give Mr. Adams or Mr. Wall, preferably both, as much time as I reasonably could.

"I'll just call home, and see if there's anything I should pick up while I'm in town. I promised I would. And it'll take me a few minutes to close the library."

He nodded cheerfully, and returned to the shelf of local-interest books, so that I did not have to worry much about concealing the slip of paper with Mr. Wall's number, but he was still well within earshot of the telephone.

"North Salisbury Auto Repair."

"Hi, Daddy, it's Joanie. I'm just leaving the library. I've done the basic chores here, and people aren't coming in in this weather. Is there anything I should pick up?"

"Joanie, are you in danger?" Mr. Wall asked.

"Not right away. An old friend of Miss Peterson's turned up at the library, and I'm just going to bring him to see her at the fort, and I'll be home in maybe an hour and a half. You're sure I shouldn't bring anything?"

"Nick and Tom left for the abbey about five minutes ago. Do I understand that you are going to the fort, and then home, if no one intervenes there, and you are bringing a suspect with you?"

"Yes, Daddy. I'll be careful. See you in a little while."

"I'll call Martin, and try to raise Nick, and follow you as closely as I can. If you hear me yell, 'drop,' you hit the ground flat and fast, and roll away from the suspect. Have you got that?"

"Ok, Daddy. Bye now."

I wasted as much time as seemed reasonable, tidying up behind the circulation desk and wondering who in the world Mr. Wall had been before he was a garage mechanic; and then I went for my parka and boots.

"Sir? I don't know your name. I'm Joanie O'Connor."

He smiled, and again began to put on his own coat, which saved me from shaking his hand.

"How do you do? Irvin Smith."

May God rebuke him, we humbly pray.

I turned off the lights, and we went out into the fog. What use Mrs. Crawley might be I could not imagine, but this was about the last possible second for her to appear. She did not. I locked the library door, and pocketed the key with a mental apology to Mrs. Redfern. The air was still impenetrable pale grey, with little spheres of brighter grey for the streetlights.

"I spend too much of my life behind a desk," Mr. Smith said. "It isn't really cold any more, and it's nice to be out."

"Oh? What do you do?"

"I'm an insurance adjuster, over in Hartford." I thought I heard him having a private joke with himself over that one, and shuddered a little. Insurance adjuster, meaning he thought he was on his way to protect the interests of some of his policyholders, the moles. What in the world was I going to do with him if we got to the fort and Martin and Mr. Adams (or Mr. Adams' reinforcements) were not there? Could I really bring him home? Agnes was one thing; this was one spy too many for my house. I'd have to act surprised at Miss Peterson's absence. And I'd have to let him go. I could not think of a plausible reason to invite him home, and I didn't want to.

I walked as slowly as I thought could be believable.

"It must be kind of a tense job, insurance adjuster."

"It has its ups and downs. The worst part is that a lot of it seems petty after a while. I keep myself occupied with a hobby for local history, but I've pretty much exhausted the possibilities in Farmington, which is where I live now. I've been wanting to find an old place in the country for some time. Do you like living here?"

"Yes. I don't think I'd be happy in a city or a development, although I suppose some of it's what you're used to."

"Some of it. But some people just aren't suited for city life. Look at this, now."

I was looking, and trying not to be obvious about it, for we were passing the garage.

"You don't even get a really decent fog in the city," Mr. Smith said, and for a second I practically liked him, a little, for under normal circumstances I like unusual weather, myself. Then we passed the place where Agnes had been shot, and I remembered who had done the shooting.

We were silent for a minute. There was still no traffic, and there was still no visibility. Once we passed the last streetlight, we could see only a few paces ahead, and navigated by the division between the darker surface of the highway and the lighter surface of the shoulder, where we walked.

I thought of asking how he knew Miss Peterson, but I very much did not want to start a verbal fencing match with him.

"How large a farm are you hoping to find?"

"I'm kind of up in the air. If I buy fifty acres or more, I can probably rent most of the land to a farmer, right?"

"Possibly. I think that sort of arrangement is more common in the Midwest, but you might find someone."

"Maybe I'd be better off with a just a few acres," he mused, "but I really want an old house."

"An old house will keep you very busy," I warned him. "Are

you handy?"

"Not very: desk jockey, remember? However, I imagine I can find people who know what they're doing."

"Where are you taking me, by the way? Where is your fort?"

"In here. This is a Benedictine abbey; our fort in its woods."

We turned in at the abbey drive.

"Do the monks know?" He sounded amused.

"They're nuns; and don't worry: they know. They like hearing our reports on the woods."

I hated giving him even that much of my friends, but I thought it best to keep talking, keep his attention focused ahead, in case someone was following us. *And do thou, oh prince of the heavenly host, by the divine power . . .*

"We just cross this field, and if it weren't for the fog you could see the beginning of our path. Our house is just down the hill, through the woods."

I hated telling him that, too . . . *cast into hell Satan and all the evil spirits who roam the world seeking the ruin of souls.*

"I think I see the beginning of the path now." I pointed, and he naturally peered ahead. Twenty yards, fifteen, and we'd be in the woods, with less chance he'd look back.

"Yes; there it is. My brothers and sisters and I started building our fort ten years ago that is, my big brother and I began it; now mostly the little ones play in it . . ."

And then we were in the woods, and I could stop talking, as we concentrated on avoiding the worst of the slush and mud. Not talking gave me time to notice how frightened I was. Part of it was certainly the plain social fear of being found out leading on a grownup to make a fool of himself; but most of it was the more vague and far more potent fear of what he might do if I failed to deliver him neatly into stronger hands than mine.

I strained to hear whether there might be (friendly) footsteps behind us: nothing.

He negotiated the path neatly. So, the KGB or the CIA had basic woods skills. Or both. Big deal. I remembered that soft feet in the forest mattered a whole lot less in the age of ICBMs than in the age of catapults and sappers. I led him around the mock orange without comment, but with the heartfelt wish that I was back in a simple day like the preceding Saturday, with Tom administering an oath of secrecy to Agnes.

There was no sound from the fort, but there was a faint roar of adrenaline in my ears. They felt cottony, in fact, with the closing-in sensation of a fever faint. I tried to slow my breathing as we approached.

"This is charming," said Mr. Smith. "A real, old-fashioned fort."

"Hold it right there," said a voice behind us. I spun around, and so did Mr. Smith, and Joe Fredericks tackled him. I backed to the wall of the fort; the scuffle was over in five seconds. Joe lay struggling rather feebly with an invisible enemy just in front of the door; the black umbrella lay beside him. Before I thought about doing anything Mr. Smith pinned my right arm up behind me, and pain shot along my shoulder.

"Walk in quietly," he said, so I did. Joe inchwormed part of the way in behind us, and lay in the doorway.

Mr. Smith surveyed the empty fort, and relaxed his grip just a little. I wondered why the canvas curtain was rolled up at the back window.

"Estelle Peterson," gasped Joe. "Sorry. Wrong. Sorry. Tell." And then he lay still.

St. Michael the Archangel, defend us . . .

"Where is she?" asked Mr. Smith, and lifted my arm again, just a little.

"She who?" I asked, stupidly, and knew it was the one time I was going to dare him to lift it further. He did, and the pain was actually less than the different roar around my ears.

"Estelle Peterson. Where is she? This—"

He held something in front of my face; oddly enough, it registered only dimly as an automatic pistol. He was holding it to show it to me, not aiming it at me; and a gun looks a lot less effective from the side, unless you have a thing about them. Most of my attention remained on my shoulder and neck. Oddest of all, the one thing I saw clearly was that he was so certain of his status and of mine that the safety was on.

"Let go of her and hold the gun out to your side, slowly."
He turned slightly, and we could both see the barrels of a shot-gun pointed in through the back window. Behind it was Mrs. Brown.

"Let her go, and hold the gun out to your side," she repeated, in the voice that was accustomed to bring Jimmy and Joey, quaking, to the bar of maternal justice. "Now," she added, in a tone that so completely expected obedience that an East Moldavian who had never heard a word of English would have complied on the spot. Mr. Smith gazed at her with unbelief.

"It's only a twelve-gauge," she said, "but the casing of the shell has been slit right around, just above the brass. At this range it would land in one large piece, and with considerable force. I want you to move both your hands well out, away from your body. It is true that I have never shot a man before, but I have shot lots and lots of clay pigeons much farther away, and I have also shot dogs that I liked, and I don't like you. Let go of her now, and hold your arms out, both of them."

He thought about it for just a second more, and she twitched the end of the gun just a little, and he complied. I ducked down and walked carefully away, without getting between them.

"Who the devil are you?"

"A citizen. This is a citizen's arrest, mister. Joanie, is the safety on his gun?"

I nodded.

"Open your hand, scum, and just let it drop. That's right. Now keep your hands out there. Now you can raise them very slowly, and put them on top of your head. I would be about equally happy to shoot you and bury you; in fact I am almost wishing you would give me an excuse. Move the hands onto the top of the head right now, buster.

"That's better. Joanie, take a look at Joe."

I knelt beside him, looked, and shook my head at Mrs. Brown.

"All right, scum," said Mrs. Brown, very quietly. "Now, listen carefully. There isn't any capital punishment in this state right now, so if you hold still and behave like a good scum, you can look forward to long, comfy time somewhere with your dental

bills covered. If you so much as breath wrong, I will have no compunction at all about assuring the safety of that minor over there.

"Joanie, pick up his gun. I know you know how to work a gun."

I nodded, and rose slowly.

"Mrs. Brown, that will not be necessary," said Mr. Wall. His
own gun was already pointed directly at Mr. Smith as he walked
in. He held it there from about two steps away, and continued,
"Why don't you come around in now, Mrs. Brown, and we'll see
what we can do to secure the situation."

She did, and Mr. Wall bent down very smoothly to pick up and
pocket Mr. Smith's gun. The muzzle of his own never moved from
its focus on Mr. Smith's chest.

"Joanie, is there any rope or stout cord around?" Mr. Wall
asked.

"In the sea chest," I said faintly, and walked slowly and carefully to it. All I could think of was not to foul up Mr. Wall's line
of fire. It seemed to me that if I stepped to within a foot of the
direct line the world would end. It took an eternity, but I got the
twine that Mary had used to repair the table. The others simply
waited in their insane tableau.

"Mrs. Brown, are you as good on knots as you are on ringing a
shotgun shell?" asked Mr. Wall.

She smiled faintly.

"I didn't ring the shell. It was Mary. You can come in in just a
minute, Mary. Mary has apparently read a fair amount of sporting
fiction, including some valuable stories about what you do if you're
out after duck and encounter a bear. I can do a decent knot, Mr.
Wall. How nice to see you, by the way. Hands out to the side, scum,
slowly, and then behind you. That's right, there's a good scum."

The next person wasn't Mr. Adams or Martin, either. It was Len
Laurio, also with a gun drawn; but he put it away as soon as Mrs.
Brown finished with the knots. He and Mr. Wall nodded to each
other.

"Uh, Mr. Laurio," I dithered, "I don't know if you know Mrs.
Brown and Mr. Wall."

They nodded again. "A pleasure, Ma'am," said Len Laurio. "I
have the honor to know your husband. Marine?" he asked Mr. Wall.

"Sixth," said Mr. Wall, "but most of the credit goes to the civilians. And you?"

"Third," said Len Laurio. "A pleasure, sir."

And then we heard a helicopter overhead, and we had only to sit quietly and wait for Martin and Mr. Adams. Mrs. Brown let Mary come in. Mary looked grimly at Mr. Smith, nodded, then walked over to Joe's body, knelt and crossed herself, and began to pray, silently.

"I'm sorry, Joanie," Mr. Wall said, keeping his eyes on his prisoner.

"Sorry?"

"I was as close behind you as I dared to get, but poor Joe was waiting at the entrance to the abbey drive. He was watching for you, I guess, or maybe he had been watching for Nick and missed him; and he didn't see me. So I had to wait, to give him a little distance. It just wasn't safe to make a noise right then.

"I think he must have overheard me talking to Nick, back at the garage. Nick figured out his medical question, you may as well know; but I'd guess you won't want to tell many other people, not now."

I heard Mr. Wall's explanation as though it were coming from very far away, and I watched my little sister saying prayers.

"Joanie?" said Mrs. Brown.

"Yes?"

"Mary is doing a very obviously useful thing right now, and it was very smart of her to raise the alarm with me, and bring me here. And sure, she gets lots of points for ringing the shotgun shell. But you have done very well, too. You mustn't think you have failed, you know."

"Sure, Mrs. Brown. Thanks."

"Joe got to be a man for the first time in his life. Some men never do."

"I understand."

"Probably not, but you will."

Len Laurio was regarding Mary.

"She did what, that little girl?"

Then, finally, Martin and Mr. Adams appeared; and it was wonderful to let the grown-ups have explanations together.

Only a little later, Len Laurio and Mr. Wall rigged a stretcher out of a couple of saplings and our ground cloth to bring Joe up the path to the abbey. Mrs. Brown and Mary and Martin and I followed; and Nick and Tom met us at the top of the path.

Mrs. Tonypandy was waiting in the middle of the abbey drive. She was enormous in a brown quilted down coat; she didn't look smaller than her usual self, at all, the way family usually do at wakes and funerals. Mr. Wall and Len Laurio stopped beside her, and she looked down at Joe. The fog had lifted, but I could not see her face from where I stood.

"He's never been nothing but trouble," she said after a short pause. "Never nothing but trouble to nobody."

I passed Mr. Wall at his end of the stretcher and stood beside her.

"Mrs. Tonypandy," I said, very gently. "Joe saved my life. He got killed saving my life."

She didn't turn to me. She looked one more moment at Joe's face.

"Must've been an accident," she said, and turned away, and walked down the drive.

CHAPTER 13

ON DECEMBER 28, the Feast of the Holy Innocents, Martin and the twins and I set out early for the abbey. We went by the road. It was a clear, cold morning, with a simple, ordinary fresh fall of snow looking normal on the ground. We caught up with Mrs. Brown and Nick about half way between our drive and the abbey one.

"Do you know," said Mrs. Brown, "I began with the assumption that there must have been six or eight moments at which you people ought to have called in whatever adults were available; but as I thought it through, I couldn't identify a single moment at which you should have and could have, except for when you did. Obviously I cannot like the precedent, but I am compelled to admit you did all right."

"How can you say that?" I asked. "What about Joe?"

She smiled and shook her head.

"I tried to tell you before. That was a twisted, wasted life, and a good, clean death," she said. "You know better than to suppose that dying is the worst thing that can happen to a man."

"What would have been worse, for Joe?"

"If Miss Peterson had died, that would have been worse. Worse for Joe, I mean; much, much worse. And let us remember, please, what she might well have done, if you children had not intervened. You won't be easy about it, Joan; but from Joe's point of view, things worked out well."

We turned up the abbey drive, and Nick nodded at the manila envelope under my arm.

"Another essay?" he asked.

I nodded.

"I couldn't work for a while, but the day after Christmas I kind of made myself. It's OK, I think. Not brilliant, but the Abbess says

I have to get used to being workmanlike first. Are you ready for your exams?"

"I fear so. I may never have another imaginative thought; I may never yield to another frivolous impulse; but yes, I am ready. Bring 'em on."

We came to the abbey door, and Mary knocked.

"This is really stupid," said Tom.

"Hush," said Mary, and Sister Maura let us in.

"*Deo gratias*," she said, and led us into the parlor. There were little fires on both hearths, as before, and Mr. Adams already sat near the grille on the visitors' side. He nodded to us.

Tom planted himself in front of him.

"Mr. Adams?"

"Yes?"

"Who was Irvin Smith?"

Mr. Adams regarded him gravely, but one corner of his mouth twitched.

"I'm sorry, but that's need-to-know."

Tom sighed.

"I was afraid you'd say that, but you can't blame me for trying."

But then the Abbess came in on the other side, with Sister Andrew. Then came Miss Peterson, and Agnes, and Sister Mark.

I handed my essay through the grille to the Abbess. Sister Maura unlocked the gate, and Miss Peterson came out first. She looked at us.

"Well, I suppose it was a little more exciting than I hoped," she said. "But it will be good to get back to work. Joanie, could you help out for a few extra afternoons, until I get things sorted out?"

"I'd be happy to. Are you really feeling all right?"

"Right as rain. I have had a splendid visit; and I am ready to get back into harness. Apparently I shall have to spend a week or two in Virginia—" she glanced at Mr. Adams "—looking at pictures and so forth. But I imagine you and Mrs. Crawley can manage, more or less."

"More or less, but we'll be happier when you're back to stay."

"So shall I, Joan."

Agnes came out next, and shook hands with Mr. Adams. Then

she turned to us.

"I can never thank you enough," she said, "and I'm not going to try, because I don't want to embarrass you out of being friends. Mary, if you ever want a perfectly awful job, talk to him." She nodded toward Mr. Adams, who smiled faintly.

"What about me?" demanded Tom.

She regarded him gravely.

"You are an outstanding citizen," she said. "Lord knows what you will someday be; in all probability an outstanding something or other; but not a spy, Tom. Trust me. You'd hate it. Remember? You're the one who's bigger and smarter." And she winked at him.

Tom burst into tears, and hurled himself at her middle. She caught him cleanly, and hugged him, and rumpled his hair. Then she looked up at Nick.

"I owe you several apologies," she said.

"Not a bit of it," said Nick. "I am a ass, and you are a lady. But—" and he half held out his hand, palm up in the approved manner.

She smiled, and gave him hers, and he bowed over it. Then he fished her revolver out of his inner jacket pocket, and offered it to her. She nodded, and took it, and turned to give it to Mr. Adams.

"You'd better take this, Ed."

"Apparently."

"I don't think we were wasting our time, you know."

"I know."

Finally Agnes turned to me.

"You don't see the sense of this?"

I met her eye, and didn't trouble to disguise my skepticism.

"In general, I do; in this particular case, since you ask, no."

"It is less than obvious. But now I won't have to worry that what I do will be wasted by somebody else's mismanagement. I don't mean Ed, and he knows it; but I've found a boss whose judgment I trust. Does that make sense?"

"I suppose."

"You'll come and visit?"

"Certainly."

"Then we can talk about it again. Remember what we said

about being certain of your calling? Getting shot in your town is the best thing that ever happened to me. OK?"

"OK."

Then Agnes turned away, because the Abbess and Sister Mark and Sister Andrew were still waiting, on the other side of the grille. She knocked at the side of the gate.

"What do you ask?" said the Abbess.

"To try my vocation," said Agnes, quite steadily, "as a Benedictine."

"Enter, in the name of the Lord."

We watched her through; she bent down so that the Abbess could kiss her. Then the Abbess led her to the door across the cloister side of the parlor. Agnes didn't look back. Sister Mark shut the door behind them and Sister Maura let us out into the sunshine.

"Oh, rats," said Mary.

"Which rats are those?" asked Nick.

"That leaves the rest of us," said Mary, "to figure it all out on our own."

ABOUT THE AUTHOR

ELIZABETH ALTHAM has been teaching at Our Lady of the Sacred Heart Academy in Rockford, Illinois, since 2000. Before that, she served several years as managing editor of *The Latin Mass* magazine; her articles have appeared there, in *Sursum Corda* and in *Homiletic and Pastoral Review*. In 1993 she appeared on EWTN's *The Abundant Life*, in a symposium in defense of Pope Pius XII.

When she began *The Misplaced Spy*, Mrs. Altham was a home-schooling mother working part time for the journalist William F. Buckley Jr. Her family's move from Connecticut to the Midwest led serendipitously, or otherwise, to the teaching position at the academy. In 2006, the Acton Institute named the academy one of its *Top Fifty Catholic High Schools* in the nation; in 2009 Hillsdale College awarded it the *Salvatori Prize for Excellence in Education*. Mrs. Altham hopes to continue teaching there until she is ninety-five.